MAMA SAID

STORIES

|||||||||||||||||||||||||||||||

KRISTEN GENTRY

|||||||||||||||||||||||||||||||

WEST VIRGINIA UNIVERSITY PRESS · MORGANTOWN

ISBN 978-1-952271-98-4 (paperback) / 978-1-952271-99-1 (ebook)

Library of Congress Control Number: 2023010669

Cover and book design by Than Saffel / WVU Press
Cover image: *Illusions of Peace* by Tonnea Green / simplyartbynea.com

Stories in this collection appeared in slightly different form in the following
publications: "Mama Said," *riverSedge* 32, no. 1, Fall 2019; "A New World,"
Jabberwock Review, Fall 2016; "Grown Folks' Business" (originally published as
"Matching Sheets"), *Columbia Journal Online*, November 2013; "Introduction,"
Specter Magazine, no. 3, November 2011; "To Have and to Hold," *Meadowland
Review*, Fall 2010

Dedicated to my mama, Cheryl, and the Sublett family's past,
present, and future generations of mothers and mothering women

CONTENTS

MAMA SAID

The JFK Bridge links Louisville with Jeffersonville and hovers over the Ohio River, which is brown, not blue, and this has always made you sad. You have seen documentaries and news stories about pollution, watched large pipes barreling plant and factory waste into rivers, oceans, streams on TV screens at school and at home. You have seen the ways that people destroy the world around them, destroy one another, destroy themselves. It is easy to cry about this and everything else—your mother has taught you this.

Last summer at Waterfront Park with your cousin Zaria, you imagined a couple trying to create a romantic moment on the riverfront during the day with all that brown water unmasked and the face of the Colgate clock on the Indiana side dark and sullen like it knows there's nothing about Clarksville worth lighting the sky red.

"It's like dead dogs and shit floating all in the water," Zaria had said. You conjured a golden, non-descript mutt, bloated, X-eyed, drifting on the current, past the Belle of Louisville and two lovers sitting on a blanket spread on a patch of grass, sipping from wine glasses, and you laughed until your stomach cramped, and you couldn't meet Zaria's eyes without starting all over again.

Last night, after hanging up the phone on your mother and what she'd told you, you reimagined the scene, and your mother replaced the dog drifting on the river. Nothing about that scene made you want to laugh.

You were not surprised when your mother told you she's dreamt of disappearing into the Ohio. A type of vanishing is what she's been looking for all along with the sleeping, the Vicodin and OxyContin. Since you were thirteen, you have had the same nightmare about coming home, peeling back the comforter and sheet shrouding your mother, holding your breath as you check for hers and find that it has stopped. When you search for a pulse, her wrist under your thumb is still warm. You are minutes, maybe seconds, too late from saving her.

You have always known your fears are your mother's fantasies, but you've been polite enough to keep your dark thoughts to yourself.

You are starting to realize that you have no solution for your mother's depression. There is nothing you can say. Nothing you can do. You will never save her.

You don't want to believe this.

This is your whole problem.

"You can't fix her. She's got to get better on her own," Zaria has told you this a million zillion times.

You know this is true. It's the whole reason you moved to Bloomington—one hundred miles away from your mother—to attend Indiana University instead of just going right near downtown to the University of Louisville. Her sadness is extensive and destructive, a hurricane you had to escape. You think it's not fair that even when you are being selfish your mother controls your actions.

You'd gone home the break weekend, your first full weekend home since school started because you rarely got full weekends off from your job cashiering at Kroger. Your mother said the two of you would go to the movies, and you'd really been looking forward to it. You hadn't been to a movie together since you were a kid, and she used to make funny faces at you with her eyes crossed and lips poked in a duck pout, back when you weren't the one doing all the work for a smile or burst of laughter.

She slept all weekend, and when you were in your car early on Monday morning, ready to leave, and she was walking down the driveway toward you, you wished you could run her over and she wouldn't bleed or die, just know how mad you were.

She wore hospital scrub pants the gray blue of storm clouds and a faded red "Orlando" T-shirt from a family vacation seven years ago when you were eleven and she and your father were still married, but barely happily so. A small hole about an inch to the right of the tail *o* of "Orlando" exposed the side of her breast. The hair tornadoing from the top of her wrap cap ruffled in the cool breeze. Her face was dull and needed washing.

The rushing click of heels on pavement drew your attention to the next-door neighbor, Carla, who threw an absent-minded frown of curiosity before catching herself and lifting her mouth in an awkward smile, her hand in a stiff wave that only you returned.

You were embarrassed by your mother's appearance and rudeness. Carla was nice, and you'd hoped she and your mother, both middle-aged single mothers, could be friends. Carla went out some nights in red cowboy boots and made her thick, frizzy hair even thicker and frizzier with teasing and hairspray, which seemed to indicate a mildly aggressive, fuck-what-you-think sort of self-assurance that you wanted to rub off on your mother. Carla could have been someone your mother could talk to and get her excited about leaving the house, someone you could call to go and check on her when needed. You weren't sure if your mother had any friends who'd continued to stick around with all her dodging and sometimey ways.

She squinted up at the sun as if confused by it, crossed her arms, and clutched her elbows in her palms like she would break apart if she didn't hold herself together.

"I'm gonna miss you, Jay." Her shaky words fell to you.

She was crying. This is to be expected with your mother and her depression. She usually cries stoically, silently, alone. What you call her thug tears. But that day, when she finally looked down at you, she broke wide open, and there were hiccups and snot and pain blown right into your chest.

You'd wanted her to feel the disappointment you felt, but you watched your mother, folded like a love letter you've desperately wanted to read all your life, and you shut off the car and wrapped her in an awkward hug as both of you limped back into the house and settled onto the couch.

She told you she felt guilty about not being there for you, not just this weekend but during your early teenage years when she was preoccupied with the back and forth of taking pills and then trying not to take pills in rehab. She told you she wasn't currently using (you'd wondered), but she thought about it because of the depression; it had always been there.

"Always?" you asked her, recalling those goofy mother-daughter moments.

"You know, I grew up poor, country, black—dark-skinned black—and it wasn't easy. Even when I was little, sometimes it was hard to find something to be happy about. So, yeah . . ." Your mother paused and nodded, like the weight of what she was about to say and what it prophesied for her future was settling over her. Her face was somber with the accepted defeat by a formidable opponent.

"Always," she finally answered, and you felt a hopelessness

all your own creep inside. It must have bled onto your face because your mother said, "I do feel genuinely happy sometimes. *You* make me happy." She grabbed your hand. "You make me very happy . . . and proud." She smiled, sheepish and close-mouthed.

You didn't believe her. She'd had you for eighteen years and had still said "always." You thought your mother's game was weak and sloppy, but her hand was warm and squeezing yours, and her smile reached her eyes.

You told her to let go of the past. "*Now* is what matters. We're here now, together." You told her, "I'm here for you."

After everything was said, you sat quietly, uncomfortable with what you now knew until your mother was snoring beside you. She slept often, but never snored. This was reassuring. She was in a peaceful sleep. You covered her with a blanket and waited until she woke up to leave. You didn't want her to feel abandoned.

The next Friday, you surprised your mother and drove down, even though you were scheduled to work on Saturday and had a test on Monday, math, which you were failing, driving down your GPA and putting your scholarship in danger. You thought you and your mother could catch the movie you missed last weekend. When you arrived at five o'clock, she was in the bed sleep, wearing the same old T-shirt. She said she didn't feel like going anywhere and that you should have called. You left and went to Zaria's apartment.

"You can't fix her. She's got to get better on her own,"

Zaria told you for the million zillion trillionth time. "I know it's hard, but you can't sacrifice your life for hers."

Zaria understands your situation because she has her own situation with her mother Dee and Dee's crack addiction. While your mother gets ghost with sleep that stretches for days, Dee gets gone ghost, floating around West End corners, alleys, and boarded-up houses.

Zaria's words weren't revelatory, but they were true and solid, the whisper of your intuition given voice, finally louder than your fears and guilt. You nodded and said, "I know," and felt a soft, pink piece of yourself quiver with the effort of hardening.

"Mama, look." Malik, who stood hunched over the coffee table coloring with fat crayons, smacked Zaria's thigh. He pointed to his half-colored page of a smiling orange airplane that appeared to be grounded on a green nest.

"That looks good, but, baby, the sky's not green. Look." She pulled the blue crayon from the table. "Blue," she said and handed Malik the crayon. She pointed to the blank space around the plane, circling the clouds. "This is the sky, and the sky is blue."

Malik shook his head. "I don't want blue."

"Okay, it's your picture, just remember the sky is really blue. I don't want you getting your colors mixed up."

He frowned, his three-year-old face contorting into grown-man seriousness as he tried to figure things out. "This is blue?" He traced Zaria's path around the page.

"Yes. That is the sky, and the sky is blue," Zaria repeated.

He sighed heavily, exactly the way he'd no doubt heard Zaria sigh many times, before returning to the picture to scratch blue on top of the green, around the orange airplane, through the clouds.

"Mama, look," he finally said and stepped back to show her what he'd done, how he'd painted the sky for her.

Zaria gasped in exaggerated awe. "That is perfect! A masterpiece!" she exclaimed, and Malik beamed in the wake of her smile.

Melissa's mother, Beverly, had a heart attack.

No one saw it coming.

Even if your mother doesn't jump, you will see death approaching her from miles away. Zaria expects every phone call to be a strange white person telling her that Dee has overdosed. These alone are reasons not to touch Melissa, to keep your arms folded around your own chest, reasons to hate her, but you have more.

Zaria had Malik when she was sixteen. Dee was somewhere getting high while Zaria was pushing him out. Zaria is already a statistic, but you will not let her join the ranks of teen mothers who've done something tragic and/or stupid because they felt overwhelmed and trapped in motherhood.

Zaria works part-time at UPS and attends Jefferson Community College full time, making steady progress toward her associate's degree in social work. You are always watching her for signs of mama burnout. This summer when you weren't working, you took Malik to the park, out for lunch, to spend the night with you at your father's house. Zaria hasn't been on many dates since Malik was born, which is probably a good thing since a shiny car and wavy hair still turn her head, but you push her to go to Applebee's with friends, out to the movies. You tell her to wear a tight dress and go to clubs so she can dance and feel bass pumping in her stomach. You don't want her to forget herself.

Sometimes you think you understand those teen mothers who've done the tragic and/or stupid things. You are nobody's mother; nonetheless, sometimes you still feel trapped. You feel a recklessness burrowing to your core.

The Monday after the disappointing visit with your mother, you left math class feeling dazed and dumb. You didn't have the official confirmation yet but knew that you'd failed the test.

On Wednesday, your mother called while you were at the math study group you joined on Monday. You didn't want to answer, but she rarely calls you. She was crying. Another problem you couldn't solve. Exhaustion swept into your bones, but you remembered what you'd told her ("I'm here for you"), the way her smile reached her eyes when she'd told you you make her happy. You told everyone you were going downstairs to the lobby to take the call. They said they were getting hungry and taking the studying to Mama Bear's for some pizza. You stayed behind.

You remember Beverly from move-in day. She had a blond bob and was dressed for function in a breezy beige linen dress with thick-soled hiking sandals, in contrast to your mother, who wore jeans on an eighty-five-degree day because she thinks her legs are too fat and cursed as soon as she walked into the dorm room's stifling heat.

"Unh unh. I'll be back." She dropped the shopping bags full of the new bedding she'd bought for you, and her flip-flops, obnoxious with Coach *C* logos on the footpad, slapped the linoleum tile as she walked away.

You and Zaria stood just inside the doorway. The baking room grumble-hummed with the efforts of the old air conditioner perched in the window, struggling to make a difference. Melissa leaped from the bare mattress of the twin bed she'd claimed for her own.

"Oh my god! Which one of you is JayLynn?" Heat marked her face with the tender pink flush of a double-cheek smack, and her blue eyes zipped between you and Zaria, who exchanged a look with you because Melissa was legit bouncing, on her toes. Zaria smirked as you hesitantly revealed yourself.

"I'm so happy you're here. I thought something had happened to you. I was hoping we could go to the induction together and grab lunch before," Melissa said, "but I gotta eat something now. Where's your purse, Mom?"

"Check under some bags. It's here somewhere," Beverly tossed the words to Melissa before turning to you. "Are you excited?" Her grin was all teeth and a little disarming. It seemed to push: *be excited!*

"Yeah," you replied and smiled a shaky smile before crossing the room to sit your bags on the other bare bed.

"I'm starving," Melissa groaned.

"You are not starving," Beverly corrected her. "You ate breakfast."

"Yeah, *hours* ago." Melissa hunched over, pawing around pink and purple plastic storage bins and white garbage bags. Her denim shorts dug into her thighs, and you predicted that she would struggle with the freshman fifteen.

Beverly rolled her eyes, and you liked her a little for that. Zaria dropped the box she was carrying by your feet.

"Are you her sister?" Beverly asked her.

"Big cousin," Zaria clarified.

"Are you a student here too?"

"No, I attend JCC in Louisville."

"Oh." Some of the chirp in Beverly's voice died, some expectation zapped. "But you can still help her navigate the transition to college. Living on campus is one part—a big one—but there's also adjusting to classes, syllabi, the different professors, maintaining a schedule." Her voice rose in singsong as she listed the adjustments, casting her words to Melissa, who was preoccupied with the triumph of finding Beverly's purse, a brown, hardware- and logo-free, leather sack bearing a hard-worn patina, from which Melissa pulled granola bars and a large freezer bag full of grapes after plopping back on the bed.

"Y'all want some?" she offered.

You and Zaria declined. The grapes were bright green and jewel shiny. You weren't hungry, but you wanted to squirrel handfuls of them into your mouth until your cheeks puffed. You felt like the Trix rabbit or Hamburglar or some other pitiful character whose hunger was always being taunted by something they couldn't have. Your mother had stopped at McDonald's for breakfast before heading to Bloomington late, setting out at eight-thirty for a two-hour drive that made you late for the ten o'clock check-in, and she had not bothered to pack snacks.

Melissa shrugged and ripped a granola bar's packaging open with her teeth. "My period must be coming. I just wanna eat everything. God, I'm glad it didn't come today. Trying to move all this crap in the heat, and I'm all bleeding and bloating and gross?"

"Melissa, Jesus." Beverly frowned. "Nobody wants to think about that."

"She's a girl, Mom. It's not like she doesn't know what I'm talking about. Plus, we're roomies. We're gonna know *so* much about each other after this year." She grinned at you.

Zaria raised an eyebrow that said, *This white girl is gonna be something.*

Beverly and Melissa volunteered to help you and Zaria bring in the rest of your things. You found your mother in the car sipping a can of vending machine Coke, blasting the air conditioning, and listening to the radio. James Taylor sang over a folksy guitar.

"It's just so hot," she whined through the open window.

"Yeah, Mama, it's August," you said.

She didn't register your sarcasm.

"I thought I was going to pass out." She sighed, laid her head back on the seat, and closed her eyes, which prevented her from seeing you roll yours.

You were tired of her being so weak, always run down and worn out when you needed her.

She opened her eyes slowly, as if coming to. "I'll be ready in a minute."

"Beverly and Melissa are helping me," you said in hopes of hurting her feelings, letting her know that you would be fine without her. Beverly, Melissa, and Zaria were pulling your belongings from the trunk. Beverly dragged a turquoise plastic storage container identical to Melissa's past the car's driver's side and called to your mother, "Don't you worry about it. We've got it. You cool off." Her calves were tight with muscle.

"Roomies help roomies, no problem," Melissa said. She hugged pillows to her chest and marched behind Beverly.

Zaria shook her head at Melissa and followed with more boxes.

"Well, they seem nice," your mother said. "You want to come in and sit with me for a minute?" She patted the passenger seat and smiled, but her eyes held a seconds-away-from-crying gloss. You didn't want your mother's tears here, even though you understood that most of those tears were for you. They said, *I'm proud of you. I love you.* But you also knew some of those tears were for her because you were leaving her, maybe because she was lonely, possibly because the tears were for reasons that you and no one else would ever understand.

"I gotta get going," you said. "I'm already late."

You carried all the tears your mother had ever cried, the words she didn't say, with the rest of your stuff.

You turned eighteen last month in October. You are an official adult, but you don't think you have spent enough time as a child. Too much of your life has been spent mothering your own mother. Making her meals of chili dogs, just-add-water pancakes, and Hamburger Helper that she sometimes ate and sometimes didn't. Telling her to brush her teeth, take a shower, put on clean clothes. You are so tired of all that and so scared not to be doing it.

The day you met Melissa, she told you Beverly was her best friend. She said she and her mother had always been close. Some nights they had mother-daughter slumber parties, and they stayed up late watching romantic comedies, talking, and laughing over brownies and popcorn. You wanted to end the conversation here, but Melissa kept talking and explained that she never realized her mother was her best friend, the one she could really trust and tell anything until recently. Her former best friend, Caitlin, slept with her ex-boyfriend, Jason, the night they all graduated high school.

"They were at a party that I didn't go to because my nana and uncle were in from out of town. She said they were drunk and it 'just happened.'" Melissa made air quotes with her fingers. "But I didn't buy it. I always thought they were too close and jokey-jokey, so I called her out on her bullshit and we stopped talking. I kind of thought we would be friends again after I calmed down. I mean, I've done some stupid things when I was drunk too, you know?" She paused like she was waiting for you to ask what so you could trade stories, but you don't.

You don't have the kind of stories she's looking for. You don't like to drink and have never been drunk before. You don't like the idea of losing control of yourself, even if you thought you could afford to do so. You're afraid you're genetically prone to addiction. You are not about to tell Melissa this or that you lost your virginity at fourteen because you wanted to see if your mother would notice, worry, wake up. You only agreed to walk to the student union with her to get some pizza. You didn't ask to hear any of the shit she told you. All you did was be the fool and take the bait and ask, "Who?" when Melissa was like, "I hope I don't see that bitch." And then she started telling you about Caitlin and how she was attending IU too, and they'd planned to be roommates before that fateful night.

"Next thing I know, I'm at Sonic one day and here they

come walking out together with some slushies or milk-shakes or whatever, and they're trading cups and sipping and tasting and that's how I know Caitlin's a liar. What happened between her and Jason wasn't '*accidental*.'

"I couldn't believe it. When I was little, Mom was always telling me, 'Be nice to other people, and they'll be nice to you.' And I kept telling her, 'You lied, Mom. You lied.'"

Beverly's words via Melissa's mouth caught your attention. Your mother had never told you anything like that. As a poor black girl in rural Kentucky, your mother learned from her mother not to suppose much from the world; she never expected anyone to be nice to her no matter what she did.

"I feel awful for that now because Mom is an angel. She brought me food when I didn't want to eat. Lay in the bed with me while I cried and cried. It was horrible. I wasn't even gonna come here, but they have one of the best under-graduate business programs, and she told me if I was going to succeed in business and in life, I had to get tougher, stronger, and not let people keep me from my dreams. She's really helped get me through. I mean, I'm still on Zoloft, but it's not that bad," she lied.

Melissa showed you her schedule so that you could "link up"—her words, not yours—in the gaps for lunch, studying in the library, or "whatever"—another one of her words. She had classes Monday through Friday, but by October, she was only going to class once, maybe twice, a week.

Around mid-September, she ran into Caitlin at Burger King in the union, and Caitlin was wearing Jason's necklace.

"It's just a cross necklace, but I *know* that necklace. That's how close I was; we almost bumped into each other. She didn't even say excuse me and had the nerve to look at me like *I'd* done something to *her*."

You felt bad for Melissa. In the pauses between her words, you tossed her clichés about other fish in the sea and lying down with dogs and waking up with fleas, but when these didn't seem to work, you backed up quickly from Melissa and her situation and maintained your distance. Even when you were grabbing meals for yourself at the union, you refused to bring her food so she could stay in the bed and sleep.

Melissa called Beverly every day at nine-thirty on Beverly's first break at the post office, right as you were heading out for your first class on Monday, Wednesday, Friday and as you were going to shower on Tuesday and Thursday. You are sure that Melissa talked about you like a dog when you were gone, that she told Beverly you were standoffish, rude, selfish, mean, possibly a bitch.

But it is necessary for you to be all these things. You care. You are not inhumane, but your actions are bigger than Melissa. She is practice, strength training. You have learned how to close the door on her crying when you leave—for work, the library, dinner with other friends—without looking back.

—

Despite Melissa's worsening condition, from what you can gather, Beverly didn't urge Melissa to come back home. In a tinny voice from the receiver of Melissa's cell phone, you heard Beverly encourage Melissa to see a counselor on campus, go to the doctor and ask about increasing her dosage of Zoloft.

"You've gotta be stronger, honey," Beverly said, the words sore-tender like she knew they wouldn't work even as she spoke them.

You hope Beverly is resting in peace.

Yesterday, when your mother told you about wanting to jump, before hanging up on her, you'd asked, "Why'd you tell me that?"

"I don't have anybody else to talk to." Here your mother's voice quivered and she began to cry, but when she'd told you about jumping, her words had been solid. Stones.

"Well, you need to get somebody else. I'm your fucking daughter. I don't want to hear that shit."

This was the first time you'd cursed to your mother. As soon as the words hit your ear, proof that you'd birthed them, something inside of you broke. But this break reinforced rather than weakened, like the sway needed to keep bridges standing.

You are terrified of heights and can't swim, so the gentle roll you swear you feel when you're in the car, in the middle of a bridge, trapped in traffic, snatches your heart, squeezes your lungs, blurs the world like a movie fade-out. Sweat prickles under your armpits, and you tell yourself, *This is what makes it work. This is what keeps it from falling.*

Now, Melissa cries and you watch.

"Oh my god! I can't do this. I can't be here without her. Oh my god!" she wails.

You are looking at Melissa and seeing your mother, forever fragile and pulling at you even when her arms aren't outstretched.

You want Melissa to learn the truth. People aren't always nice. The world is rough. It requires tough skin and sharp teeth.

You are on your way to math class. So many students bombed the last test that the professor has agreed to give the exam again today and drop the lowest grade.

You tell Melissa you are sorry, you have to go.

You are shaking by the time you reach the classroom. When you see your professor, you break down in tears and tell her your mother has died. She gasps and walks you and your tragedy to the hallway so you won't distract the other students. She hugs you. You sob and smell the soapy scent of her shampoo as she tells you not to worry about the test, the class. You can reschedule. Take care of yourself.

Your words are not true, but your tears are. You can only use this excuse once, you know, and cough up a whole new round of tears thinking about your mother jumping, having to explain yourself to this professor hugging you like you're her daughter. It's hard for you to gather yourself, but you eventually do. You stop at the bathroom and rinse your face, breathe. In. Out.

When you return to the room, Melissa is still crying. You sit beside her, give her your shoulder, and lie about how everything is going to be okay.

When you were in third grade, a white boy named David, who stood behind you in line, started pulling on your plaits. You told your mother about David and how he was a stupid bully who had a brown front tooth and shoes that were beat-up and gray when they should have been white. Your mother sighed and said, "You never know what other people are going through."

She's told you this many times since then. These are your mother's sage words for navigating this life, her way of telling you to be merciful, her way of telling you to forgive people for all the harm they would do to you.

A NEW WORLD

Parker stares at his niece Zaria's stomach, covered by a stretched-out white tank top. Her belly is a dingy full moon creeping on the horizon of the kitchen table. She carries a whole new person, a whole new world. Zaria, sixteen, sits with Parker's daughter, JayLynn, who is fifteen and wears a new hickey on her neck. It's smaller than the last one, which was actually two, neighboring islands that were fading by the time Parker saw them. The new one is the size and shape of a fingerprint. It glows red like the legs of the woman in the champagne glass on the sign for that strip joint on Seventh Street when you pass it at night. Parker can't remember the club's name. It's next door to a liquor store that's next to another strip joint. And there's another one a little ways down. They go on and on down Seventh Street, heading away from Churchill Downs. The legs of the woman in the sign spill over the glass's rim. One stretches out, kicking the dark.

The hickey demands Parker's eyes when they're not on Zaria's belly or the sad dinner and dessert he packs in saved, doubled-up plastic bags from Kroger. He's eager to streak out of the house and get to his job at Louisville Gas & Electric, someplace where he can make things work. He's a stationary engineer and runs the boilers that create the steam that turn the generators and bring light and warmth to people's homes. On his lunch break this evening, he will eat the canned beans and franks, the package of bright orange cheese crackers with pasty peanut butter, and a roll of lemon crème cookies while he jokes and complains about wives along with Jim and Terry like he's still got one.

Claudia called him last month after seeing the first hickey(s), like it was his fault, asking him what the hell he was doing over there. *Over there*, like the house and life she'd lived with him was far, far away. He hates this and his understanding of that sense of distance from places and people once known, hates that his wedding ring is coupled with dropped pennies, a fallen button, and other junk stored in the top drawer of his nightstand for unlikely repairs and reuse. Once Claudia finished yelling, Parker told her he'd never let any boys come over and hadn't seen any hickeys, but he figured JayLynn's boyfriend was who had marked her up. He's never met him, but he knows his name. Michael is always popping up in JayLynn's conversations with Zaria. She swirls his name in pink and purple ink on notebook paper. Parker didn't tell Claudia that as much as she sleeps, the boy could have walked right into her apartment. He and JayLynn could have snuggled up in her bed and watched a whole movie before they started kissing and Parker doesn't want to know what else. Part of him itched to say this, but the much bigger part didn't want to fight or hurt Claudia and suggested dinner as a solution. She'd come over, he'd cook, and they'd sit down together to eat and talk to JayLynn.

"She's already having sex, Parker." Claudia sighed. "I'm taking her to the doctor next week to put her on birth control." After that, Parker said nothing he remembers, nothing coherent or helpful before Claudia hung up. He appeared as dumb and naive as she believes him to be, someone who couldn't save anyone from anything.

The girls are talking about ways to induce labor. Zaria's due date was July 17, nine days ago.

JayLynn runs her finger down a page of the library copy of *What to Expect When You're Expecting* spread open on the table. "We can take a walk," she suggests before crunching into a slice of her frozen pizza.

Parker cracks ice from a tray and drops the cubes into his extra-large thermos. He doesn't jump in to ask if the girls intend to take this walk soon or what they plan to do if their efforts are successful since he's about to leave and there's no telling what street Zaria's mother, Dee, has lost herself on chasing today's highs. Dee and Claudia, sisters,

spend their days disappearing, each in their own spectac-
ularly common ways. If Claudia is home from work when
Zaria's contractions begin, she will most likely be buried in
her bed covers and won't answer the phone. She might even
have the ringer off. Parker doesn't know much about the
baby's father, Travis, but from listening to the girls' conversations, he's learned that the boy has pretty hair that Zaria
wants for the baby, but no car.

Zaria groans and slumps in her chair. "I'm tired and it's
hot. I just walked from the bus stop to get here. Does the
book say anything about taking a nap to induce labor?"

"You know it doesn't, but the way you snore could probably get him out of there. I'm surprised he hasn't already
pushed his way out. The last time you slept over I swear I
wanted to punch you. Matter fact, I hit you on the arm and
you still didn't wake up."

"Leave me alone, I'm pregnant." Zaria rises to reach for
the family-size bag of Cool Ranch Doritos she brought
with her. Half of her arm is lost as she digs for a chip.

The girls' hunger is relentless. They are always eating—
fat dill pickles that smell up whole rooms, bags of barbecue
Grippo's potato chips, fish platters with lots of fried batter
crunchies from Long John Silver's (where Travis works),
and frozen pizza. Parker is forever buying frozen pizza.
Sometimes it seems he's spent his whole life carting the flat
red boxes from his truck to the house, as if Claudia and her
fried pork chops and greens were only a vivid, delicious
mirage. When he looks at the girls, he feels like he's stepped

into a carnival of mirrors. Claudia and Dee ghost on their daughters' faces. They roam in their eyes and mouths, in the tiny moles marking their cheekbones. Crack has hollowed Dee, snatched her few meaty parts. If Parker didn't know about the baby and how the world works, he could believe that Zaria's rounder cheeks and chin, her swollen breasts, and all that belly are the stolen pieces of Dee. He can imagine Zaria picking up the trashed chunks and patting her mother onto herself like makeup, rubbing her in like lotion.

He is thankful JayLynn doesn't have her mother's body. Claudia in a pair of red shorts—the cocoa-butter sheen of her coffee skin stretched tight over the just right muscle-to-fat ratio of her thighs—led him out of his booth at Blue's restaurant and away from his plate of the best fried chicken he's ever eaten. JayLynn is skinny, a straight line with no brake-smashing bumps, but today it seems she's doing her best to show what she's got in lace-trimmed, blue-jean shorts so short he's grateful for the strip of extra material the lace provides even though it reminds him of nighties and bedroom whispers. Her hair is pulled up in a bun on top of her head, as if she's showcasing the hickey right along with the tiny gold-plated Nike earrings she begged him for last Christmas. He regrets buying them and supporting the company's slogan to *Just do it*.

The Wednesday before last, JayLynn left her new birth control pills on the bathroom counter. Parker thought she'd be back the next day to get them, but every morning he's been brushing his teeth glaring at the butter-colored plastic compact. He thought that when JayLynn came over yesterday afternoon that would be the end of that, but this morning he scrubbed his mouth into a slobbery white foam and spat staring at the compact. He imagined its pale yellow spread on nursery walls and crib bedding. He opened the compact to find the "THU" pill still nestled in its slot.

"It is Fri-day!" the DJ on the radio announces as Parker fills his thermos with tap water. Some of the cubes snap and split clear bolts of lightning on the inside when the water hits them. "TGIF am I right, y'all?" JayLynn's boombox, perched on the kitchen counter, is always playing some song about sex or love or both, reminding Parker of all he's lost. When the girls sing Mary J. Blige's "Not Gonna Cry," they begin quietly, but by the time they reach the song's climax about no guarantees in love and not getting the part about being left, the words are rising from their guts, their eyes are shut tight, and they belt that song like women who have been married to lying sons-of-bitches for years and years. JayLynn can carry a tune, but Zaria has the worst voice Parker has ever heard. He thinks she must be tone deaf. It's painful to hear her cracking love songs into pieces.

When the DJ fades into the music, Parker recognizes the intro of Bone Thugs-N-Harmony's "Tha Crossroads." He's no more relieved to hear this than whatever song would have the girls singing about shaking butts or broken hearts. When the synthesizer zigzags the intro, the girls don't gasp and jump to turn up the volume. "Tha Crossroads" is the only video that plays when they watch The Box. Over and over, the Bone Thugs walk down streets with friends who vanish before their eyes, lost to another world. The song plays on B96.5 (the only radio station JayLynn and Zaria will listen to) at least once an hour, making every day funereal. The girls are getting over the hype, but they sing along. Even half-heartedly and without knowing most of the words, they get the haunting sentiment of loss and vulnerability just right.

Claudia moved out in November, two months after she left rehab. Clean of the Vicodin, she said to Parker, "This isn't working," and Parker thought it was just the depression talking. The words weren't backed with the passion he thought someone would have if they were really planning to get a divorce. Yet, she got a job at the plasma center downtown, packed, left, and Parker thought it could be a good thing, that more physical space could help Claudia work out whatever was going on in her head. He now knows that was stupid. As if she actually needed to wrestle her demons, launch into a tornado of fists, elbows, and feet rumbling through room after room. As if she had a better chance of winning without him jumping in and helping her fight.

He stayed in the house, in the Shively suburbs, surrounded by homes decorated with leftover Halloween pumpkins whose carved smiles melted to rot. For Christmas, he bought a real tree like he always did, and he and JayLynn filled it with the ornaments he pulled from the basement. When he came home from work, he vacuumed the fallen needles and watched his neighbors' candy-colored lights blinking out of synch in the cold black.

Claudia and JayLynn moved to an apartment in the Highlands, just off Bardstown Road with its stretch of cafés, bookstores, and vintage boutiques roamed by punk rock white boys who look like whips of black licorice, white girls with pink hair, black girls wearing blue lipstick. The shops sell "Keep Louisville Weird" bumper stickers to remind the outsiders and outcasts to stand proud and firm.

Claudia hired a divorce attorney in February and Parker followed suit. He signed the papers without a fight, as if he'd never loved her, because he loves her so much. He wants her to be happy, but when he asks JayLynn for updates, he finds that nothing's getting better. He knows Claudia's embarrassed about stealing pills from the hospital and regrets losing her nursing license. He likes to imagine she misses him.

When he came home from the grocery store yesterday to find JayLynn on the couch, she reported, "She's still depressed," in a bored monotone before he could even greet her or ask about Claudia. JayLynn used *What to Expect When You're Expecting*, resting on her lap, as a makeshift table as she painted her fingernails in steady black stripes.

"Somebody drop you off?"

"No. TARC."

"I told you I don't like you catching the bus. I could have picked you up. I was just out." He walked to the kitchen, set the bags on the table, and began putting the frozen pizza, milk, and eggs into the refrigerator.

"I can ride the TARC, Daddy, it's fine," JayLynn called to him. "I'm not a baby. Plus, I told you I don't want you coming to get me anymore because you can't ever just honk the horn and wait. You always gotta knock and come in and peek around and knock again at Mama's door and beg her to talk or get coffee, and it only makes things worse. Plus, asking her to get coffee is lame anyway because neither one of y'all drink it, and the whole thing is just sad."

Parker left the rest of the groceries on the table and went back into the living room so JayLynn could see him when he said, "It's not sad; it's love. I love your mother," but she was wiping a black smudge from her pinky with a neatly folded pad of toilet paper.

She spoke while looking down at her hands. "I know, but she don't want all that. Plus, it ain't helping her and you're playing yourself, doing all this loving for somebody who ain't trying to love you back."

Parker has heard JayLynn throwing her two cents to Zaria about running back to Travis after he's spent days ignoring her calls and pages. She says, "Wouldn't be me. You a good one." All this tough love disappears when they're talking about Dee. "She'll be back," JayLynn says when Zaria tells her how many nights Dee has been gone. "It's the drugs, it's not her," she said when Zaria told her Dee found the money Travis gave her to buy baby stuff. She forgives their mothers for all trespasses. When she visits Parker, she never stays longer than two nights before returning to the apartment to check on her mother. Parker is sure Jay-Lynn likes Michael and wears all that greasy-looking, strawberry-scented lip gloss for him. She probably thinks she loves him, but she doesn't love him enough to go running across town just to be there while he sleeps, not enough to do things she said she would never do.

The word "sex" from JayLynn's mouth sends a tremor through Parker's hand. Some of the water in the ice trays he's refilled splashes onto the floor.

"Shit," he curses so softly the girls don't notice.

"It's too hot to do it," Zaria whines.

Parker sets the trays in the freezer and goes to grab a paper towel.

"Look, it's summer, it's hot, get over it. I'm sure they got air conditioning at Travis's house. I don't think you have to do it for that long," JayLynn says.

"The book says you're supposed to have an orgasm to get your muscles contracting and stuff and that would probably take a *looo*ng time. You know Travis be like . . ." Zaria rat-a-tat-tats on the table with her fist, and the girls burst into laughter. Parker winces at the knowing tinkling in the notes that float from JayLynn. "The doctor said the man's thing doesn't hit the baby's head, but I don't see how it doesn't, especially now. The baby's probably, like, right down there, all ready, and I don't want him traumatized with Travis beating on his head, denting it all up. Plus, I ain't even feeling

Travis like that right now. I told you, Cindy said she saw him walking down Broadway with some light-skinned girl the other day."

Parker wipes the floor and wonders when the idea of his daughter having sex won't startle him so much, though he's already grown more accustomed to it than he'd like. The girls' conversations around him have gotten increasingly frank. With Zaria's pregnancy and JayLynn's birth control pills, he guesses they figure there's nothing left to hide; they've laid their cards flat. Bluntness has risen in JayLynn like a fever.

Last night, she was curled on the couch with her knees nearly tucked under her chin, gazing at the TV in a blank way that made Parker's stomach turn. When he asked her if something was wrong, she told him, "Cramps. I'm bleeding in clumps," without taking her eyes off the TV.

"Jay," he'd groaned before he could stop himself.

She laughed. "I know. It's gross."

He feels bad about that groan, the chastisement. He acted like a boy. He should have handled the situation better, been comforting like she was when she looked up at him, said, "I took some Pamprin. I'll be alright," and gave him a quick, close-mouthed smile before turning back to the TV. She drops this token of reassurance that she's not her mother and only gets a normal kind of sad when he catches her contemplating things he can't see in the tumble of boiling water as she prods a block of Ramen noodles with a fork or lying on her bed staring into a book. Claudia used to lock their bedroom door, and Parker had to open it with a bent bobby pin, but JayLynn always keeps her door wide open. He can walk right in. He knows he should be happy about this. She wants to talk the darkness away so it won't catch them too. She wants to know that they're okay, but they're not, and he doesn't know what to say about that.

Now, he drops the paper towel in the garbage and watches JayLynn's black fingernails flash as they flip through the book's pages. She's the one who checked the book out from the library. She reminds Zaria to take her prenatal vitamins. She wouldn't just forget to take her birth control pills, not with Zaria big and pregnant, the baby any minute away. The abandoned pills are another card face up, plans being announced.

The baby JayLynn's trying to have is for Claudia. It's a last-ditch-effort baby, a poked-hole-in-the-condom-when-he-left-the-room baby, what Parker and his friends used to call a Jesus baby—a baby that will fix all the problems, save the world. This phrase was coined before any of them had kids, when they could laugh at somebody else who had gotten the wrong girl pregnant, when losing a woman didn't turn them into piles of shards. Parker has only seen one successful Jesus baby.

When his friend Buggie's girlfriend, Theresa, came up pregnant, everybody but Buggie knew what that was all about. They humored him when he bragged about his super sperm busting through the fortress built by years of birth control pills. Theresa was a decent girl, so nobody said anything. She was good for Buggie, too good for him really. No one knew why she'd want to stick around with him, but she gave him a son that straightened his wandering eye and made it see all her magic. They're still married, both happily, it seems.

Sometimes Parker thinks if he could do it all again, he would flush Claudia's pain pills down the toilet, get in her face and yell instead of convincing himself she knows what she's doing. He wishes he hadn't loved Claudia like a puppy, all pant and rollover. Sometimes when he can't stand the open space in his bed and spreads himself wide to fill it, he feels all his regrets buzzing neon yellow.

But he keeps doing stupid shit. Keeps walking past those birth control pills and not saying anything. He could live with the discomfort of knowing he's still the same coward, but he knows he's worse than that.

He has imagined the child JayLynn could have. Claudia will blame him. Even if he doesn't tell her about the pills on the sink (and he never will), she will make the baby his fault. He will deny, defend, and take all her insults like bullets. He will accept their lodge deep inside of his white meat. Claudia's anger will fade like a headache when she sees the girl with JayLynn's baby face—big, glossy eyes and dimples poked into cheeks.

JayLynn had a grown woman's belly laugh at eight

months. She would laugh so hard at Claudia peek-a-booing at her that she would sigh, slumping back sideways into her swing with a crooked grin on her face, catching her breath after the surprise of her mama returning to her world. Claudia loved this, couldn't get enough of it. She would always call him to watch, and he never got tired of hearing her and JayLynn's laughter jumbled up and spilling out.

Parker has dreamt about him and Claudia together as grandparents, showing JayLynn how to change a diaper, helping her bathe the baby in the sink. He's seen Claudia rocking from side-to-side, gathering calm from the warm, milky smell of the baby's crown. He's given the baby Jay-Lynn's laugh. He's heard Claudia calling to him, seen her playing peek-a-boo and laughing so hard she's unable to steady herself for another disappearance.

"Come out, come out, little one!" JayLynn is bent down speaking into Zaria's stomach. Her mouth nearly touches the small knob of Zaria's belly button. "You're gonna be so cute and fat and squishy, and I'm gonna eat you all up."

Zaria puts two fingers to JayLynn's forehead and pushes softly, slowly, nudging her backward. "That's probably why he's staying in there. Back up, weirdo."

JayLynn turns back to her plate and takes another bite of pizza. "But he's gonna be so *cute*!" she squeals through her mouthful.

"Alright, girls. I'm gone." Parker grabs his lunch and thermos. "Call me if you need me." He plants a kiss on each girl's forehead. When JayLynn raises her head for him, he gets a closer look at that damn hickey.

"I just wish you were having a girl," Parker hears her tell Zaria as he walks to the front door.

"I know. Me, too."

"*I'm* having a girl."

"You get what you get," Zaria says.

"Well, I'm getting a girl."

"Alright."

"I'm serious. You have to do it in the missionary position right after your period every day until four days before you ovulate and eat a lot of—"

Parker closes the door. He will talk to JayLynn as soon as Zaria leaves. He will figure out what to say.

JayLynn calls Parker at ten, an hour before his shift ends, to tell him Zaria's having contractions, they called Dee, and now they're at the hospital. He's surprised that Dee was at home and more surprised to see her at the hospital when he arrives. She looks worse than he remembers. He saw her just a couple weeks ago when she dropped Zaria off, but her deterioration is like a stunning beauty that slaps like new every time. Even her hair—brushed into a stiff, dry ponytail—is skinny.

Dee cocks an eyebrow. "What you doing here? They said it's okay for Jay to go to the delivery room when it's time, though I don't know why she wants to. Ain't nothing pretty gonna happen in there."

Parker doesn't tell her he's come to see how things play out because the baby already seems to be working miracles. "Support." He shrugs. "I was up anyway. Just got off work."

Dee smiles, showing her rotting teeth. "That's real nice."

Parker wants her to close her mouth. It's hard to look at her.

"The doctor said she's got a while to go. She's still dilating and worrying my nerves, about to drive me crazy. Travis ain't even up here. We been calling and calling. His mama said he ain't home, and she don't know where he is. Ain't that something?"

Parker wags his head in a that's-a-shame shake.

"Come on down here with me. I told this girl I was gonna get her a Popsicle." Dee starts scooting down the hall and Parker walks beside her. "You're a good man," she says, smiling again. "Claudia's stupid."

After they reach the nurse's station, Dee asks one of the three nurses for a Popsicle and turns to Parker. "She just did this because she hates me."

"Claudia?"

"No, Zaria."

For a second Parker thought Dee had answers about his marriage that he didn't. He manages to climb out of that disappointment to offer her reassurance. "That's not true," he says.

"She thinks it's gonna be easy. Like it's a doll."

"Naw." Parker shakes his head and chuckles. "It ain't easy."

"That's what I try to tell her. She thinks I don't know nothing. *Nothing*. All that kid stuff is out the window."

"Sure is."

The nurse returns with a Popsicle and hands it to Dee, who holds it out to Parker. "Give this to her. I need to go get something to eat. The chips from the vending machine ain't cutting it."

Parker doesn't move. "I can pick you up something to eat." He stares into her eyes and sees the itch crawling all over her.

"Naw, I got it. I'ma be back."

"Dee . . ." He's never spoken to her about the drugs before; it's never been his business.

"I'm coming right back. She ain't even ready yet." She sets the Popsicle on the counter and turns to leave.

Parker grabs her wrist and speaks quietly, "Stay." This word is a plea, and he hates the way it sounds, the way he always sounds—nice, understanding. But he doesn't understand. Nothing makes sense. "You are killing yourself." As he says the word "killing," he feels the tight scrunch of his face, the rise of his top lip and nose. The face has to contort into a snarl, teeth have to be bared, to speak it clearly, to emphasize it. He needs her to get it. "*Killing* yourself," he repeats, "and that shit's not worth it." His eyes are locked with hers, but she breaks the connection to flash squinted eyes down to his hand wrapped around her as if trying to make sure what she's seeing is real.

"Nigga, you crazy? Get the fuck off me."

"Don't—"

"Get the fuck off me!" Dee's raised voice gets the nurses' attention.

"Is there a problem?" The redheaded nurse reluctantly rises from her chair. She looks young and afraid but prepared to handle the situation.

Embarrassed, Parker releases Dee. He watches as she stomps away in her beat-up shower shoes, cursing to herself, and disappears through the double doors. The nurse's chair creaks as she sits back down.

JayLynn pokes her head out of Zaria's room. When she sees Parker and no Dee, she looks confused and hurries down the hall. "What happened? Where's Dee?"

"She left," Parker says.

"Just now?" Her eyes dart in the direction of the double doors.

"She's not going to stay," Parker says to keep her from bolting down the hall.

"What'd you say?"

"I asked her to stay."

"But is that what you *said*? 'Stay'? Was she just about to leave and that's when you came?"

"I said she's not going to stay. Let her go."

"Don't get mad. I'm just saying, you're not the best person for persuading people." She sighs. "You're right, though. She was probably gonna go anyway. Zaria's gonna be so hurt."

"That baby wasn't ever going to make her stay."

"But you would think she'd be thinking about being there for Zaria and seeing her first grandbaby being born."

"Dee needs help."

JayLynn nods slowly and looks grave. "Yeah."

"A baby's not going to help your mama, either."

JayLynn's eyes flash to the nurses before she whispers, "Dee's a crackhead. Mama's not taking those pills anymore; she's just depressed. It's different."

Parker's not surprised that JayLynn doesn't deny her plan, she's hidden nothing, but he's startled by her conviction that the plan is reasonable.

"Your mama's an addict, just like Dee." He hates admitting this, but knows he needs to speak the words for himself as much as for JayLynn. "Just because she went to rehab doesn't mean her problems with drugs are all over. It's not that simple. And depression is a serious illness. It's more than being sad, Jay."

JayLynn rolls her eyes. "I know that."

"Well, act like you know the next time you want to jump in bed with your boyfriend without taking your birth control." The words come out harsher than Parker intends, but he adds nothing soothing.

JayLynn swipes the Popsicle off the counter. "I gotta take this to Zaria."

"Do you hear what I'm saying?" Parker asks.

"Yeah," JayLynn mumbles and glares at the floor.

"Do you *hear* me?" Parker leans forward and bends down so her gaze falls on his eyes staring up at her.

She wipes the tear sliding down her cheek with the heel of her hand not holding the Popsicle. "Yes, god." She rolls her eyes again. "This is melting." She raises the Popsicle.

He feels the jarring smack of déjà vu as he watches her walk away.

Zaria snores loudly over the juicer infomercial playing at whisper volume on the TV mounted in the corner of the room. Parker watches JayLynn staring down at Malik in his hospital bassinet. Parker's so tired, his eyes are burning like the room is full of smoke. He appreciates the way this helps to nearly blur JayLynn's hickey into nonexistence, but he wants to go home and sleep. Before sleep, he wants a shower. He needs the clean slate, the fresh start. He wants to wash last night. All his hope has gone foul and embarrassing, like his breath.

He called Claudia last night.

He was relieved when Zaria turned down his offer to stay in the delivery room because it would be too weird, but he thought she should have somebody other than JayLynn, who wouldn't be prepared for the shit, the blood, and all those other intimate and uncomfortable smells. More than this, he was lonely and missed Claudia, and it was dark and he wanted to follow the day's opportunity to the end of its unraveling. The phone rang and rang. Claudia must have heard it. He told himself that was it, the last time, but watching the sun rise, dousing the city with light, made him itch. Every day spins a new world of possibility; that spool of thin thread seems to have no end. There is always another day, another hour, another minute when he thinks, *Maybe now. Maybe today.*

But right now, he sits in a new day stinking with yesterday, and JayLynn doesn't want to leave while Zaria is asleep. He is tired of everything being his problem. He doesn't want this for JayLynn even though she seems intent on this fate.

"Was I that little?" JayLynn looks at him.

"Smaller," he answers. She already knows this. She was a preemie, born nearly a month early.

"Were you scared?"

He smiles as he remembers. "Terrified."

"Was Mama?"

"Oh yeah. You know how your mama worries."

JayLynn's mouth twitches in a quick frown before her attention returns to the bassinet.

The baby manages to find rest in Zaria's noise until he doesn't.

"I'll get him," JayLynn says when Malik starts mewing.

"Alright, now. Be careful." Parker rises from his chair to stand beside her. "Hold his back and neck."

JayLynn's movements are stiff and slow as she takes Malik in her arms. The baby manages to work his fists out of his blanket's loose swaddling. One wrist is wrapped in the mate to Zaria's hospital bracelet. Parker thinks about this link— the thick, inescapable knot of mother and child. He thinks the sunrise must scream to JayLynn. *Go! Go! Go! Now!*

Now! Now! Save her! He imagines this is the call of every mirror when she only wants to brush her hair or wash her own face and sees her mother's staring.

Parker warns, "No book can prepare you for this," though this is weak, hardly a deterrent against a baby, and certainly not convincing proof against JayLynn's undying faith in their magic. Learning how to hold a baby is easy, and JayLynn demonstrates this by gathering Malik securely in her arms and cradling him to her chest. When she softly kisses the top of Malik's head through his thin beanie and breathes his warm, baby scent, Parker can see how much she already loves him and how so much of that love is tied to her wants and wishes. She can't fathom him not being just as irresistible to Dee who hasn't seen, smelled, or held him yet. To JayLynn, he is a bundle full of firsts and cuteness that could keep his grandmother amused, proud, home, happy, and Parker is grateful that he hasn't stopped fussing.

"Hey, little man. It's okay," JayLynn whispers, but Malik's whimpers turn to tiny, sputtering coughs. She bounces slowly, bending at the knees, and taps his back. "Hey, hey, hey," she coos while Malik tries to shake his head from her palm. He finally finds the air he needs to grow his coughs into wails. JayLynn looks to Parker for help. This is another opportunity to teach a lesson. He will take every one he gets. He will not and does not step in to take the baby.

He only offers, "He's probably hungry," and he and Jay-Lynn turn to Zaria, who doesn't stir. Her breaths fall heavy and undisturbed.

A SATISFYING MEAL

When Smoke, an outsider—like me—at the Thompsons' Thanksgiving dinner, says the N-word, it's like the Temptations' Christmas CD playing in the background is a record, and his "nigga" scratches right through all that classic, classy black soul.

"—niggas out here is on some—"

My boyfriend, Nigel, is unfazed, but his mother clears her throat, plants her palms on the table, and gathers a swell of breath in her chest. "*Please*," she bellows over Smoke's rambling and Eddie Kendrick's falsetto as her eyelids flicker, "do *not* use that word in my house." She flashes all her teeth in something barely smile-ish. The flickering stops and her eyelids remain shut as she inhales again, I assume, gathering calm to stop herself from calling guards to remove Smoke from her home and feed him to some lions she's got roaming around the backyard. With the intricately wrapped Kente cloth crowning her head and the raucous of gold bangles lining both wrists, she looks like she can command that kind of power even though her eyeliner is crooked.

"Wha?" Smoke is confused.

Nigel's Aunt Janice, Smoke's girlfriend, raises her over-arched eyebrows. "The N-word?" she offers. Her words, intended as a gentle reminder, translate to me like, "Duh, nigga." She seems annoyed that she had to pull herself away from the apparent bliss of her yams to address Smoke's ignorance.

Nigel had brought his nephews some books we'd found at the Salvation Army near campus back in Bloomington, and Malcolm had been sharing one aloud, showing off his reading skills, when Smoke interrupted him to tell everybody why it was so important for kids to read, like he's not the one at the table who needs to rest in a library for a good while, at least until he stumbles on a book that informs him you shouldn't wear your coat and doo rag at the table, especially not during a holiday dinner. For somebody who spent most of their life on the streets and in prison, Smoke isn't very good at peeping the scene. I'm just an English major. I don't worry about whether I'm going to make it to twenty-one, but I'm capable of the close studying it seems like you should be able to do if you're trying to dodge bullets and police. This is my first meeting with the Thompsons, but even if Nigel hadn't told me, I can clearly see from his sister

Tammy's floppy afro, the references in her sons' names (Malcolm and Marcus), and Mr. Thompson's research interest in the Black Power movement as a professor of Pan-African studies at the University of Louisville all up in the titles lining the room's floor-to-ceiling bookshelf that the Thompson home is a "No 'nigga' zone."

"I'm sorry." Smoke holds both hands in front of his chest in a "Don't shoot" pose. Dark trenches crease his palms. "I wasn't trying to offend. My apologies."

Mrs. Thompson opens her eyes and nods a regal acceptance. Malcolm, who wears an obnoxious cloud of eager-to-please, stares at Smoke, glances down at his book, and appears to consider whether it's in his best interest to continue including the man as a target in his efforts to impress.

Mr. Thompson's sour face tells me there's a clot of words waiting on his tongue, but he drinks some iced tea and forces them down. I'm wondering if he thinks Smoke's not worth the breath of a lecture when he turns to me. "Nigel tells us you're a writer. What do you write?" he asks.

I straighten in my chair, my spine setting stiff against the ridging of the intricate wood carving. "I write features for the school newspaper."

"Yes, he told us that, but he also mentioned that you write fiction. What sorts of conflicts do you examine in your work?"

There are too many eyes on me to cast the vicious look I want to throw at Nigel, who waits with everyone else for my response. I'm in a fiction workshop this semester and won't let him read my stories even though he's begged.

"I explore the black experience from a number of different angles," I say, which is not untrue and more than I usually offer Nigel before telling him his questions are killing my art.

"Okay," Mr. Thompson chuckles. "The black experience is vast. What about it are you exploring?" He gives a half-encouraging, half-condescending grin that says, *Come on, now, girl. You're smarter than that.*

I take a long drink of iced tea before I respond. "I'm exploring the struggle."

"Mmhmm." Smoke nods like he knows exactly what I'm talking about.

I focus on him as I continue because I'm afraid to see the Thompsons' expressions. "My work explores the multifaceted struggle of being black in white America. The effects of slavery, Jim Crow," I glance back at Smoke, "mass incarceration." I sound like those kids in class who spew bullshit for participation points and think they're passing as smart. I know I'm clarifying nothing, though Smoke keeps nodding.

"Yes!" He claps once, punctuating his exclamation.

"Well, it looks like you've got one enthusiastic fan for your work right there." Mr. Thompson grimaces a fake smile before turning his attention to his grandson. Marcus claps his dimpled hands and wiggles in an unsteady dance as Mrs. Thompson spoons him dressing. She and her daughter chorus the deep-down laughs of mothers whose hearts are full. It's a rich sound I want to sop up like gravy. I want to stuff myself with it.

"You are a mess, boy." Mrs. Thompson's face glows so fiercely she looks celestial. Just watching her lights my chest with warm tingles.

I excuse myself to go to the bathroom. On the way, my cell phone buzzes at my hip. Its bulk in the front pocket of my blue-jean skirt is hidden by the drape of my hand-knitted poncho, another Salvation Army find. With the bathroom door closed, I read the text from my cousin Zaria: *Yo mama ain't here with the greens. U call her?*

Dinner at Aunt Yolanda's started an hour ago at two. I call Mama's cell and house phones. Both ring and ring until message systems kick on.

No answer, I reply. *Maybe she's on her way.*

She returns, *:(*

On the drive to Louisville, Nigel and I listed the foods we couldn't wait to eat. He said his daddy's turkey, and I said my mama's greens. He said cornbread stuffing with gravy, and I said, "Mmm, yes." I said chittlins drenched in hot sauce, and he said, "That's slave slop." Then he asked how I could eat that shit, did I know I could actually, potentially eat some shit if they aren't cleaned well, and I made a show of rubbing my belly and licking my lips.

He fake-retched. "Don't be trying to kiss me after you eat those things."

Back at the table, I stare at my plate full of food unsure how I'm going to eat anything with my stomach so knotted while Smoke drones on. "Coming up, my mama was always telling me to keep my head in them books and be my own man, like him." He nods across the table to Nigel, who is decked out in a thrift-store ensemble he calls "*Miami Vice* Prom": a powder blue tuxedo paired with a ruffled pink button-down, navy ankle-length trousers, powder blue socks dotted with pink flamingos, and mahogany, all-up-in-the-corner-roach-killer oxfords polished glossy enough to blind. "I love your whole vibe, man. The hair, the 'fit. You're doing your thing." Smoke scratches absently at the patches of black naps on his face struggling to connect to a beard and stares at the short dreadlocks sunbursting from Nigel's thick roots. He appears to be imagining the different Smokes he could be.

"Thanks," Nigel says, continuing the business of shoving down turkey and dressing.

"Nigel, slow down before you choke." Mrs. Thompson frowns. "Show JayLynn you got some home training."

Smoke laughs, and I spot the gap of a missing tooth two spaces behind a canine. "It be like that sometimes when the food's good," he says.

"It *is* like that sometimes when the food is good." Malcolm smiles primly at me as he speaks.

Everyone but Tammy's husband and I laugh at Malcolm's revision of Smoke's poor grammar.

Smoke takes Malcolm's words as enthusiastic agreement and chuckles. "See? Little man knows." His thick black leather jacket creaks softly when he stands and reaches over the table for the porcelain bowl of green beans.

"Unh unh. Sit down." Mrs. Thompson's bangles clink as she intercepts his hand with her arm. "If it's too far, somebody will get it for you. Just ask." She passes him the bowl.

"Thank you." Smoke sits and gets to scooping green beans onto his plate. "You know," he says to Mrs. Thompson, "you remind me of my mama."

She returns the oily sheen of her blank face and Smoke explains, even though nobody asked, "She was always correcting and teaching even when I wasn't listening. I thought me and my boys knew everything, but I was just a dope selling dope. Mama said bullets don't have no name and she was right. I ended up getting shot all in here." He leans to the right and points with two fingers, sweeping up the left side of his body from hip to armpit. "Three bullets. Learned some tough lessons, man."

Nigel drinks some iced tea, clears his throat, and swipes his cloth napkin down his mouth before speaking. It's an action sequence I imagine he learned from his father over a lifetime of dinners. There's something professorial about it, a self-assurance of the truth and importance in the words about to be spoken. "The point is you learned from them. I hear you went through some rough stuff, but you can't move from that past if you're always talking about it."

"Right," Tammy's husband's agreement is bright and eager with encouragement.

"Hmph." Smoke considers Nigel's words. "College man got all the answers." Something unsteadies his grin.

Mrs. Thompson frowns at my still-full plate. "Are you not enjoying your meal?"

"No no!" I insist, plunging my fork into a pecan-crusted chunk of yam. "It's all delicious," I say, and it is. The turkey is the best I've ever eaten. When Mr. Thompson brought it to the table, it was so perfectly brown and shiny and Thanksgiving proper, with its legs crossed and tied, I thought it was a shame we had to eat it.

"She's gotta save room for chittlins." Nigel smirks at me.

"Chittlins?" Smoke's eyes light up. "Where?"

"Not here." Mrs. Thompson tunes her face up like just the word brought the chittlin stank crawling on top of the onion, sage, and rosemary rising from the table, the cinnamon spice of her air freshener plug-in.

"At my aunt's," I answer reluctantly.

"Aw man. Thought y'all was holding out on me. You eat yours with hot sauce, a little potato salad on the side?" Smoke asks, and I hate that he's grinning like he knows me.

"To be honest," I return to Mrs. Thompson, "I'm not feeling well. My stomach is a little queasy."

"Well, the food was stored and cooked properly, and Nigel didn't mention that you had any food allergies." Her frown deepens.

"Oh no no! I'm not implying that the food is the reason. I just—"

"You was just in the bathroom and now you telling us you nauseated?" Nigel's aunt hums a little accusatory tune before asking, "Is it anything else you wanna tell us?"

All forks pause as eyes rush to me.

"We got a bun in the oven?" Smoke raises his glass in anticipation of a toast.

"Man, put that glass down." Nigel shoos Smoke's hand back to the table. "Ain't nobody pregnant."

"I'm just saying," Nigel's aunt says, "it's only been three months and she's coming to meet the family. It's kind of fast."

"Love don't have no time limit," Smoke declares.

"You are being careful aren't you, Nigel?" Mrs. Thompson asks. Worry melts her frown to a sadder expression.

Nigel rolls his eyes and sighs. "Yes, Mama."

But the worry persists on Mrs. Thompson's face as her eyes snatch at me in lingering glances. She doesn't need lions. She picks me in pinches without touch, breaking me apart, squinting to see what I'm made of.

"Goddamn, that nigga can talk!" Nigel says as soon as we're back in his car. On the radio, "All I Want for Christmas" is closing with Mariah Carey's piercing high notes.

"Your mother thinks I'm a ho," I say. "Your aunt too."

"My aunt ain't got no room to talk. She only with old

dude for when the lights go out. You see she wasn't paying him no attention."

I understand that it's an attempt at my defense, but am disappointed that he offers no reassurance that I am, in fact, not a ho. "Your daddy thinks I'm dumb." I continue sulking as I check my phone. No missed calls or texts from Mama.

"I don't think he thinks you're dumb . . . Maybe evasive. Why do you act like that when somebody asks about your stories?"

"Because talking about what you write ruins it."

"But you've already finished them."

"I'm revising."

He sighs and buckles his seatbelt. "Where am I going?"

I tell him to take 264 West to Bells Lane and go down Algonquin until it turns into Southwestern Parkway.

"Got it." He turns the radio up and sings along to James Brown's "Santa Claus Go Straight to the Ghetto."

I check my phone again as he drives out of the J-town suburbs and cruises onto the expressway.

Nigel and I discovered we were both from Louisville during class introductions on the first day of Literary History earlier this semester. After class, we stood in the hall sharing stories about standing downtown and feeling Thunder Over Louisville fireworks rumbling through our feet, gawking at the ass-shaking on Broadway during Derby cruising. We'd spent our teens wasting Saturdays at the Jefferson Mall and Showcase Cinemas, summer days pruning at Kentucky Kingdom's Hurricane Bay before spinning dry on rollercoasters. Even though we grew up in suburbs thirty minutes apart—me in Shively, him in Jefferson-town—between the two of us, Louisville felt as small as the hallway, and I wondered how we hadn't met before. In the dining room crowded with the Thompsons', me, and Smoke (who'd proudly declared he was born and raised in the West End), Louisville grew huge, became an expansive container of multitudes. That vastness spreads in Nigel's car, feels like it's elbowing us apart.

"Where are you going?" I ask when he turns right from Taylorsville Road onto Hurstbourne Parkway.

"Walgreens," he answers. "I want to get your moms a little gift. Make myself look good." He winks.

"You don't need to do that."

"I know," he says.

"No, really. Don't worry about it. I'm sure she'll like you."

"Let me do this," he insists, parking the car. "Help me pick out something she'll like." He unbuckles his seatbelt. I don't move.

"It's Walgreens," I say. "She won't like anything."

"It's just a little something, JayLynn. To show that I'm thoughtful. I would get flowers but every place else is closed. Why are you being so difficult?"

"I'm not being difficult," I say, even though I know I am. "I just know my mama, and I don't want you to waste your money."

"Don't you worry about that."

Now, I sigh and unbuckle my seatbelt. Inside the store, I direct him to a box of chocolate pecan clusters and the section of blank greeting cards. I've long since stopped counting on cards to express the words I need to say to my mother. As Nigel pays and folds his change into his wallet, I resist the urge to check my phone despite what I already know. It hasn't buzzed with a call or text. There is nothing new, I remind myself as Nigel tucks his wallet back into his coat pocket and guides me forward.

Mama hasn't been to a family gathering since last Christmas.

Partly, this is because she was busy leaving her apartment off Bardstown Road and all the hustling she'd done there to pick up her life. She'd sought therapy for her depression, gone to rehab for the opioids, pleaded before the Kentucky Board of Nursing, and after a couple years working at the plasma center, she could finally ditch all the ashy elbows attached to sad stories and return to a job on Hospital Curve—this time at Norton's.

The other part of the reason why Mama hasn't been to a family gathering is because she doesn't want anything to do with them niggas. She bragged to Aunt Sandy and Aunt Yolanda about her new house in Middletown with the four bedrooms, two and a half baths, finished basement, fireplace in the living room, granite-topped kitchen counters, and everybody got all excited about a Memorial Day barbecue on Mama's deck, which was presumptuous and stupid because all of the calls Mama didn't answer should have made it clear that she'd moved to get away, not bring the party with her. She'd drawn a thick dividing line in the miles of highway stretching before and after the knot of Spaghetti Junction.

After weeks of missed calls, Aunt Yolanda asked me to talk to Mama about hosting the barbecue, and when I did, Mama laughed. "Hell no. I'd have to batten down the hatches so Dee won't steal me blind. And what she won't steal Maxine'll be begging for." She shook her head. "It's always some shit and I don't feel like dealing with it here or there, but they're definitely not bringing it here. Nope." She took a blessed and unbothered sip from her sweaty glass of Coke.

"So what do you want me to tell them?" I asked.

"Tell them the truth. I don't care." She shrugged. "It's the truth."

I told Aunt Yolanda Mama said she was tired, and we had the barbecue in Aunt Yolanda's backyard like we always do.

Mama doesn't realize she's a shit starter just like Aunts Dee and Maxine because she's never around to witness the shit she starts. She'd been using the "tired" excuse for months, and after Labor Day, everybody was sick of it. For Thanksgiving, we agreed it was best to assign Mama something supplementary and easy for anyone to pick up in the event of her anticipated no-show. Aunt Sandy called her in the beginning of November to leave a message telling her to bring some rolls, but Mama answered. *And* volunteered to make the greens. She's the only one who can make them just right, spiced with a soft heat and seasoned to the edge of too salty with enough jowl bacon that a bowl of them can be a satisfying meal.

We were all surprised, but I was also relieved. Too often now when I call Mama her voice is thick with listlessness, like a record dragging on the wrong speed, a sad song I've heard too many times before. I imagine her burrowed under her plush comforter, weighed down by the disappointment that the thousand-thread-count of her sheets, the house, and all the glossy stuff in it aren't delivering the dream life she'd filled with white people who invite her to dinner parties filled with more white people who toast to all the good things that white people—and now she—have to toast about. In her fantasies, I think Mama and these white people talk about Oscar-nominated movies and award-winning books that fill my English professors' syllabi. These white friends don't automatically throw the latest movie or novel about slavery or the struggle growing up in "the hood" into conversation because Mama's black, and this is because they are tired of hearing about slavery and black struggle just as much as she is. *Can't we move on?* They shoo away four hundred years like flies.

I think the day Aunt Sandy called Mama was just lonely. I spent the summer in Bloomington working my gig at the university library and made my own move out of the dorms and into an apartment in June. After Nigel and I got together, it wasn't hard to choose a good time staying put with him over a questionable time with Mama after traveling for two hours. Nigel suggested we drive home together for Thanksgiving, grab two meals—one with his folks, one with mine—and return to Bloomington that night since he has to work on Black Friday and I have a story revision due the Monday after break. I thought it was too soon to be meeting families, but Mama said she was coming and I wanted to believe her. I also didn't want to explain my reservations—Mama's depression, the possible return of her addiction.

"This Christmas" is on the radio, and Nigel is straining his voice to keep up with Donnie Hathaway. The houses lining the Bells Lane exit are squat and dingy even in the soft purpling of the afternoon. Some of them wear chain-link fences, but most of their lawns are balding and all of them look vulnerable. We crawl past the wastewater plant's huge white tanks as Nigel brakes over railroad tracks and potholes pockmarking the road.

"It always smells like a fart back here," Nigel says.

"Yeah, it does."

"This should be making you hungry. Getting you all fired up for those chittlins," he teases with a grin.

I smile back at him and sing, "Mmm mmm mmm."

Every time Mama takes this route, she scrunches her nose, shakes her head, says, "God," and the curse is soft like an unfinished prayer, gratitude for the blessing of just passing through.

"These potholes are deep," Nigel says. "You could really fuck up your rims. But it's already Thanksgiving so nobody's about to fix them anytime soon." He sighs. "I guess they figure they ain't got to worry about it if it's just niggas driving back here."

"Probably not," I say.

After Nigel parks in front of Aunt Yolanda's house, he turns to me with puckered lips. "You'll wanna kiss me now because you won't be able to do it later," he explains.

I smack him on the shoulder and he laughs. "Nigga, please," I say. "You know you'll want this."

He shrugs. "Maybe."

I lean over and kiss him deep, with tongue. He tastes like sage and cinnamon. I reach over the console and rub his crotch. He protests when I stop. "Maybe later." I grin, happy to have the upper hand.

With the chittlins funk and all the heat from cooking, walking into Aunt Yolanda's living room feels like stepping into a bathroom after somebody has taken a dump and then a long, hot shower.

"Smells about right," Nigel whispers as he follows me to throw our coats on Aunt Yolanda's bed.

"Shut up," I say and reach for the hand not holding his gifts for Mama, lacing it to mine. The warmth of his fingers clutching me back is reassuring as I lead him into the kitchen. "Everybody, this is my boyfriend, Nigel!" I announce.

Aunt Dee, who sits at the table, stretches her "hi" into a flirty, two-syllable song and grins like crazy, revealing teeth that look like gnawed-on Tootsie Roll nubs. She likes them young, which is basically how she ended up with those fucked up teeth. Five years ago, when she was thirty-five, she got a twenty-four-year-old tenderoni who showed her a good time with a crack pipe.

"Calm down," Zaria tells Aunt Dee, rolling her eyes at her mother before greeting Nigel with a cheesy, sneaky grin like she knows his secrets, which she basically does because she's my best friend and I tell her everything.

"Hey, everybody!" Nigel waves, sending the box of candy into an arc in the air.

"Oooh! Turtles!" my little cousin Angel chimes. "Can we have some?"

Another cousin Macy, four, rushes to Nigel, her red patent leather Mary Janes and hair beads clicking. She reaches for the candy.

"Maybe you can have some later," he denies them sweetly. "This is a gift for JayLynn's mother. Miss Brown?" Nigel looks expectantly into the crowd of strange faces.

Waylon, Zaria's big brother, stands against the counter. He nods what's up to Nigel, glaring with suspicion. "You might as well hand that over," he says. "She ain't here and ain't gonna be here."

"She might be on her way. She said she was coming when I spoke to her yesterday," Aunt Sandy says. Angel sits on her lap even though she is six and too big for that. Angel's hair is free from its usual braids and plaits. She leans back onto Aunt Sandy's chest, smashing her bush of curls against the bush of curls in Aunt Sandy's Diana Ross wig, and they look like a double-trunked tree, like mother and daughter, even though Aunt Sandy is the golden color of wood beneath bark and Angel's mother is Aunt Maxine, who's not in the kitchen, possibly not here either.

"You know Claudia ain't coming," Aunt Yolanda says before distracting Macy with an offer of yellow cake slathered with a thick paste of caramel icing. "If she wasn't gonna be here or cook or nothing that's all she had to say."

"She's coming," I insist. "She's just running late." I take the card and candy from Nigel, ignoring the confusion on his face as I place his gifts on the counter beside a store-bought pecan pie.

"Nigel!" Zaria exclaims. "It's so nice to finally meet you. I've heard so much about you. Good things. *Great* things." She grins, more at me than Nigel, as she adjusts herself in her chair, crossing her arms over her chest. Her boobs are damn near cresting out of her sweater. It's a blessing her ass is flat, though she's probably wearing a short, tight skirt; I can't tell because she's sitting in the corner. Aunt Yolanda has the kind of butt people write songs about, and if Zaria had an ass like that, she'd probably just stop wearing clothes altogether. Nigel already knows about her son, the pregnancy at sixteen, so there's no need for him to calculate Malik's three years from Zaria's twenty, glancing back and forth from the table to the floor where Malik sits with his back against the refrigerator sending his Ninja Turtle through a series of backflips on his knee. Still, I'm ashamed of what looks like Zaria's ho-ish ways and glad for the second time today that I'm covered up even though Nigel's seen everything I've got.

"Looks like I need to go up to IU to see what they got going on up there. Get my groove back like Stella." Aunt Dee snaps her fingers to the R&B song floating from the stereo in the living room and laughs, showing her horrible teeth again. I wish she had a teaspoon of Mama's self-loathing so she'd be ashamed enough to cover her mouth.

"What is this nigga wearing?" Waylon blurts like he's finally put his finger on what's wrong with Nigel. He leans back against the counter. Even underneath his University of Louisville sweatshirt, it's clear that his arms are jacked. He folds them over his chest so his biceps plump just right, so Nigel—tall, thin, and without one muscle to lump up his clothes—can see exactly who's the boss dog, the big dick in the room.

"Waylon, shut up and leave that boy alone," Aunt Yolanda steps in to cut the bullshit. "Nigel, have a seat, baby." She rises, pats her chair and Nigel sits. "You hungry? Fix him a plate, JayLynn," she directs before he can answer.

"Ain't no more chittlins." Zaria's cuts her eyes at Aunt Dee, who catches the look but acts like she's too busy enjoying her slice of pecan pie to see.

"What?" I lift the lid on the five-gallon pot and find a golden broth of chittlin juice. Scraggly survivors float in the greasy slick.

"Ain't no more chittlins?" Aunt Maxine comes upstairs from the basement as if on cue. She's always been theatrical. With the large fork resting on the stove, she stirs the chittlin juice, banging the sides of the pot in her search for meat before grabbing a strainer spoon from a cabinet drawer and filling a Styrofoam plate with scraps. "It's plenty in there," she says.

Aunt Maxine and Aunt Dee cleaned and cooked the chittlins as contribution to the meal since neither one of them has a job or the intention of getting one. Everyone expected them to take some off the top when the cooking was done because they always did, but it had never been this bad.

"Everybody else put in money for four buckets, and when they brought them in, it looked like they'd already eaten half," Aunt Yolanda tells me.

"They shrink when they cook, Yolanda!" Aunt Maxine shrieks. Her scorched voice breaks into unevenly pitched pieces. She's always yelling even when she's not mad or trying to prove a point. It might be because she's the baby and had to fight to be heard.

"Ain't that much shrinking in the world, Maxine."

Aunt Maxine notices Nigel as she's sprinkling hot sauce on her chittlin findings, pretending to ignore Aunt Yolanda. "Look at this pretty young thing." She grins. Miraculously, her teeth are still intact. Some can argue that

Aunt Maxine is still beautiful though five years ago there would have been no question and that beauty could have taken her somewhere. Today, she wears a floral pillowcase as a headwrap and her signature lipstick. It's green in the tube and turns fuchsia on the lips. She wore that ninety-nine-cent lipstick on a date with Wesley Snipes after serving him lasagna at the Spaghetti Factory during his break from filming *Demolition Man*.

Zaria and I wanted to hold the kind of magic that would have rich and famous men seeking us out, but when we tried Aunt Maxine's lipstick, passing the tube between us, it looked like our lips were screaming. It was too much, even for two adolescent girls who filled days dreaming of being too much in hopes of catching boys and our mothers, who were slipping away from us. We smashed toilet paper across our lips and walked around with quiet stains.

"That's Nigel, Jay's b*ooo*yfriend," Angel sings.

"Cute." Aunt Maxine eyes Nigel as she slurps up a forkful of chittlins. "Mmhmm," she hums while chewing. "Real cute." She pauses to swallow. "Let me ask you something, Nigel. Would a handsome brother like yourself have a few dollars to give to your future auntie-in-law?"

"Maxine!" Aunt Sandy snaps.

I want to die. Mama would have died twice if she was here.

"She's just playing," I tell Nigel.

"No, I'm not," Aunt Maxine says before sucking up more chittlins.

"Go sit down somewhere!" Waylon points her toward the basement like she's a dog.

Angel runs to fold Aunt Maxine in a hug and yells, "Don't be mean to my mama!"

"That's right, baby. You tell them. I'm just talking to my new nephew." Aunt Maxine turns up the sugar for Nigel, "You don't have two, three dollars for your auntie?"

"No, I don't," he lies. I recall the change folded back into his wallet at the store. "Sorry." He gives a pained expression, like he wishes he could help. He must know why Aunt Maxine wants the dollar, how she will spend it. With her gouged cheeks and that pillowcase nesting on her head, it's not hard to tell.

Aunt Maxine frowns. "Come on, niece. You can do better than that. Not even a dollar in his pocket." She dismisses Angel to go play and returns to the basement to watch TV.

"We're so sorry about that," Aunt Sandy apologizes to Nigel. "I can't believe her."

"I can," Aunt Dee chimes and scrapes the last bite of pie from her plate.

"It's okay," Nigel says.

"No, it's not," Aunt Yolanda replies.

"I saved you some chittlins and put them in the fridge," Zaria tells me. "It might be enough for y'all to share."

"Naw, I'm good," Nigel says. "I don't eat chittlins."

"You one of those brothers who don't eat pork and be out on Eighteenth and Broadway selling those *Nation* papers and bean pies? Cause you look like one of those bean pie-selling niggas," Waylon says, suspicion returning to his face.

"I eat pork," Nigel says, "I just don't like chittlins."

"Me neither. The shit is disgusting." This common ground seems to relax Waylon; he loosens the fold of his arms and pauses before offering, somewhat reluctantly, "Try some ham." He perks with pride as he brags, "I smoked it myself."

"There's dressing," Aunt Yolanda points as she speaks. "Sweet potatoes and macaroni and cheese in the oven, deviled eggs in the fridge, greens in that other pot—"

"*Canned* greens," Zaria clarifies.

"Right. I been waiting all day for Claudia and those greens," Aunt Dee says, eager to throw some blame on somebody else.

"She's coming," I say.

"I been calling and she's not answering. You spoke to her today?" Aunt Sandy fluffs up her wig though it is more than big enough.

"Not yet," I admit.

"You haven't heard from her today? Somebody needs to make sure she's okay," Aunt Sandy's voice is high with alarm, her yellow face one big, bright frown.

"What's wrong with her?" Nigel asks.

"Claudia's alright." Aunt Yolanda waves away Nigel's concern.

"She's coming," I repeat, pulling my phone from my pocket.

Waylon sucks his teeth. "Nigga, please."

Nigel excuses himself to go to the bathroom.

"Your mama is officially on my shit list over this," Zaria says.

I'm pissed too, but more worried. In my ear, Mama's line rings and rings the first and second time I call. She's probably sleeping. I'm trying not to think about what could be helping her sleep so deeply when Nigel returns. I glimpse his back pocket during his reach for a piece from the hacksawed ham and note the subtle bulge of his wallet, apparently pulled from his coat in Aunt Yolanda's bedroom during his trip to the bathroom. I know I shouldn't take this personally, but I do. I'm embarrassed and feel insulted, like I'm the crackhead, thief, a nigga that can't be trusted.

One day before our literary history class began, while Dr. Cameron was sorting books and papers on a table at the front of the room, blond buzzcutted, baggy-jeans wearing Josh was listening to his iPod on full volume, blasting a song I'd heard so many times that summer that I didn't care if I ever heard it again.

The rapper growled, "*Got my finger on what?*" and Josh answered, "*This trigga!*" Before the rapper's question, "*Never scared cuz I'm who?*" had unfolded from the tinny earbud speakers, Nigel stared Josh dead in his green eyes and said loudly, clearly, "You bet not," and Josh said nothing as the gravel of a chorus of men shouting, "*That nigga!*" fell heavy in the room.

Dr. Cameron let us spend most of that class debating whether Josh should be able to say the word "nigga" if, in Josh's words, "his heart was in the right place." Dr. Cameron, who's white and knows what's good for him, made the argument that no one no matter their race should use the word because of the history it carries. Nigel had a different stance that he tried to explain, but the rest of our white classmates (everybody else in the class) who were trying to prove they weren't racist (everybody else in the class) jumped in and took over.

"Josh, *your* great-great-grandfather probably kept *his* great-great-grandmother enslaved and called her the N-word while he *raped* and *beat* her and now you want to say the word because you want to be '*down*' or whatever?" This came from forever-eating-a-fruit-cup Mindy. "Not cool, bro. Not cool." She popped a pineapple chunk into her mouth.

After class, Nigel and I met up to shake our heads at white people and ended up walking over to Mother Bear's for pizza. He told me his parents side with Dr. Cameron, Oprah, and Dr. Cornel West who maintain that even when the "er" is dropped and "nigga" is used among black people, the whippings, lynchings, and cross burnings are irrevocably tied to the word's core.

"I say the word," Nigel explained, "cuz nobody can tell me I can't. It's a word used to talk about black people—me as a black man—so I'll say it and use it however I want."

"And how is that?" I asked.

He looked confused. "You're black. You know how we use it." He bit into a slice of pizza.

"If we're gonna have a conversation about the word let's have the conversation. Different people use it different ways. How do you use it?" I repeated my question.

He leaned back, tilted his head, and ran his hand down his jawline, over his trim beard as he thought. "Sometimes when I say 'my nigga' I'll be speaking generally, like 'Pass the salt, my nigga' so that 'my nigga' is like 'my man,' 'my dude,' but not like 'That's my *man*.' But you know it means that, too—'my nigga' as a close friend."

"Why not just say 'my dude' or 'my man'?"

"I do. 'Homie,' 'dawg,' 'ace,' all that, but 'nigga' is right in there, too. A nigga is that friend who's like blood. Like, y'all are connected on the deepest levels. Maybe y'all grew up together, been through some serious shit, but you can communicate and understand beyond words and the trust is never questioned."

"Would you ever call somebody who wasn't black your 'nigga'?"

"Unh unh." He shook his head. "They gotta be black. That's part of the distinction. I guess I should have said that, but I thought it was implied." He sipped some ice water before adding, "But I will call a non-black person '*that* nigga.' For example, 'That nigga Josh almost got his ass kicked today' so 'that nigga' means ignorant motherfucker. When I say 'nigga' like that, it's equal opportunity, not just for black people. But I won't say it *to* that non-black person like I would another black person. I said it to you, but I wouldn't go up to . . . let's say, Jill and say it."

"Why not?"

"Cuz it seems like giving consent for them to say the word and use it that way in the context of black people, and then it gets too close to the demeaning way some of them use the 'er' original." He chomped a huge bite from his slice.

"How is it different when you're using the word in a demeaning way to describe black people?" I ask. "It goes back to the history. How do you reconcile using the word with that history?"

Nigel nodded, held up a finger. He chewed furiously, trying to finish his mouthful so he could speak. He was polishing off his second slice, but I was barely halfway through my one. After a couple gulps of water, he cleared his throat, wiped his mouth with a napkin, and said, "I'm black so I recognize the complexity of blackness. It's like a relationship with a sibling. I can tease my sister, criticize her, but nobody else can because they aren't *in it*. White people ain't in this." He traced his finger back and forth across an invisible track that bridged his chest to mine, stared into my eyes with a laser gaze, and I didn't realize I'd lost myself in the connections he'd drawn between us until he blinked and I was just me again.

"I mean, look," he said. "You're right. 'Nigga' is used for love and hate. Good and bad. The word's history is deep, and I'm not trying to ignore it. I can't. *Nobody* will *ever* be able to erase it. *I'm* just saying . . ." Here, he pressed his hand to his chest and I told myself to stop being stupid for feeling left out, my chest an abandoned field. "... for me, 'nigga' is a magic word like 'Shazam!' It transforms and restores power. Josh can't use the word any way he wants in front of anybody he wants, but I can and do. I don't care if there's white, purple, green people around."

And it was clear that he didn't. I'd heard everything he said, but there'd been a simultaneous interpretation of his conversation playing in my head that sounded like "NIGGANIGGANIGGANIGGA." I was squirming inside, wondering if any of the white people (everybody else in the restaurant) had heard him say the word, hoping they hadn't.

"Out of respect I don't speak the word in front of my parents, but they're the only exceptions. What about you, Oprah?" He grinned. "You're all interrogating me. I bet you don't even say the word."

"Sometimes," I blurted in defense.

It was kind of true. In middle and high school, I'd tried the word out around cousins and black friends, but it never felt right. From my mouth, the word was stiff. It was always asking, never telling or hugging or joking the way it was when my daddy threw it around with his friends and my uncles out of Mama's earshot. Mama's aversion to the word was not about upholding respect or pride for blackness but erasing it.

"Liar." Nigel gave me that stare again. "Say it."

"What?" I acted offended, all pearl-clutching white woman.

"If you say it, say it. I'll know if you're telling the truth."

I played with my hair, pulling at the tight curls, gathering courage. I'd recently cut off my long, permed hair for a short natural. I wanted the word to work all the magic Nigel spoke about when I looked at him and said, "Nigga, please."

He busted out laughing. "You definitely don't say it."

"Shut up, nigga," I said a little louder, with a harder lean on the "N."

"Hmm." Nigel raised his eyebrows. "Better."

Nigel and Waylon are talking shit about their rival football teams' head-to-head scheduled for next week when Aunt Dee says, "Let me see the phone, Yolanda." She wiggles her fingers in an inpatient "gimme" motion.

Zaria glares at her mother. "Who you calling?" She cradles Malik in her arms, rocking him side-to-side as he feigns the thumb-sucking sleep of a baby.

"My friend to come pick me up."

"Sandy's taking you home," Aunt Yolanda says.

"I'm ready to go," Aunt Dee whines. "I'm tired."

"We all about to leave here in a minute since you and Maxine ate all the food," Zaria says.

"Yolanda, where's the phone?" Aunt Dee pushes extra exasperation into her voice.

"I don't want no shit in my house, Dee." Aunt Yolanda's eyes darken. "Whoever you calling can't come in here."

"He's coming to pick me up," Aunt Dee insists. "He ain't got no reason to come in here."

Aunt Yolanda frowns and goes to get the cordless.

"It's just killing you to sit still and spend some time with your family, ain't it?" Zaria scowls at Aunt Dee over Malik's fresh haircut.

"You're gonna see him later, Dee," Aunt Sandy attempts to mediate.

"No, let her go." Zaria rocks faster in her frustration, though she's trying to act unbothered. Malik's eyes pop open, and he pushes his way off her lap.

"I'm *gonna* go," Aunt Dee says.

"Nigga, what you mean?" Nigel shouts. "Do I gotta tell you again that we're undefeated?"

There's that word. From Nigel. For the first time in front of my family. And I'm telling myself it's a good thing that he feels comfortable enough to say it, but I can't help feeling startled and letdown.

"Nigga," Waylon replies, "y'all ain't nothing but a bunch of bitches."

"Come on, man," Nigel chastises, gesturing to Macy and Angel.

"I wasn't talking to them." Waylon shakes off the admonishment.

Nigel sighs, but they continue their banter. The kids settle into a corner of the kitchen with a pile of Macy's toys.

The rest of us shuffle through the sales ads scattered across the table, sharing our idle wants, until a car horn blares.

"Alright, people. We're out of here." Aunt Dee shoots the peace sign and calls downstairs to Aunt Maxine, who rises from the basement wearing her coat.

Angel drops the Barbie doll she's dressing and runs to Aunt Maxine. "Where you going, Mama?"

Aunt Maxine smacks a kiss on her forehead. "I'm going with Dee. I'll be home later."

"You said we were going to decorate the tree when we get home." Angel stands slumped like someone has slipped the bone right out of her shoulders.

Aunt Maxine stares at Angel, but her body faces away from the kitchen, toward the front door. "It's too late for that, baby. We'll do it tomorrow."

"But Mama, it's not late. It's only . . . ," Angel's eyes flicker to the digital clock display on the stove, ". . . five thirty-six and I don't have to go to school tomorrow."

Aunt Sandy offers to decorate the tree, but Angel's not listening.

"What about drawing names for Christmas? Y'all ain't drawn names yet," Angel says. It's a decent effort, but an ultimately doomed stall tactic. Still, Aunt Sandy tells Zaria to write everybody's name down.

"For what?" Zaria asks. "So everybody can *not* be here for Christmas too? I'm sick of this."

"What you talking 'bout? I'm here!" Aunt Dee slaps her chest.

Zaria ignores her.

"I been here all day, waiting on Claudia. *She's* the one ain't here."

"You still ain't heard from her, Jay?" Aunt Sandy asks though she knows the answer. I've been sitting right at the table with her, my phone not ringing. "Somebody needs to make sure she's okay." Her alarm from earlier returns, ringing with my own fears humming heavy in my gut.

"Claudia's fine just like Yolanda said," Aunt Dee says. "She was over my place last week." She acts like this should clear any worries, but everyone knows the only reason why Mama would venture to the Beecher Terrace projects. "She'll move when she wants something."

"Ain't you got a ride to catch?" I say, the proper grammar I been holding on my tongue all day gone.

"Don't get mad at me. I'm just saying."

"Well, just don't say nothing else about my mama, nigga," I throw the word hard, *G*'s grunted from my core, the humming place that holds lists of the endless things I can't control. Hot blood storms in my ears, swirling with the tornado siren of Angel's steady wail.

"I'm out of here. Come on, Maxine!" Aunt Dee stomps out in her beat-up fake Timberlands.

Aunt Maxine kneels on the floor, trying to clear Angel's face of tears. She wipes so hard the heels of her hands drag Angel's cheeks flat. She coos stupid shit about how Angel shouldn't cry because she's so pretty.

Three more honks blare. Aunt Maxine stands. "I gotta

go." Angel is crying so hard she's hiccuping. "Stopstopstop." Aunt Maxine fishes through her purse.

Macy rises from the floor and goes to Nigel. "Hey," she taps his thigh, "can my cousin have some of your candy now?"

He looks at me. I grab the box from the counter and begin peeling the plastic.

Aunt Maxine finally pulls a tube of green lipstick from her purse. "Hold onto this for me," she directs like she's commissioning Angel with some grand duty. The rest of us throw looks at one another like "What the hell is that supposed to do?" Angel keeps hiccuping and crying, but she nods solemnly and holds onto the tiny wand as she watches her mother leave. The berry stain of Aunt Maxine's lips blooms on her forehead. She looks like she's been painted to participate in some kind of ritual.

I apologize to Nigel when we get in the car and explain on the way to Mama's. Before I get to the parts about the opioids, rehab, depression, and the John F. Kennedy Bridge, Nigel is driving fast, sensing the urgency. We barely gave the car time to warm up, and the words leave my mouth as ghostly puffs, haunting the air between us.

"It's not your fault," he says. We're at a stop sign in Mama's neighborhood and he tries to look me in the eyes, but I'm staring through the living room window of a house down the block. A Christmas tree is lit with tiny white lights and decorated with silver bulbs. It is simple and perfect.

When we pull up at Mama's house, I don't invite Nigel to come with me and he doesn't ask. Mama answers shortly after my second round of pounding against her front door. Her face is puffy with sleep.

"Why are you beating on the door like that?"

"Because I didn't know what might've happened to you!" I shriek. She is unfazed by my worry and I wonder if she's on something right now. I can't tell. I could never tell.

"Come in, it's cold." She folds her arms tight against the November chill.

"Nigel's waiting in the car." I point to the driveway. "You were supposed to come with the greens. Everybody was waiting on you."

"I didn't feel like it." She scratches at the top of her head, digging a finger into the thin polyester of her wrap scarf.

"I wanted some greens," I say. This desire sounds stupid, juvenile, not warranting the lump in my throat crowding everything else I want to say.

"I can still make them," she tries to soothe, mend. "You and Nigel can spend the night and I can make dinner tomorrow."

A small part of me almost believes she will and wants to accept her offer. Instead, I cough and sniff the tears forming, acting like I'm catching a cold, and say, "We have to go back tonight," because we do and I don't want to give her another chance so soon.

She asks, "Did you bring me a plate?"

"No," I reply, finding satisfaction in delivering this disap-pointment, a response that Zaria's always reminding me is a full sentence. Still, I add, "Aunt Maxine and Aunt Dee ate all the chittlins," as explanation, though there was a sharing portion on the plate Zaria saved, the plate that she ran out of the house to give to me before I left.

"Figures." Mama rolls her eyes, and I'm suddenly impa-tient to get away from her. I rush a goodbye, draping my arms around the hard knobs of her shoulders in a flimsy hug.

In the car, Nigel asks, "That's what you write about? Your mother?" I can see him processing, rewinding conversa-tions, inserting this new knowledge, reassessing.

"Pretty much," I say.

"Why didn't you tell me?"

At the Thompsons', everyone went around the table and said what they were thankful for. When it was Smoke's turn, he stammered before grinning a stupid grin and saying, "I'm just happy to be here, man. For real. All the sh— I mean, stuff, I done been through. So many of my ni— uh . . . homies ain't make it. These streets just sucked 'em up." He shook his head solemnly. "I'm thank-ful the Lord blessed me with another day to be here and y'all opened y'all's arms to me. I'm sitting at this table and ain't nobody fighting and yelling or drunk." He chuckles at a memory. "It's people in love, and I'm one of 'em." He beams at Nigel's aunt, and she gives him a drowsy, watery smile. "Y'all got the new generation and raising them up right." He nods to Malcolm and Marcus. "It's just beautiful, man. I ain't got a bad thing to say. This is a real blessing." He looked around the table and smiled at everybody, and I hated him for saying what I was thinking and making it sound like some nigga shit. When it was my turn, I kept it short and tried to sound grateful, but not like I wasn't used to the ordinary miracles of eating dinner on china, a thirty-year marriage, mothers who mother.

Now Nigel asks, before I can answer his first question, "What kind of nigga do you think I am? This is not gonna scare me away. I love you." He reaches for me and the console between us makes the hug awkward. I tell him I love him too, mumbling into his coat. I adjust and squeeze his shoulders, trying to bridge the distance.

I told Zaria I didn't want the chittlins, and I know later I'll wish I hadn't. I'm sure Zaria will take them. She'll probably call me tomorrow and tell me she was so happy I left them, that she warmed them up and they tasted so good.

A SORT OF WINNING

Patricia regretted assigning a written final. She strode down the rows of cross-legged students spread down the length of the gym's hardwood, delivering tests, ready to get the whole thing over with so they could play dodgeball—girls versus boys—and she could hit somebody. She'd nearly single-handedly secured an undefeated record for the day, whopping boys in the chest, back, feet, sending them tumbling like bowling pins.

"Miz Hines!" Darius raised a wide hand attached to a long arm before unfolding the rest of his body into a brown tower. "I don't have a pencil." He sang a loud, lengthy yawn as he reached under his T-shirt to scratch absently at his chest. His lifted shirt showcased four-square abs and a scraggly trail of pubic hair leading to the blue boxer briefs worn at least six inches above the basketball shorts dangling on his hips. He leaned back, yawning again, louder, arching his back, thrusting his pelvis forward.

"Stop it." Patricia rolled her eyes. She believed last year's scandal of Mary Kay LeTourneau's confession to a sexual relationship with her sixth-grade student, a child more than twenty years her junior, continued to give hope to Darius and the other patchy-bearded, husky-voiced upper-class man-boys at Central High who called her Fine Hines when they thought she couldn't hear. The sad, weak game they threw at her faced long odds like her mother's chemo and radiation treatment, which had ended three months ago, and suggested they imagined an easily surmountable ten-year age gap between their wet dreams and reality. Patricia had little hope for her own impossible dreams so now especially she had no patience for horny boys and their dumb ones.

"What?" Darius's mouth twitched up at the corners. "I need a penc—"

"Put your shirt down and pull your shorts up." Patricia ignored the snickering while Darius threw the laughing boys a knowing glance. "You know Coach Snyder wouldn't let you wear them like that on the court."

Darius unleashed his grin in all its girl-getting glory before tugging his shorts to his waist. "For real though. I need a pencil."

She inhaled deeply, gathering patience and the gym's smell of dried sweat on rubber. "Don't play with me, D." She gave him the mechanical pencil from her jacket pocket.

"Never." He took the pencil and scrunched back into a large nest of limbs on the floor.

Patricia decided he would be her first target.

When she reached Maya, the girl blocked her with a raised hand. "No, thank you." Her face cradled a sarcastic smile as tight as the rubber bands that held her long, thin braids and sometimes littered the maple floor like tiny, black worms. She popped up from her seated position and made her way to the bleachers. Patricia could tell Maya was relishing this, her final show of defiance after a semester-long war. Her legs stretched long in short running shorts, and she switched with visible effort to make her butt jiggle so Darius, the heart of her hate for Patricia, could see.

Maya was convinced Patricia wanted that boy even though Patricia's husband, Gerald, taught English upstairs and their pecks caught in stairwells and corners were often the target of romantic sighs and dramatic gagging by colleagues and students alike. Maya had likely read the exchange with Darius as flirty banter. They thought everything was foreplay. Patricia figured that Maya had only done the little activity she'd half-assed—talking to her spotter while she splayed idly on the weight bench, twerking during dodgeball—to offer her body to Darius in a variety of displays. Their faith that their bodies would always deliver what they wanted was inspiring as much as it was exhaustingly naive.

What Patricia wanted was to run until her body burned and delivered her to a new horizon dawning strange and hopeful. What she did was drift through the students hunched over makeshift desks of binders and hardcover textbooks, past the walls crowded with senior sendoff messages to athletes on the football, basketball, baseball, volleyball, tennis, soccer, and wrestling teams. A rainbow of neon posters screamed goodbyes: *YELLOWJACKETS 4-LIFE! FIGHT, FIGHT, FIGHT! Float like a butterfly, sting like a bee, go be a champion just like Ali! We'll be missing you! Good luck!* Each step in her polyester jogging suit was animated with a short swish like a scythe whipping back and forth, eager to gain purchase. Later, she would flit about her mother's hospital room making adjustments that didn't matter—watering the lilies she'd bought, straightening stacks of magazines and books, tossing the food containers, cans, and paper bags her father had left because he was forever leaving things undone in his wake.

A tap on her shoulder brought her surfacing from her thoughts to find JayLynn holding out her test. She took it and checked her watch. She'd frequently been losing time and attention. Barely five minutes since she'd started the timer. She'd set it for thirty minutes but doubted most would need that much time. The questions covered nutrition, rules of the sports they'd played, proper form of exercises they'd done. They were easy, all short answers because Patricia didn't like multiple choice, a game of chance that allowed poor students to luck up on a good grade. She believed in hard work, blood, and sweat.

A glance at the test revealed that JayLynn had only answered the first five questions—all correctly—before stopping.

"Here." Patricia stretched her arm, holding the test for JayLynn to retrieve. "You didn't finish," she said like the girl had made an honest mistake though there were additional questions she must have seen, plus a whole back side and second page. She liked JayLynn and was willing to give her an opportunity to reconsider whatever she thought she was accomplishing.

"I'm done," JayLynn said flatly.

"No, you're not," Patricia replied, her voice an equally steady plane.

"Yes," JayLynn glared, "I am."

"This is an F, JayLynn." Patricia held the test up as if showcasing the failing grade, a weapon she didn't want to yield though she knew it would barely scar. JayLynn had no doubt calculated the risk for this protest and tallied damage no worse than a B−. Nothing that would prevent her approaching graduation or scholarship to Indiana University, for which Gerald had written a recommendation. JayLynn was a favorite from his AP class. He read her essays with his fine-tip pen largely at rest, sipping his coffee and humming his approval. JayLynn's athleticism, however, was not impressive, for the most part. She contorted herself into zigzags socking volleyballs into the net and airballed granny-shot free throws, but the girl could run. She smoked in relay races, her skinny legs pumping and powerful. Patricia believed in A's for effort and, until now, JayLynn had earned just that. It was clear from her reluctant approaches and relieved concessions to the bleachers to laugh and talk with Maya that she didn't like sports, but mustering the strength and motivation to act precisely because she didn't want to had appeared to be the whole point for her.

But now, she said, "This is PE . . ." and paused, considering her words before concluding, ". . . it doesn't matter." She seemed apologetic, as if Patricia had forced her to reveal this truth.

Patricia had to concede that the test was wack. Heartless. Pointless, she thought as she watched JayLynn's skinny legs make their way to Maya on the bleachers. Sauntering like that with basketball shorts swinging around her knees, they looked foal-weak, easily broken. There was so much breaking in the world. JayLynn knew this, and Patricia guessed this little rebellion was her way of fighting against it, a sort of winning. She got it, but there were more constructive ways to channel the anger and sadness that she knew burned the same as anger, all of it churning in your stomach, a growling engine seeking any reason to rev, roar.

"I'll race you," Patricia threw the words at JayLynn's back.

The other students who hadn't made their meddling in this conversation obvious until now raised their heads with their classmates, all catching the whiff of the new scent, a potential power shift, swirling in the air.

"Oh shit!" Darius giggled behind his fist.

"You're not serious," JayLynn said.

"I'm so serious," Patricia said. She was cocky at just the anticipation of competition.

Her blood rushed and she buzzed, solidly alive. She tried not to think of her mother's face whittled to the hard fact of bone. Each body taught its own lessons. Of power, weakness, and wonder. Blood creeping through underwear, staining a whole day. Dicks rising to an unknown call, leaving boys covering, cowering. The body is a temple. The body can eat you alive. Nothing but the body could highlight these points.

"*I'll* race you!" Maya stood.

"No thank you." Patricia couldn't hide her smirk at karma's quick return, the sense that she was teaching a useful life lesson. She didn't even flinch when Maya said, "No this bitch didn't!" though the class chorused a two-octave "Ooo-oooh!" and watched her with wide eyes, awaiting her response. She put her hands on her hip and turned to Jay-Lynn. "One lap around the track."

Darius approached Patricia and rested his forearm on her shoulder. At six-foot-two, he stood a good seven inches taller than her. "What we win?"

"We?" Patricia shifted her shoulder and his arm slid off the slick polyester of her jacket.

"We doing students against teacher and Jay's our representative, right? You know I'm on your side." He licked his pink lips, grinned, and rubbed his hands together. "But I'm a businessman."

"I didn't say I was gonna do it." JayLynn folded her arms.

"She don't wanna race *me* cuz she knows I'll whoop that aaaass!" Maya yelled.

"If *JayLynn* wins," Patricia began, "everybody gets an A for the semester."

"Psshh." Maya sucked her teeth while her classmates chattered excitedly. "So what? Like my girl said, it's PE."

"Shut up, girl," Darius told her. "I'm failing everything else. I need this A."

"But what if she loses?" Latisha cried. She was a junior shooting for a spot at an ivy league college, and she never let anybody forget it. Patricia often wanted to shake her. Tell her there were more important things than grades, like warming yourself in the sun while there was still light and growing a personality worth being around. "I can't concentrate. Will we get extra time to finish?"

"If she loses, you'll get an A, too, okay?" Patricia told her, making no attempt to hide her exasperation. "Everybody will get an A!" She raised her hands in an exaggerated gesture of triumph to cheers, tests flapping into the air like released doves.

"Then what was all this for anyway? I could have been studying for my science test." Latisha stood, holding her test like a customer requesting a refund. "What's the point?"

"Ex*act*ly!" Maya smacked her thigh on the word's second syllable for emphasis and, likely, to draw Darius's attention to that expanse of her skin. "JayLynn, you gone beat her real fast so we can at least get that out of all this?"

"Dooo it! Dooo it! Dooo it!" Darius began a chant that the other students, minus Latisha, picked up.

"Okay, alright," JayLynn finally relented.

"Aww shit! We 'bout to smoke this bitch!" Maya shrieked with melodramatic amusement, tossing her head back. JayLynn chimed into her mean-girl laughter.

Yes, Patricia had challenged her to a race, but her purpose had been to teach JayLynn how to push forward amid situations and people she couldn't control. Ultimately, she'd imagined them on the same team, making strides toward a similar victory. She stung with hurt feelings, even though she knew it wasn't logical for her to feel deserted.

JayLynn's mother wasn't dying, but in an essay written in February for Gerald's class, she explained that sometimes it was like her mother was dead.

"Shit." Gerald had taken off his glasses and pinched the bridge of his nose. "Read this," he'd said, pushing the paper into Patricia's hands.

The title "How to Be Normal" was centered and bolded at the top of the page. JayLynn began:

It's hard to smile when Mama doesn't. It used to be easy. It was something I took for granted, something I never thought about. Now, I think about smiles, smiling, all the time. I also think about laughter. I study both of them, and sometimes, I study so hard that I forget to do them myself.

Patricia found herself—a scared daughter—in JayLynn's words and swiped at her tears as she read about the "gray slate" of JayLynn's mother's face, her hospital scrubs donned for days until they and she appeared "wilted," her locked bedroom door that JayLynn "watched expectantly for signs of life."

On days when Patricia was tired after she'd stayed up all night watching her mother sleep and not sleep, Jackie's eyes creeping open and falling shut like curtains, she rolled out the TV and VCR to play Richard Simmons' *Sweatin' to the Oldies* because Simmons's wispy afro, short shorts, and the corny music kept the students endlessly entertained. She looked forward to watching JayLynn laugh and shimmy off the shroud of her mother's depression. Maya bounced into flying leaps, grapevines with extra strut and whooped it up, exaggerating the fun she was having without Patricia leading the activity, and Patricia tried not to hate her.

Her mother would say that every bitch is a woman going through something. She was willing to grant all women grace in word and deed, even though she said reasons never stop bitches from being bitches. Jackie knew this because she could herself be a bitch sometimes—a beautiful bitch with seashell pink manicured nails and pressed and curled hair nestled on her shoulders, the prissiest bitch—and she had her reasons. But her bitchiness was often hidden so deep in her smile, tucked behind her straight teeth and under her tongue like a razor, that it rarely cut.

On Christmas Eve, at Jackie's request, Patricia had dropped her father's presents—socks and underwear—at his apartment, along with a package for his girlfriend, Terry. Her mother usually bought Terry a nice sweater or scarf, a gift intended to show how much more class and refinement she had, and always a bottle of perfume, as if to say, "And you stink too, heifer." In return, she received jingly earrings, cheese and summer sausage baskets, pairings of cheap nail polish and lipstick—gifts plucked thoughtlessly from some clearance bin or dollar store. Jackie never kept them; their confirmation of Terry's inferiority appeared to be gift enough.

Patricia's father had given Jackie his annual gift of a one-hundred-dollar check, money from their still-joint bank account, shoved in an envelope signed, *Love, Bruce.* Patricia had caught her mother tenderly running her thumb across the rushed scrawl before—she was happy to see—dropping it into the trashcan beside her bed. She hated her father for the scraps he left her mother to relish: old military uniforms and dress shoes still in the closet, biweekly spring and summer visits to mow the lawn, a fall drop-by to rake and bag leaves, house calls to fix what had broken.

Bruce moved out when Patricia was seven. In the cave of his apartment with the light struggling through small, north-facing windows, the shadows seemed to cast guilt on everyone. Patricia felt like an accomplice eating spaghetti dinners and watching Disney movies with Terry and her father, a traitor helping them paint the picture of a happy family like her mother didn't exist no more than a ten-minute drive down Dixie Highway. Even when she tried to make things difficult within her mother's requests to be nice, her father appeased her most unreasonable requests. No bedtime, cake for breakfast and lunch, her own cup of beer to drink while watching the basketball game—all were granted with Bruce's warning not to tell her mother. "It'll be our little secret." He'd wink.

Of course, she'd tell and Jackie would pull a towel from the dryer, snap, fold, and say "What your father does at his place is his business" or smile like she knew exactly what Patricia was doing, kiss her forehead and say, "I love you, and your father does too. I trust that he's not going to let you do anything that would really hurt you."

The weekend visits with Bruce stopped when Patricia was fifteen, bristling with attitude and done with pleasantries, though he called every Friday trying to justify a situation that was plain wrong, simple as winning or losing, being dead or alive.

"Me and your mama hashed this out years ago. I love her. Always have, always will." Patricia caught the sound of the TV in the background, Terry's shrill laughter. "I'm always gonna take care of her, both of y'all. Anything she needs. We just don't always mesh well and your mama knows that. She's fine."

Jackie now depended on Bruce's health insurance and a cut from his hefty army pension, but she hadn't always needed to rely on him for money. She'd been a homemaker since Patricia had been born, but before that she'd been a teacher. Patricia knew her mother's biggest bind to Bruce wasn't financial. On her decision not to divorce, Jackie had said, "I play to win," offering a sports analogy she thought Patricia, dense with muscle from junior varsity basketball, would understand. But she couldn't understand her mother wasting time and beauty pining for her own husband, never bringing home more than a phone number she wouldn't call, crawling into a bed she had to warm by herself after locking all the doors and reactivating the security system with codes Bruce had set. That was losing, and Patricia hated losing.

Maya was an upfront bitch. A loud bitch. A bitch's bitch.

She wielded a ferocity Patricia could respect, even targeted at her, if it wasn't rooted in jealousy over a boy who reluctantly gave her the energy it took to turn his head and witness her parading for him. Apparently, he was bored. Been there, done that after last year's junior prom, and now Maya was sprung. Open, the girls said. Gone off the dick is what Patricia had caught Darius and other boys saying. "Get off my dick" is precisely what he'd told Maya one day during the basketball unit when she was supposed to be guarding him and yanked at his arm, trying to whisper into his ear. Patricia felt bad for the girl, but she was too young to be that dumb, limiting herself to that disrespect, and too stubborn to hear sincerity, not condescension or strategy when Patricia tried to help and told Darius to leave Maya alone.

"She gone be looking so stupid when you win!" Maya told JayLynn. "I can't wait!" She cackled and smirked at Patricia. The smooth bronze of her face was interrupted by a deep dimple that slashed into her left cheek. It was an alarming smile made more chilling by the beauty still clear in all that hate. Patricia could imagine it in an advertisement, plastered on a billboard for a pop that all the girls would drink.

"I'm glad that if I can't kick her ass, it's gone be you." Maya's anger shone, cut. It was alluring, a diamond, and Jay-Lynn watched her intently as she spoke, her face pointed toward the white core of its radiance, gathering its brilliance to blaze her own fires.

"We're heading outside!" Patricia announced, and Camile rushed next to her, walking in step to her right, as she led the class.

"I'm thinking about cutting my hair for the summer, kind of like yours." Her eyes flashed to Patricia's permed pixie cut. "What do you think?"

"Cut your hair if that's what you want to do," Patricia answered.

Camila gasped, swept her hair over one shoulder, and held the long tail in both hands protectively as if Patricia had scissors ready to cut. "What if it's ugly?"

"You got a funny-shaped head," Darius, on Patricia's left, said. "It's a possibility."

Camila gasped again, tightening her grip. "Shut uuup!" To Patricia she asked, "What if Angelo doesn't like it? Does Mr. Hines ever say he wants you to have long hair?"

"It's hair. It'll grow back if you don't like it. But that's all you need to be worried about—whether you like it." Patricia pushed the door open and was hit with the smell of grass, mulch, and rain waiting in clouds decorating the bright sky. "If Angelo doesn't like it and acts silly over some hair, you don't need to be with him anyway."

Reenah, who walked to Camila's right, nodded. "That's deep."

"Yeeeah," Camila said, uncertain. She petted her hair, and the tiny diamonds on her promise ring caught the sunlight. She and Angelo had been together since seventh grade. Forever, the kids said.

Somebody said, "Ooh, it feels good out here," and Patricia felt like she was doing something right, bringing them out into the world, teaching them something different.

"Those shoes are dope. You just get them from J Mall?" Reenah asked. "I went last week and didn't see those in none of the stores."

"Mall St. Matthews," Patricia offered, recognizing Gerald in the group circled on the green beside the track. He stood and dusted the back of his khakis before heading toward the track's edge.

So many of the girls were eager to anchor themselves to something, someone they believed to be bigger than themselves. Patricia sensed that her visible attachments—her marriage to Gerald and wardrobe full of the students' favorite athletic brands—were major factors in her fast rise as a student favorite in her year and a half at the school, the reason they believed her opinion was one they could trust in many, if not all, situations. She resented the way Gerald's presence seemed to invalidate her advice to Camila to be her own woman.

"Ay, Mr. Hines! Your wife and JayLynn fitting to race!" Darius reported. "It's going down!"

"What?" Gerald chuckled nervously. His brows wrinkled in concern.

"I thought it would be fun." Patricia shrugged.

"You should get your class to come over and watch," Darius suggested.

"Why JayLynn?" Gerald asked Patricia.

"I told you she can run. It's just for fun."

"Yeah, that's what you just said." He watched Patricia's students thundering onto the bleachers on the other side of the track. "Fun," he croaked suspiciously. He stretched the word like he did before every argument that began with him repeating a word or phrase she'd said, swirling it on his tongue, judging its meaning from all angles as if analyzing a passage from one of his assigned readings.

Patricia muttered, "Don't make a big deal of out this, Gerald," before sending Darius to tell JayLynn and the class there would be a ten-minute warm-up. JayLynn was already doing quad stretches.

Gerald called to his students, "Y'all can go join Mrs.

Hines's class for the show." He directed them up and out of the grass with a wave toward the bleachers. He reached for Patricia's hands, and they stood much like they did on their wedding day when they exchanged vows. He waited until they were out of the students' earshot to speak. "Our parents can't be here forever in spite of how much we want them to be."

Patricia rolled her eyes. "I know that, Gerald."

"I don't think you really do."

"Why are we talking about this?" She retrieved her hands and crossed her arms.

"I went buck when I lost my father," Gerald said.

Patricia sighed. Gerald's father died of a heart attack when he was thirteen. Afterward, Gerald joined a gang. She knew this.

"I'm not proud of the way I acted," Gerald continued. "All that shit amounted to nothing and left me feeling so *tired*." He looked at her like there was a lesson in his words he was waiting for her to pull out. She hated when he did that.

"I did so much fighting against what was. If I would have just sat my ass down and given myself time to think and process, those years after Pops died would have been easier on everybody."

"I don't need a lecture," Patricia said.

"I'm not giving you a lecture. I'm talking to you. I know it hurts; it's gonna hurt. I miss Pops every day."

"I know, baby." She'd seen him pouring fingers of his

father's favorite whiskey, thumbing through photo albums pulled from the bookshelf. "But it's not the same. Your father has been gone for years. My mother is still alive."

"Damn, Tricia." He shook his head. "Not everything is a competition." He sighed and headed to the bleachers.

Patricia let JayLynn choose the race official. She made a good pick with Caleb, a gentle giant from Gerald's class who liked everybody and everybody liked. All three met at the starting line, and Patricia and JayLynn stood on their marks against a whooping crowd.

"You got this, Miz Hines!" Darius yelled.

"Smoke her, J!" Maya replied.

Patricia glanced at the bleachers. Gerald sat silently.

When Caleb gave the go, Patricia shot off. Sky and grass blurred as her legs rushed her over the track. There was only its infinity, stretching before her. The wind she created in her ears. Her heart a fist in her chest. Her breath controlled, steady. And then there was JayLynn padding behind her, beside her, maintaining her breath just as she'd taught her. Patricia thought this would please her, but she was annoyed by JayLynn's intrusion on the spell her body was casting. She huffed and pulled ahead. Maybe she was being a bitch, but she had her reason. She'd hovered over Jackie yesterday, listening, feeling for her breath. A whisper of warmth from Jackie's lips, like a sound you had to strain to hear, floated ghostlike against Patricia's ear, carrying a quickly unsettled relief. She gasped now, faltered.

And JayLynn whizzed past her, legs churning, tense with muscle, solid, healthy.

"Go, Jay!" Maya screamed.

Patricia only spoke about her mother with family and Gerald. None of their colleagues knew because she didn't want to give updates rehashing details of Jackie's cough-laugh, fuzzy head, or the bitter odor that had attached itself to her and seemed now to be rooted in her bones, her nails that Patricia polished for her, painting everything as pretty as it could be.

She wouldn't cry. She scrambled to recover, running faster, harder. Her arms and legs zip-zip-zip-zip-zipped in her jogging suit, the scythe relentless as she trailed JayLynn's heels and eventually caught up. They tore down the track shoulder to shoulder until JayLynn pushed forward, dug to some deeper level and barreled ahead.

"Oh shit, Jay! Go, girl!" Darius yelled.

"Naw, naw, naw. Don't try to be on our team now. Cheer for your girl," Maya replied.

"She's doing it, though! Look at her!"

"I know, that's my girl. Get it, Jay!" Maya screeched.

The bleachers exploded when JayLynn crossed the finish line. Caleb grabbed her hand and thrust it into the air, declaring her the winner.

"Girl!" Maya raced down the bleachers.

"Congratulations." Patricia extended a hand to JayLynn. She smiled and batted her eyes, fighting the threat of tears.

"Thank you," JayLynn panted, placing her hand in

Patricia's. Her face was flushed red, effervescent. Her triumph melted into alarm as she noted Patricia's wobbly smile and flickering lids. "What's wrong?"

"She just mad cuz she lost," Maya, now standing beside JayLynn, answered.

Patricia shook her head, denying the tears now falling. She held onto JayLynn's hand and squeezed softly. "Keep smiling. And laughing. You're gonna be okay."

JayLynn looked confused until Gerald approached, placing his hand on Patricia's back. Her eyes seemed to flash with realization. The essay. And her face darkened. She yanked her hand from Patricia's.

"You don't know me," she said, but the words were toothless, muttered before she walked away with Maya on those skinny legs, past Darius.

"Miz Hines!" His voice rang with disappointment. "What happened out there?"

Bruce was asleep in one of the two chairs in Jackie's room when Patricia and Gerald arrived at the hospital. The room smelled like fried chicken, gravy, and salt pork.

"Hey, baby." He stretched. "I bought some dinner." He pointed to the paper bucket and a plastic bag on the rolling tray resting against the wall.

Patricia nodded. "Thank you."

Gerald leaned down to greet Bruce in a loud smack of hands, a hearty slap on the back.

"I couldn't eat a bite." Bruce yawned. "My nerves are a

wreck. I got the nurses to bring in a cot. Figured y'all might be here a while. Doctor said it could be any time."

Patricia stood by the bed. "Hi, Mama." She brushed a hand over Jackie's curls. They were dry. "I'm here." Jackie's eyes remained closed, her mouth slack in a way she would never tolerate in health. "Catching flies" she would have said.

Patricia knew that beating cancer didn't involve punches and kicks, but she couldn't help feeling that her mother—who'd gone on to do what she'd always done after her initial diagnosis—cook, clean, try not to be lonely—had gone about things all wrong. Her first chemotherapy treatment had been on the Tuesday morning after Thanksgiving. Patricia had prepared to take the day off, but Jackie told her not to worry; she'd made arrangements with Bruce. After work, Patricia had gone carrying soup and sandwiches and found her father propped up in her mother's bed with his shoes off. He and Jackie were laughing and watching *Sanford & Son, his* favorite show. Styrofoam food containers crowded Jackie's perfumes and lotions arranged on the dresser.

"What did you eat?" Patricia asked Jackie, throwing an accusing glare at Bruce.

"Your father picked up some fish dinners. I could only eat a hush puppy, but it was still good." Jackie smiled.

Patricia sat carefully, gingerly on the corner of the bed, eating her turkey sandwich and feeling like a third wheel. When she called the next day, Jackie said proudly, "Your father spent the night. Slept right beside me." And he did following each of her appointments, until they ended and in-home hospice care began. Patricia imagined her mother hanging onto Bruce's arm as they walked into the hospital, his words filling the sterile, white space in the treatment room, his hands helping her into bed. Patricia wondered if all those years holding on had been worth a few midnight hours. A laugh and a tuck-in. Patricia didn't think so.

"Let me get your brush and I'll moisturize your hair." Patricia stroked Jackie's hand.

"It's in that purple bag." Bruce pointed.

Patricia knew that because she'd packed the bag, but she tried not to act surprised that her father knew.

He sighed. "I'm gonna miss her."

"I bet you will," she said.

Patricia had told her mother not to worry about Christmas gifts, especially for Terry, but Jackie had insisted. Patricia didn't have her mother's refined, ladylike taste and she'd wandered the mall, unsure of what to buy until she passed a woman wearing Jackie's favorite perfume. She bought the big bottle and had a store employee wrap it up. She imagined Terry spraying it on her wrists, dabbing it behind her ears, the scent of gardenia ghosting through her father's dark apartment.

ORIGIN STORY

Zaria saw it in the dresser mirror while she was rummaging through a garbage bag full of pajamas and underwear. At first, she thought it was a bird. A bird she could handle, though she watched it fly a quick circle over her head, and she crawled toward the window, imagining Tippi Hedren swarmed with thrashing feathers and squawking beaks that left her bleeding and undone. The black, winged creature reached the window before Zaria and floated to the bare curtain rod to hang upside down as if to announce, "I'm a bat, bitch." This—a rabies-carrying flying rat planted in the room she'd spent the afternoon painting sunburst yellow—was too much and Zaria screamed.

"Mama?" Malik shrilled from his bedroom across the hall.

"I'm okay, baby," Zaria said. "Stay in your room. There's a bat in here."

"A bat?" He was standing beside her in seconds. "Wow!" he whispered. "That is so cool!"

"Didn't I tell you to stay in your room?"

"But I've never seen a real bat before."

"You've never had rabies before either, and I'm trying to keep it that way."

"What's rabies?" Malik asked.

"If the bat bites you, it'll make you sick. You'll go crazy like a wild animal, and then somebody'll have to shoot you, so go to your room."

Malik chuckled like she was the crazy one. "Nobody's gonna shoot me. I'm just a kid."

"Malik." His name came out as a plea instead of the warning that Zaria had intended. All day she'd been painting, cleaning, and telling Malik to sit down or get up to clear toys, Popsicle wrappers, and half-eaten sandwiches.

"Besides, he wouldn't bite me. He's just a little fella not bothering nobody."

"Malik, what did I tell you?" He trailed her as she stepped outside of the bedroom to turn on more lights to the hall, the stairs.

He gasped sharply.

"What? What?!" Zaria's eyes darted about the hall, flashing to the bat, still and unbothered in her bedroom.

"It might be Batman!"

Zaria sighed. "Batman doesn't turn into a bat."

"You don't know. He might. It might be a new trick so he can sneak up on his enemies."

Malik was seven, an age when the fantastic was undoubtedly real. It was intriguing to live in a world constantly shifted by his imagination. She usually indulged him with stories about the tooth fairy, Spiderman, and Camtron (her Toyota Camry who Malik informed her was an Autobot who would reveal himself if the situation were dire enough), but she was tired now and didn't feel like explaining Batman's capabilities to disprove his "Batman as bat" theory. In the hallway walking Malik back to his room, she saw a dark flash, another bat flying downstairs in the living room.

"Shit," she cursed.

"What?"

Zaria pointed.

"Holy cow! This must be the lair to the bat cave!" Malik pushed against the wall before kicking it.

Zaria smacked him upside the head. "What the hell is wrong with you?"

"I'm looking for the secret door."

"Get in your room like I told you." She pushed him toward the open door. He landed just before the threshold of his room where the white stars from his nightlight faded in the hall light.

"What are you gonna do?" Malik asked.

"Go!" Zaria yelled, and he finally obeyed.

Zaria stared at the bat hanging on her curtain rod. It seemed to be settled in for the night, insistent upon fucking up her new life. She breathed deeply, gathering courage, before snatching her cell phone from the dresser and re-treating into Malik's bedroom.

"So you calling me now?" Ameer answered.

"I've got bats," Zaria replied. "In the house," she clarified. They hadn't spoken in two weeks, and she didn't expect him to hold details of her life like her moving date.

"You got rats?" Ameer asked.

Zaria hated when he tried to talk to her over his music. She was annoyed that he was playing it so loud at one o'clock in the morning and wondered where he was going, though she tried not to be bothered by this curiosity. "Bats! I said 'bats.' Turn that shit down."

The fisting bass fell silent.

"Bats?" he asked.

"Yeah."

"Plural?"

"Yeah."

"How many?"

"I saw two, but it might be more. I didn't wanna know. Malik and I are in his room."

Ameer laughed.

"Look, I'm pissed and scared right now, are you coming?"

He asked for the address and assured her, "I'm on my way, baby" before hanging up.

The way he called her baby made her feel loved and uneasy.

—

When Zaria passed her bedroom to go downstairs and let Ameer in, she saw that the first bat was still hanging on the curtain rod. She crouched low, afraid that the second bat—reeling in the living room, seemingly gleeful for having the space all to himself—would end one of his dizzy figure eights by divebombing on her head.

She opened the door to the skunky funk of weed floating from Ameer's clothes. "Have you been smoking?" she asked.

"Wooow," Ameer marveled, taking in the scene. His voice suggested wide-eyed animation, but his heavy lids rested in a lazy drape.

"Are you high right now?" she whispered the word "high" leaning closer to him so he could hear. The smell grew stronger.

"Look, Zaria. I didn't plan this. You called me; I came. It sounded like an emergency."

"But you're high! I don't want you high around my son!" The bat zoomed past her, whipping the air right by her ear.

She shrieked and dropped to the floor, holding her ear.

"Mama!" Malik called, running to the steps.

"Go back to your room, Malik! I'm okay."

"Hey, l'il man!" Ameer waved.

"Ameer!" Malik ran downstairs, ignoring his mother's instruction. "You gonna help us find Batman?"

"Uhh . . ." Ameer extended a hand to Zaria, which she

reluctantly accepted, rising to her feet. "I'll do whatever your mother wants me to do," he said, staring into her eyes.

Zaria didn't want to call her brother. She hated asking Waylon for favors. He, a couple of his friends, and her cousin JayLynn, who'd driven down from Bloomington, had helped her move yesterday, and Waylon had complained the whole time and scowled up at the sun when he wasn't doing that. He was often moody, zipping from jokes and laughter to a stone face as if receiving a reminder of all their mother's debts owed to him and steeling himself from being stupid enough to give again. Dee had smoked up hundreds taken from Waylon, crying LG&E cutoff, but then Zaria would come home after school to find her TV, radio, bedroom light not working, her mother gone. Malik's father, Travis, was good for nothing, as dependable as her mother who she wasn't inviting into her home to bring the same old shit into her fresh start.

She stared back at Ameer, into his drowsy eyes all stupid, sad, and hopeful, and her stomach clenched with anger. She hated feeling desperate, like she had no options. "I need these bats out of my house," she relented. Silently, she vowed to get stronger, man up, to avoid a situation like this in the future. It was a promise she'd made many times before when helplessness had fallen on her like a stone. A promise she always intended to honor until another impossible problem made it clear that she hadn't. She hadn't found the time to learn the necessary skills, hadn't imagined all of the scenarios or gained the muscle.

The bat whooshed by again and all three ducked. "Damn." Ameer scratched the top of his head, ruffling a patch of tight, black curls as he took in the scene. He did this when he was thinking, like a cartoon character. Usually, Zaria found it endearing, but now he reminded her of a doofus character on a sitcom. "Any windows open?" he asked.

Zaria shook her head.

"Where's the broom?"

"Don't kill it!" Malik cried.

Ameer assured Malik he wasn't planning to kill the bats. "I'm just gonna run them out of here so y'all can sleep tonight without Dracula all up on your neck." Ameer wiggled his fingers around Malik's throat and clavicle.

"It's not Dracula; it's Batman," Malik corrected him.

"How you know?" Ameer threw a knowing glance at Zaria.

"Because I know."

"Well, 'scuse me, then." Ameer smirked.

Zaria placed her hands on the bony knobs of Malik's shoulders, guiding him back toward the stairs. "Don't be smart. You don't need to be down here anyway."

"I'm not being smart, Mama. I'm just saying I know it's Batman."

"Alright, Malik." Zaria wanted him to shut up. Sometimes he could be embarrassing when she was around Ameer, who made her feel like she wasn't being a good mother by entertaining Malik's fantastic imagination though, unlike Waylon, he had never said anything to indicate his disapproval. When Malik started spinning tales about Camtron, Waylon always cut them short. "Cars can't come to life," he'd say. Zaria knew Malik could get on other people's nerves, and she felt that sometimes Ameer's daughter, Yaniece, tolerated Malik with the tempered patience of an adult more than five times her six years.

Though Yaniece spoke to imaginary people, her most frequent invisible companion was her husband, Cosco. She was often squeaking about his inadequacies. Why couldn't he take their daughter (a doll named Lolo) to the park or get her some juice or just help her out sometimes, dang? One day on the way to the park, Malik told Yaniece about Camtron. Yaniece stopped fussing at Cosco about getting a better job to toss Malik the absent "mmhmm" of a tired mother slogging through a rush of kid babble after a long day at work. She jerked Lolo upright onto the seat and demanded her to sit still. She screamed at Cosco to get out of her face.

"Hey hey, baby girl." Ameer reached into the backseat to give her leg a light tap. He looked at her through the rearview mirror as he spoke. "Don't be so loud. You don't have to yell at the man. Give him a chance. He's got a job, working at Dizzy Whizz, right? He's trying. Why you always on his case?"

Yaniece sat quietly. Her chubby cheeks sagged from the weight of her frown. Zaria could tell by the wrinkle of her forehead and the pensive look in her almond eyes that

Yaniece was considering Ameer's question. She thought it would be more beneficial for Malik to contemplate real-life situations like that instead of waiting for a car to become a robot.

Now, he repeated, "Don't kill it!" as Zaria handed Ameer the broom.

"I got you, man." Ameer raised a hand for Malik to chill. "I'ma need your help."

"No, you're not!" Zaria protested. "Bats carry rabies."

"Ain't nobody 'bout to get no rabies, Z. I got this," Ameer said.

"That's what I told her," Malik chimed.

Zaria rolled her eyes. "You didn't even know what rabies was. Go to your room."

Ameer turned to Malik. "Your mama's just scared. But that's why we're here to protect her. Go check all the rooms upstairs. Tell me how many bats you see."

"There's just the one in my bedroom," Zaria declared.

"I got this," Ameer repeated before continuing his instructions to Malik. "After you check the room, close the door behind you."

"Aye aye, Captain." Malik saluted and ran to the stairs.

"Don't try to touch or talk to them!" Ameer called.

"Ten-four!"

Ameer opened the basement door, flipped on the light at the top of the stairs. "You've got to let him be a man, baby," Malik told Zaria who stood at the doorway peering down into the shadows.

"Don't tell me how to raise my son," she said, her voice steely.

Malik sighed. "Zaria," he said softly, turning to her. "I don't smoke every day. Not around you or the kids." He resumed his points in their argument as if no time had passed. "It's not a big deal."

"How can you say that to me?" she asked. "You know about my mother."

"Because it's just weed, Z. It ain't that deep. And it's me. It's me and it's weed; that's all. I keep telling you it's different." Zaria knew he didn't want to say what the weed wasn't, how things were different.

She'd never meant for things to go further than that first date five months ago. He was thirty, five years older than her, and that maturity seemed reflected in his conversation and steady employment at the Ford assembly plant. He was handsome, smart, and funny. Everything had been perfect until he'd mentioned smoking weed in one of his stories. When they were standing kiss-close at her front door, she wanted to breathe the cologne rising from his neck all night and do the easy thing, but she looked him in the eye and told him, "You smoke weed."

He stepped back, laughed, and asked if she was serious.

There was no smile on her face when she told him, "Very."

But she liked talking to him. There was nothing wrong with talking, so they kept talking. And hanging out. They introduced their children without fanfare. Yaniece was quiet at first, clinging to Ameer and mumbling her requests for juice and snacks, but she eventually dropped all that quiet to direct Malik in their games and shriek with excitement when he was finally doing something right or losing terribly. The four of them ate Sunday dinner together at Zaria's wobbly table. She heaped Ameer's plate and tapped doll-size dollops for Yaniece, a very picky eater. She'd felt a silly sense of achievement when Yaniece asked for more macaroni and cheese on their third Sunday. This tiny victory was bringing her closer to what accomplishment? When she asked herself, *How far are you willing to go with this?* it was supposed to be rhetorical chastising, a finger wagging like wiper blades clearing all her foolishness, a voice of reason, not a challenge.

"They're coming from the fireplace," Ameer announced after opening the lace-latticed screen, kneeling on the brick hearth, and sticking his head in the firebox to look up the chimney. He seemed untroubled by the bat swirling above him. It left the living room and breezed into the kitchen before returning to settle on the mantel ledge as if affirming Ameer's statement.

"But the flue is closed," Zaria said like she'd lived her whole life knowing about fireplaces and chimney dampers.

"The damper could be warped. Bats are small; they can get through tight spaces."

"Shit."

"It's not that bad," Ameer said. He hadn't found any bats in the basement, and Malik had returned downstairs with a report confirming the single bat in Zaria's bedroom. "I'll work something out."

The fireplace was one of the best things about the house. Zaria had envisioned many evenings in front of a fire. She didn't have any living room furniture because she'd refused to haul the worn-out hand-me-downs from the old apartment to the new house, but she'd be able to buy her sectional soon, before all the trees in the neighborhood were burning red and orange, and she and Malik would stretch out on the lounger with books and mugs of hot cocoa. She'd allowed herself to imagine being hugged up with Ameer, listening to the fire's crackle, making love.

Two weeks ago, she and Ameer had a rare weekend without the kids. Yaniece was traveling with her mother to visit family down South, and JayLynn had come down for the weekend and volunteered to take Malik so Zaria could have some "Mama time." She'd winked when she said it like she already knew what would happen. But why wouldn't she? Everything had been adding up to it.

Afterward, Zaria rose from Ameer's arms to answer her phone, Malik was sick, throwing up and diarrhea. JayLynn thought it might be food poisoning from the hamburgers they ate out. Zaria could almost see her cringing, shrinking with apology. JayLynn's mother's depression made her believe all the bad in the world was somehow rooted to something she'd done. Zaria told her everything would be okay; it wasn't her fault.

This, Zaria knew as she plucked her panties and bra from the floor, was a warning. A reminder, and it was her fault. She'd known better than to let herself get carried away with someone like Ameer, but he made her feel so comfortable, like she'd always known him. This was nice, but it was also one of the reasons that had given Zaria pause. After she'd rushed Malik to the urgent care center, given him the pre-scribed antibiotics, and lain him in her bed, she watched the slow rise and fall of his chest beneath his Spiderman pajamas, listened to the breath whistling through his nose, and called Ameer to tell him they had to stop whatever they'd started.

Tony had made thirteen-year-old JayLynn giggle.

"He's so cute!" she'd whisper-screech behind her hands.

Zaria had agreed but felt kind of gross for crushing on her mother's boyfriend who had hair that kept the kind of waves seen on the dudes grinning from boxes of texturizer and a perfect smile with teeth white enough to blind you stupid. Tony looked like one of the senior boys at Zaria's high school, but he was twenty-four. Dee was thirty-five, and Zaria wondered why her mother couldn't just act thirty-five and get with some thirty-five-year-old man who wore embarrassing short sets and busy sweaters and listened to the oldies R&B station while preaching about "real" music. Tony wore Air Force Ones like Waylon and kept a

copy of Dr. Dre's *The Chronic* on repeat in the house and
the car. He smoked weed constantly, which made his eyes
heavy, bedroomy. And he talked slow. Together, these features brought a sexual undertone to everything he said. Jay-
Lynn could be caught asking Zaria, "Did you hear what he
said to me?" at least a million times in one weekend. Zaria
just stared as JayLynn threw Tony's words back at Zaria as
questions "*Gimme that jelly?*", "*Save me some hot water?*"
like she was so lame for not catching the innuendo.

Tony had been skinny from the start. That didn't change.
His cravings did, though. When he first moved in, he ate
all the time. Those pretty teeth were always chewing and
crunching food down to nothing. He loved Flaming Hot
Cheetos and JayLynn hated them, but every time he offered her some, pushing the bag her way, she accepted so
she could eat something his fingers had possibly touched,
just like some Suzy from an After School Special who was
always biting her bottom lip and "I don't know about
this"ing before coughing on the first toke, wincing through
the first drink, or lying down in the backseat. Naive, just
like Zaria imagined Dee had been when she placed her lips
on the pipe Tony had kissed.

When Zaria got pregnant at sixteen, everybody thought
she'd been Suzy stupid, but Travis hadn't pressured Zaria
into unprotected sex. She thought Dee seeing her daughter
growing with child would clean her right up, but it didn't,
and Zaria had been the one left stunned. By her body's

constant spreading, stretching, softening, hardening, turning, turning in the mirror. By how much motherhood took and took and took.

It seemed like Malik had laid claim to even the memories of who she used to be days, months ago and slept with them balled in his tiny fists. Even on good days, when he smiled, revealing the white sliver of a tooth poking from his gums, or took a wobbly step and stared up at her with shiny-eyed surprise, she felt like she was losing something. Some days, her heart beat crazy for more than blood, to make a decision that wasn't weighed by Malik's needs, best interests, or wants. She got greedy for moments that spun her breathless and out of control, the way she'd felt fucking Ameer. She understood why Dee would keep chasing bigger highs and want to disappear into the wide sky she'd unlocked.

In her car racing to meet JayLynn, Malik filled all the spaces Ameer had opened. She gripped the steering wheel, frightened by how easily she could have been swept away. "Cars can't come to life," she could hear Waylon saying. She had to be the hero.

Ameer directed Malik to open the front door on his signal. "I'm gonna shoo the bat out with the broom and when it's out, you shut the door, alright?"

Zaria grabbed for Malik's arm, but he was too fast, bolting to commence his task. "What if there are more outside and they come in here?" She imagined a black cloud of bats floating across a full, white moon, swooping into her living room.

"Baby, you're gonna have to chill. I didn't see any when I was outside. Go stand over there." Ameer pointed back into the kitchen.

Zaria didn't move as Ameer crept toward the fireplace and tightened his grip on the broom. He held it upside down like a baseball bat. Before he could swing, the bat fluttered to life. He ducked and jumped back though the bat wasn't headed in his direction.

"Open the door! Open the door!" he yelled to Malik, who quickly obeyed. The bat drifted past him and into the night's watercolor mix of gray, blue, and purple as if to make them look stupid for even thinking he preferred being cooped in a house to losing himself in the bruise-colored sky. Malik hurried to shut the door.

"Good job, man!" Ameer dipped his arm low, held his hand palm up, and Malik seemed to muster the strength of his whole body to slap it with a loud smack.

Zaria kept the smile creeping on her face small and tight, but Ameer probably saw it when he turned to ask her if she had some duct tape to cover the fireplace vents. "It's just until we can call somebody tomorrow and do some research," he said. He must have read her disappointment.

She and Malik watched him pull long reams from the roll. The loud ripping was stark in their silence. It hurt to see the fireplace bandaged, but Zaria found comfort in the care Ameer took. He dragged the heels of his hands around the edges of the tape before starting in the center, smoothing down its length before adding a second layer. She didn't want to feel the relief she felt hearing him say "we"—". . . until we can call somebody tomorrow."

Two weeks ago, Zaria had called JayLynn after the fight with Ameer and relayed his point that you could have a drink and not be an alcoholic, smoke a joint and not be a drug addict. "Everything in moderation," she'd mocked him in a deep and dopey voice. She was surprised to hear Jay-Lynn say, "He's right." JayLynn's mother had wrestled with depression for years and tried to fight it with opioids. She was a year clean, and it was hard for Zaria not to feel jealous when JayLynn mentioned a conversation she'd had with Claudia, insightful advice she'd given, or something funny she'd said.

"He's a good man, Z. Has a good job and takes care of his daughter. Plus, he doesn't do it a lot. He said he smokes about twice a month or something? I mean, it's not like I'm supporting smoking weed, but . . . I think it'll be okay."

"Marijuana is the gateway drug," Zaria argued.

JayLynn burst out laughing. "You sound like a public service announcement." But she was serious when she said, "I know it is. I know what you mean. I don't even like taking ibuprofen. Sometimes when I have headaches, I just lie down, make myself go to sleep, and hope the pounding stops when I wake up."

—

The bat in Zaria's bedroom hadn't moved.

Ameer told Malik, who stood in the doorway with Zaria, to come in and close the door. "We're gonna do the same thing, but this time we're sending it out the window, okay?"

Malik nodded. "Excuse me, Mama." He needed her to move so he could shut the door.

"Oh." Zaria stepped inside her bedroom. There was something older in Malik's face. His jaw seemed tighter. His eyes glowed with determination as he carried out his order. He'd lost a little bit of baby in the short trip upstairs.

"What do I do now?" he asked Ameer.

"Protect your mama, alright, since she just *gotta* be in the room." He tossed the last few words at Zaria, rolling his eyes. When he opened the window, the bat flew to the other side of the room.

"Get down, Mama! Get down!" Malik jumped and waved his hands in front of her. The bat whizzed over their heads, zigzagging across the room.

Zaria dropped into a crouch and yanked Malik's shirt. He stumbled and fell before quickly recovering to his feet.

"I'm protecting you," he told her.

"Get down. You can still protect me from down here."

"Okay. Wait a minute." He knelt in front of her and wrapped his arms around her. "Put your head down," he ordered. Zaria rested her chin on his shoulder and hugged him back.

Ameer swiped the broom and knocked the bat onto

the floor near the foot of the bed, about three feet behind Malik. Zaria squeezed him tighter and pulled him closer to the door, away from the bat.

Malik turned left and right, trying to see which side offered the best view of what was happening. "Where is it? Where'd it go?" Malik spoke into Zaria's nose, and she smelled sour cream and onion potato chips and peanut butter cookie beneath a peppermint whisper of toothpaste.

He twisted a tight right and released Zaria to crawl to the bat. "Is it dead?"

"Don't touch it!" Zaria snatched his arm back, and he plopped onto his butt.

"I don't think it's dead," Ameer said. The bat shifted limply as he nudged it with the broom.

Zaria let go of Malik and they both crawled closer. The bat was dusty brown, not the saturated black Zaria had thought she'd seen earlier. It had fallen face down, folded into itself, and appeared wingless. She almost felt sorry for it, but it was nasty, ugly, and in her home uninvited. It and its homie had made her patch up a fireplace that wasn't even broken.

Zaria sat back on her heels. "Get it out of here."

"It's dead!" Malik screamed.

And then the bat started clicking.

Zaria and Malik jumped back to the wall. Ameer smashed the broom down on the bat, but the clicks didn't stop. They creaked and stretched, stuttered.

"What's it doing?" Malik asked.

"Echolocation," Zaria said. "It's calling for help." She was surprised by how quickly she'd recalled that information. How long had they studied bats in school? She didn't think it could have been that long. Not more than a couple of lessons. She couldn't imagine that she had paid that much attention, but the answer was there. It had been waiting all that time. What did Malik know that he didn't know he knew? What was he learning from her late-night loneliness, Travis's absence, Waylon's anger? The possibilities kept her up at night, staring until her mind blinked blank.

Ameer kept the broom pressed on top of the bat. "Shit," he huffed. The clicks chewed through the frayed straw.

"Don't kill it!" Malik jumped up to stand by Ameer. Zaria followed.

"Hold on. It's gonna be okay." Ameer raised the arm that wasn't holding the broom and dipped his face into his armpit to wipe the sweat from his forehead. He scratched his head, told Zaria to go get the dustpan, and when she returned, he swept the bat into the pan.

"You can't just throw it away!" The veins in Malik's neck strained as he screamed. "He's dying!" He was crying and hopping, unsure of what to do with his little body to change the situation.

"Calm down, Malik." Zaria rested her hands on his shoulders. He violently shook them off.

Ameer held the bat, plated on the dustpan, with a stiff

arm out to his side. "Don't disrespect your mama like that, Malik. You hear me?"

Malik looked down at the carpet, the gray blue of storm and sea brewing. He appeared to be deciding whether to wreak havoc or steady into calm.

"You hear me?" Ameer repeated, louder. The drowsiness in his eyes was gone.

The bat had stopped clicking and seemed to be waiting with Ameer for an answer.

"Yes," Malik mumbled, eyes trained on the floor.

"Speak up. And look at me when I'm talking to you," Ameer ordered. "A man always looks a person in the face when he speaks to them."

Malik brightened to hear that he was still considered among the ranks of men. He wiped his face, stared into Ameer's eyes, and answered, "Yes, sir."

The clicking resumed, on cue like applause.

Ameer jumped, and the bat bounced into the air before landing back on the dustpan. It tried flapping its wings and spun itself into a circle that almost led to a drop back onto the floor. Ameer rushed his arm through the open window and flipped the dustpan upside down. "That's not Batman," he told Malik, closing the window. "Batman doesn't turn into a bat or have special powers. He's a regular human, like you and me. He's just smart, strong, and got a lot of money to buy the stuff that helps him fight villains. That right there is just a bat. He's outside where he's supposed to be and he was moving, so he's probably not dead. But even if he is and even if he was Batman, she comes first." He pointed at Zaria. "Batman is Batman because his parents got killed by some bad guys. He don't have no mama. That's why he fights the Joker and all them, so other kids don't lose their parents. You got your mama, and it's your job to protect her."

Zaria didn't want to place herself on Malik's shoulders. Mothers were supposed to lift the burden, not become one. But she was raising a boy, a man. She knew if he didn't have grounding and responsibility, he could grow up spoiled and bitter, soft and crumbling in the face of life's smallest wrinkles. Ameer could help. She needed help, to fall into the cup of a body bigger than her own, take time trailing her fingers across it until she knew the origin story of every scar and callous. She wouldn't be stupid. She'd stay observant and ask questions, drop him quick if needed.

"Make sure no one hurts her. With their hands, weapons, or words," Ameer explained.

Malik nodded, accepting his duty, though worry still raced in his eyes. "How do I do that?" he asked.

"You'll know what to do when the time comes," Ameer assured him. "You'll learn."

Zaria watched Malik thinking, his face turning, turning.

A GOOD EDUCATION

Damon watched Tony walk the trash to the can in the backyard. He turned down all the funk from "Super Fly" to ask, "Who's that cat?"

I shook my head. Damon bought his 1978 Pontiac Bonneville a few months ago from some old man's over-crowded garage, and sometimes it was like the spirit of the seventies, curled in the light blue velour upholstery, pos-sessed him when he sat in the driver's seat. He wore white on green Nikes—the ones white people knew because of Farrah Fawcett and everybody I knew called Dope Mans because of N.W.A. and obvious reasons.

"That's Tony," I said. "I can't stand that nigga." I frowned at Damon's yellow and green Cross Colours short set that was planted firmly in 1994. "You look like a can of Sprite." Seems like Beetle would have told him not to walk around in those bright-ass colors, drawing attention. Damon was like a generic-brand chameleon, always changing to fit his surroundings and coming up a shade off.

"That's your mom's boyfriend?" he asked, ignoring my dig.

"That nigga's a bum."

It was almost three o'clock and Tony had just woken up, his basketball shorts and T-shirt roll-out-of-bed wrinkled. Sleep dragged on his heavy lids, and he looked like he was already trying to sexy-eye somebody out of their panties even though his mouth was a flat line, dead of the grin he was always working up to spin magic on Dee. Five months ago in March, when he moved in, that grin would send Zaria whispering and giggling on the phone to her friends, but even a boy-crazy fifteen-year-old could see through his bullshit and now she can't stand him, same as me. With him tired and scruffy, it was easier to see the man in his face, but he still looked like a dude me and Damon could have just graduated with.

Damon sat up, pushing his feet against the carpet near the pedals where the light blue was going brown. He leaned forward, squinted. Real theatrical since Tony's face, as he dragged the plastic can down the driveway, right toward the car and past the driver's side window, was clear as the day that wasn't sunny enough to call for all Damon's squinting.

Acting was Damon's first attempt at a long list of careers he'd planned to make him rich. He gave it up after playing Martin Luther King Jr. in a fourth-grade Black History Month production and stretching the "I Have a Dream" speech with dramatic pauses until somebody's daddy broke, hollering "Alright, we get it! Dreams. Damn!"

I thought Damon was being dramatic cuz he was getting ready to clown about how young Tony was—twenty-four, eleven years younger than Dee—but he was just doing a terrible job pretending like he was trying to be sure Tony was who he thought he was before he said, "I seen him at the spot."

He backed out of the driveway, grabbed the blunt resting in the ashtray, lit and hit it. "I seen your mother there with him, man." His choked words fell out with the smoke. They weren't surprising, but still hit like a gut punch. I maintained my composure, hit the blunt Damon passed, and closed my eyes. He sped down Muhammad Ali, past the liquor store, the tiny plaza with King's Beauty, and the grocery store with the beat-up produce and bad lighting that yellowed everything dingy. Past the gas station and Indi's Chicken like he was trying to race me to a different reality.

Makes sense he'd seen Dee. Louisville's not as big as people are always saying it is, and the West End feels like a smaller black scrap of it. I guess she thought she was taking precaution by going to the spot on Seventeenth and Garland instead of someplace closer where the neighbors and liquor store hang-outs might see, but Damon lived on Garland off Eighteenth Street. The spot was up the street from his house, and both of them were only a ten-minute car drive away from our house, maybe five if you cut all the stoplights. That's your brain on drugs—dumb.

"Slow down, man." I felt nauseous and wanted to throw up in the car just to ruin something he loved, but I knew what he'd just said, the unfolding of a future foul as the weed smoke growing between us, had already done that.

"Sorry," he said softly. The apology floated with the rest of the words taking up the small blue space that had the nerve to try to look like sky. The beeper hidden in the front right pocket of his shorts chirped. He rushed, fumbling with his shirt, to press it silent.

"What'd she say when she saw you?" I asked.

"She didn't see me. I was walking back to the spot from the store—getting some Blacks," he added, like I cared. "And I saw her car parked out front. By the time I realized whose car it was, dude was jumping in the car, and they were gone."

"So, you didn't see her." A dark, skinny hope, despite my knowing, made this a statement instead of a question.

"I barely saw the back of her. It was dark, late," he said, willing to surrender his own knowing. "She took off so fast . . ."

"When was this?"

"Mmm . . ." he hummed, doing a bad fake of trying to remember. "About a month ago, like a few days after the Fourth."

"Is that the only time you've seen her?"

"Yeah." He nodded so fast I thought he might have been lying, but he hit the weed so hard after I passed it back to him, sucking his chest concave into a half-moon, that I knew he was telling the truth.

"What about dude?"

"I seen him a few times."

"Since when?"

"Since I been hanging with Beetle." That's what he called it—"hanging."

Damon hooked up with Beetle around the beginning of the year like the whole thing was part of a New Year's resolution to get his money right, which it probably was. The persistent possibility finally added to that long list. He used to call me to "hang out" with them all the time, but I had a legit job at Pizza Hut. Customers didn't trip too much, and my manager was cool as long as everything was clean and orders were moving at a good pace, so we could cut up and bullshit, but I couldn't say I didn't think about "hanging" after getting my skinny check on Fridays, sliced even thinner after I subtracted my car payment and insurance. I couldn't sell that shit now, even though a part of me felt like I deserved a cut, something from the nothing gnawing on my moms.

Even if I really did just wanna chill with Damon and Beetle, it would have been stupid to post up at the trap spot with them, just waiting to get caught up in some bad about to pop off. I had Zaria to think about and couldn't afford to end up dead or in jail trying to find a good time with those niggas. Eventually, Damon stopped asking and the

calls dropped off. Phones work both ways, but I was clock-
ing as many after-school hours as I could and went to full
and overtime after graduation, and it's not like I had time,
or wanted, to be on the phone getting him caught up on my
life.

The car rumbled under us as it ate up stretches of the
Watterson Expressway. Curtis Mayfield crooned at a whisper.

"I mean, he's not over there *like that*," Damon added. "I
seen him at the club too when Beetle got me in. Nigga be
with all kinds of girls. Just lowdown. I didn't know, man."

"You seen him at the spot since that day you saw Dee?"

"Since when you call your moms by her first name?"

"Since she ain't been acting like my moms."

"How long's that?"

I inhaled. "A while." Exhaled. Damon was a keep-your-
eyes-on-the-road kind of driver, but I was lasering into him,
and I knew he felt it when he pinched the joint from my
fingers and his hesitant glance flashed into my glare.

"Cat came back around, but I told Beetle about it and
when man tried, Beetle broke that nigga *foul*." He chuckled.
"Said some shit that was downright wacked out." He chuckled again, puffed, passed. "Aww shit." He sighed.

He was trying to lighten the mood. Get me to ask what
Beetle said so I could laugh too, but I didn't say anything.

"Come on, man." He dropped his head to the side like
he was disappointed in me. Like I should know better, but I
didn't know anybody anymore. "I wouldn't sell that nigga no

shit knowing he's connected to my people. Your moms is like my moms . . . I mean . . . you think she's using?"

"Yeah," I said. I'd had some time to consider the clues and reach a logical conclusion.

"Damn." Damon shook his head solemnly, and his diamond earring caught the sunlight. I couldn't tell if it was real. He kept his eyes straight on the miles ahead, except for a moment when his gaze drifted to the space between us where I should have passed the joint, but that shit was mine now. It was nice to unload this secret, get some of its weight off my shoulders and onto his, but it didn't feel good enough to keep talking about it.

We rode in silence—me finishing the weed and staring out the window watching the sun battle clouds, Damon replacing the *Super Fly* soundtrack with a James Brown album and acting like he was grooving to all the trumpets' fanfare and James's grunts booming from the JBLs he'd just installed. He didn't need a system that loud; it would just bring unwanted attention, cops knocking right on one of the rattling windows. But he couldn't grasp subtlety or the concept of too much.

When he parked at Mall St. Matthews and calmed James to quiet, he turned to me, finally looked me in my eyes, and said, "I'm really sorry, brother."

I busted out laughing. *Brother?* Shit was too much. I stepped out of the car, still laughing.

Damon stood by the car. "What?" He giggled, glad for some relief I'm guessing and willing to release the moment he'd attempted, the hug he was leaning for when I opened the car door. "You're my brother."

"Come on, nigga," I said, walking toward the mall entrance.

Inside, there were all kinds of back-to-school sales. Foot Locker was packed, but they had the Jordans I wanted in my size. I sat down, slipped my right foot in that new shoe, and it made the old K-Swiss on my left foot look busted. I'd just polished them last week, and they looked like it, painted in that chalky white all creased around the toe. I hurried to take the new shoe off, stuff it with its tissue paper, place it in the box. I didn't wanna put my old shoes back on, but ditching them right at the store would have been like admitting how bad they looked. I asked the sales guy for a pair of K-Swiss.

"They're on a two for ninety special." His eyes flashed down to my feet.

"Good looking out," I said, forcing a smile. "Bring me a black pair too."

I'd saved up two hundred and fifty dollars and planned on only getting the Jordans, a pair of jeans, and a couple shirts, but the jeans I already had were fine. It's not like I was growing out of them or anything. And I could just get some plain tees. As long as my shoes looked good, I could make everything else work. I went to stand in line next to Damon who had two pairs of shoes. Even though I was bringing more to the register, I didn't feel more baller than

Damon, just needy standing in my faded black University of Louisville shirt and jean shorts, my raggedy shoes. I was glad I'd at least made it into the barber shop that morning for a fresh cut and put on some cologne, even though I could barely smell it under Damon's.

"Whatchugettin?" he asked.

I tapped the shoe illustration and description on the side of both boxes of K-Swiss.

"Classic, classic," he said. "Can't go wrong."

"And these." I showed him the Jordans.

"Those are clean." He nodded his approval. "I got them a couple months ago."

"Yeah." I pushed past my bruised ego to ask, "Whatchugettin?"

He showed me a white pair of Air Force Ones and another pair of Dope Mans (white on red), which pissed me off.

"Ain't you got enough of those?"

"Never enough," he said.

The "enough" on my mind lately had been about groceries. I'd go to the store and get a big pack of Ramen noodles, oatmeal (cuz it didn't take milk, and Zaria didn't blow through it as fast as cereal), peanut butter, bread, apples and keep that shit in my room. I hid bologna in the vegetable crisper so Tony wouldn't eat all of it. And, of course, there was always pizza.

I inched forward in line, thinking about the overdue LG&E bill. I needed to put something on that if Dee didn't. It was too hot to be without air conditioning. I was thinking about how I was gonna tell the cashier to put the Jordans to the side when Damon said, "Let me get those for you, man," so I did. I stacked my three pairs right on top of his two pairs so he had to juggle a little to avoid losing it all, and I went to have a seat on the bench outside the store.

Basketball had been another one of Damon's attempted get-rich-quick careers. He'd wanted some Jordans for his eleventh birthday, but in his bedroom, he showed me the pair of XJ900 Payless Jordan knockoffs he'd ended up with instead. His spirit was cracked, his face oozing disappointment. With his skinny body in straight-fit jeans and one of the turtlenecks his mother, Miss Liv, used to make him wear all the time, his head capped with a mini-fro, he looked like a sad Q-tip. Damon was easily bruised, like a peach, and I wasn't the only person who could sniff that sweet softness all over him even though most of the time he tried to hide it.

"I can't wear these," he whispered so Miss Liv, lying down in her bedroom across the hall, couldn't hear.

Miss Liv had worked two jobs since I'd known her. One as a package handler at UPS where she met Dee when I was seven, and one waitressing at whatever restaurant was offering the biggest tips and the smallest headache for the time being. She usually left the house tired and came home the same way.

"They don't look bad." My voice was high-pitched with

exaggerated optimism. I felt guilty for wearing my Jordans, especially since they were one of two pairs I owned, the ones that had been demoted to kick-arounds for playing. Damon wasn't supposed to wear his new shoes anywhere but school and special outings, but after I'd pumped him up about how they would probably still help him run faster and jump higher, maybe even better than Jordan, he put them on and wanted to go hoop. I decided I'd let him win.

The shoes really didn't look bad. If we lived in a world where niggas had real money, power, and respect they wouldn't go looking for it in dumb shit like pointing out whose shoes did and didn't have a little jump man or a number another man had already made great to make them feel like somebody, but the boys at the park, towers who cast their shadows on us, made it clear the exact kind of world we lived in when they stole Damon's basketball. It was also a birthday gift and the second ball that had been snatched. As the boys held it over Damon's head, sur-rounded us in a circle, and passed it between them, zipping it bullet-fast from one set of big hands to another, Damon told them he wasn't worried, he'd just get another ball, when he got rich he'd have hundreds, thousands, and his own court.

"You gone get some real shoes too?" the shortest boy said, pointing at Damon's feet. The rest of them cracked up.

I threw a punch at the boy's stomach, but it landed weakly at his hip. His punch to my gut was executed per-fectly, if not mercifully. Dude was solid and, even doubled over on the blacktop, I could tell he hadn't hit me with his full force.

"Nice try, l'il nigga." His words fell to me like loose change as he and his crew left the court. They rang with a respect that had been absent for Damon, who knelt beside me, his eyes growing shiny.

"Stop crying," I told him.

"I'm not!" he whined, his voice thick with snot. He swiped at the fat tears on his cheek.

"You gotta get harder," I said, pushing against the black-top to sit up. I brushed the grit from my hands and arms.

Damon and Miss Liv had just moved into the house on Garland. She was renting, but it was still a house. With a front porch for swinging and a backyard for barbecuing. A place where the smell of somebody else's dinner or the sound of their arguments didn't creep through the walls. It was an opportunity for Damon to start fresh in a new neighborhood without bullies, and I didn't want him to blow it. My advice wasn't wrong, but I didn't know how easy I had it.

All my aunts said me and Zaria were spoiled. We didn't get everything we wanted, but we did get most of it. Dee's "Are you crazy?" to Zaria's ask for a pair of designer jeans or laughter in response to my point to a top-of-the-line stereo reminded us of financial limits. Sometimes she would echo Miss Liv who came home from work flicking rooms dark, fussing about Damon lighting the house like he got stock in

LG&E, but Zaria and I had never worried about lights getting cut off.

I'd expected shoes for my birthday back in May. Dee had me call my job to see if they'd give me a couple free "birthday" pizzas, then asked for a ham and pineapple one for Tony. We ate pizza; they sang "Happy Birthday" over the box mix-cake Zaria had baked, frosted, and staked with candles and that was it. No gifts. Just lip service about me being a man and taking on new responsibilities.

"You're eighteen," she said. I was waiting for her to smile at this. Wrap me in a hug and tell me I would always be her baby like she'd done on past birthdays. Tell me she was proud of me. Something. It hit me that I hadn't seen her smile in a while. Her front teeth were crooked; the right tooth slightly overlapped the left, but it was a good smile. When she laughed, it was perfectly imperfect. "It's time for you to start contributing to this household." She wrapped herself tighter in her robe like she was warding off chill and my possible opposition. She was still wearing her pajamas and night scarf. Her red eyes bullseyed wide dark circles even though she'd been in the bed all morning. Her looking like that made it feel even less like my birthday than no gifts to unwrap.

It was just me and her in the kitchen. After stuffing his face with pizza and a chunk of my cake, Tony left. Zaria was in the living room on the phone. I was ironing clothes, getting ready to go out with some friends from work.

"A few dollars from every check . . . like twenty-five," she said. "One hundred dollars a month," she declared, like she'd come to a final answer after much deliberation. "Okay?"

"Okay." I didn't look up from the steam erasing the wrinkles from my shirt.

"I'm sorry I didn't get you a gift, but I been running behind," she sighed. "I was helping Tony settle some of his bills and . . ." She tossed her hands up like the situation was out of her control.

When Dee told me Tony had lost his job at Fischer, shit started making sense. I'm not dissing Dee cuz that's still my moms and she looked decent, but dude was just *slick*, and I could see it in his eyes even with the lids half-mast cuz of all the chiefing he did. It's like he was always scanning, seeing what he could get, and he could get any woman he wanted. Baddies his age, or younger, with no kids. Seems like what he wanted from Dee was a payout from her nice, steady checks; a free lay-up in the home she owned.

"You can make him get a job. 'Start contributing to this household,'" I said. At twenty-four, a man should have something more to show for himself than a couple garbage bags of clothes, a cheesy grin, and a sad story.

"He's looking for a job."

"He don't seem to be looking very hard." I moved my shirt on the board, pressed the collar smooth.

"It takes time. Good jobs don't come easy when you don't have education." I could feel her getting ready to launch into a retelling of her story as a teen mother who'd quit community college after a year and struggled in dead-end jobs before getting a customer service job at Humana and working her way up as a claims adjuster. All for the benefit of trying to make me feel sorry for Tony. I didn't wanna hear it.

"I didn't say a good job, I said *a* job. He can go down to McDonald's or something."

"McDonald's ain't gone do nothing for him, Waylon."

"It'd do better than nothing." I knew I was pushing it, but I wasn't scared of her. I'd been taller than her since eighth grade when I shot up to six-foot-one, but looking down at her sitting in that chair, she seemed smaller in every way. She was coming to me for help, and I understood that I couldn't rely on her. I was on my own now. I knew that even before I noticed my grandmother's ring gone from her finger; before she called herself "borrowing" me and Zaria's video games and the consoles, the VCR and movies; before the climbing totals on past due bills despite my "contributions"; before the twenty-five dollars a week turned into "whatever you can give" placed in her shaky hands.

When we crossed paths at the front door late one night in July—both of us still in our work clothes, but only me with good reason for it—it only took a look in her eyes to see the dilated pupils, visible in the porch light Zaria had left on for both of us, to know that everything was gone— my moms, my stuff—and there were no promises I'd get anything back.

Sitting in the kitchen on my birthday, looking shrunken, she'd sighed, "You gotta focus on what *you* gotta do." She'd seemed exhausted by offering those words, which had suddenly become the best she could give.

Damon came out of the shoe store with two big bags. He carried them to Camelot's and Radio Shack where he picked up more bags. I trailed him in my make-do shoes feeling like I guess he used to feel when he was with me. Every now and then, I saw him sneak-check his beeper.

On the way to the food court, we passed a boy, about thirteen, coming out of Bacon's moping a few paces in front of a woman I assumed to be his mother who was grumbling half to herself and half to the boy, who was obviously not trying to hear her.

"There was nothing wrong with those pants. I don't know why you're acting all silly. I'm not about to spend my money if you're not going to appreciate it. I can keep my money in my pocket." She pulled her purse strap higher up on her shoulder.

"I feel for the man." Damon laughed. "That's what it was like shopping with Moms. He's lucky he even made it to the mall. We barely made it past Value City. And Payless! She stayed pushing me into Payless shoes. I will go in there right now and cuss somebody out. Remember those And Ones?"

The laugh that raced up from my stomach was so big and sudden that I bent over, squeezing it out in a long wheeze until I could catch my breath and let it explode.

"I'm just glad I'm alive to tell the tale because those things made life *rough*."

I felt bad but couldn't stop laughing. We went to different schools, so I didn't see all the shit he took there, but I saw enough action on the weekends when I visited. Those kids in his neighborhood were vicious, but they weren't telling no lies. Those shoes were horrible.

"I'm sorry man, but those were bad."

"Nigga, I know!" he said. "You ain't gotta tell me. I was up close and personal."

We stood in the line at McDonald's cracking up so hard that white people were throwing dirty looks, and we could barely get our orders out. The girl at the register was not amused.

"I don't miss going back to school," Damon said, setting his tray on the table, his bags at his feet. "You remember Phaedra Jackson?"

I rolled my eyes. "You know I remember Phaedra."

He cracked up again.

Me and Phaedra lost our virginity on Miss Liv's living room couch surrounded by all the dollar store figurines she had planted on the tables, on top of the TV, on windowsills. It seemed like hundreds of tiny black people doing different stuff. A preacher preaching at a tiny pulpit. A girl playing with a kitten. A couple snuggled together on a bench. The whole house was cramped with the cheap shit Miss Liv bought to make her feel like she was getting something from all those hours worked besides bills paid.

A rainbow of dusty loofahs hung from the bathroom walls, rested on the back of the toilet, sat on the counter next to lipsticks and designer impostor sprays, some never opened, the tops dimly shiny with plastic wrap.

"She had you so sprung." Damon laughed.

"And Sheila doesn't have you sprung?"

He shrugged, his face melting into a dreamy grin. "What can I say? That's my baby."

"Yeah." I chuckled.

"You were pussy-sprung, me and Sheila are in love," Damon said. I wasn't in love with Phaedra, but I didn't like him being able to claim something else I didn't have yet. "Anyway," he continued, "I saw Phaedra at Walmart the other day getting stuff for her dorm. She got a scholarship to Howard."

"Makes sense," I said.

Phaedra was smart. She was always raising her hand in algebra, stretching her thick body long to answer questions nobody else knew or gave a shit about knowing. If she wasn't answering questions, she was asking them. She wanted to know me inside and out, completely, the way she studied everything, but I wasn't that deep. My interests were girls and laughing.

By the time she realized that, she was switching schools and moving on to dudes who reached as high as she did—valedictorians and salutatorians. I had no plans for—or fears about—the future. I made decent grades because if not Dee would have been on me, but I didn't get those grades by trying hard. Life was good, and I couldn't see past what was. I believed in fate and luck. The same teen-mother-struggle-story Dee told with intentions to fire me up to work hard and get a good education was the same story that led me to put my faith in luck and her hand guiding me in the right direction. She'd made it and so would I. We'd both been luckier than I'd realized, beaten statistics and now they were coming to collect.

I slid a fry through a tiny hill of ketchup. "I kind of miss Phaedra."

"I bet you do." Damon grinned.

"It's not about the boning, man. I could talk to her."

"What you trying to talk about?" He must have forgotten about my situation. A quick reminder seemed to send him stumbling to speak and avoid my response. "I don't remember you talking about all this talking when y'all were together."

"Cuz I was dumb. I wasn't ready for a girl like her."

"You were fourteen. You're being too hard on yourself. Girls like Phaedra demand a lot. They're hard to please. Sheila's like that, and you see me in the mall buying all this stuff, right?" Sheila didn't work because her parents wanted her to concentrate on her grades. She had a scholarship to the University of Louisville.

"That's an excuse, man." I looked him in the eye. He and Sheila had been together for two and a half years, way before Beetle. He fidgeted with the straw on his pop so I could tell he knew what I was getting at, but I didn't push the issue. I didn't have any better solutions. "She loves you."

"I know. I just don't want her to forget me when she gets on campus around all those Poindexters." He stuffed a plug of fries in his mouth like he'd said too much. "Phaedra's got the right idea," he declared after swallowing. "I think going to an HBCU would be the only thing that could get me excited about more school. Are you gonna miss it?"

I shrugged. "At least you know what to expect."

"Expect good things," he said and discreetly pushed the bag with my shoes toward me with his foot so that when we were done eating, I could grab the bag under the table and stand up like a man.

It was early evening when we left the mall. The sun was still trying to shine its weak rays.

"I'm not ready to go home," I said when we were in the car. It had been nice being out, really hanging.

"I got a ball in the trunk. We can hit the court," Damon said.

"You back to balling?" I didn't even try to hide my laugh.

"It's good exercise," he said. "And it helps to clear my mind."

I should have asked him what he was thinking about, but instead I said, "We're not really dressed for that."

"I'm just talking about shooting around, nothing big." He snickered. "It can't do nothing else to them shoes."

"Shut the fuck up."

We went to the court by his house. The same one where his ball was stolen and I got punched. We lost time shooting and smoking and laughing until our bullshitting was just two voices against the darkness thick enough to hide the man until he was right up on Damon.

"Where you been, man?" His skin was light, and I could distinguish his features—eyes, nose, mouth—beneath his baseball cap, but his face was still hazy in the night like a smear of clouds. "I been trying to get in touch with you all day. I was on my way to you, but since you here." He reached into his pocket and pulled out a crumpled bill.

"Not now," Damon said, just above a whisper.

"What you talking 'bout? I got the money right here; what you mean? Come on." The man sounded drunk.

"Go on." I nodded to Damon, stepped back, and rested the ball on my hip. "Take care of your business."

He sighed. "I'll be right back." He led the man across the park to his car, his white shoes glowing like beacons in the dark.

GROWN FOLKS' BUSINESS

Angel

I don't care about having to carry my candy in Mama's pillowcase. Halloween is not about the bag you carry. It's about your costume, but Mama and Auntie are in the living room fighting about the pillowcase anyway. I'm used to it. They always fighting. I'm thirsty, so I let them fight while I go get some Kool-Aid.

Like I said, Halloween is about the costume, and mine is real cute. Me and Auntie picked it out at Walmart a couple weeks ago. She said she wanted to get my costume before everything was picked over. She said leave it up to my mama to get the costume and she'd send me out with a paper bag over my head with two circles over my eyes.

I'm a fairy princess with a pink, sparkly dress, shimmery wings, and a wand with a glittery star at the tip. My shoes are glittery too, like Dorothy's from *The Wiz*, but they pink, not red, so they match my dress. They click when I walk on the kitchen floor. I'm real careful drinking my Kool-Aid because Mama let me wear some of her lipstick. Real lipstick, not Chapstick or clear lip gloss, and I don't want it to rub off on the cup. I hold the cup real close to my mouth and let the Kool-Aid fall in little red trickles. I'm real careful about that too, cuz I don't want none of my Kool-Aid to get on my dress. Auntie's always telling me how red Kool-Aid just don't wanna come out of nothing once it gets on it.

I drink all my Kool-Aid without spilling a drop and pour another cup. Mama makes it real good with a whole lot of sugar, and lemon sometimes when she remembers. I'm about to tell Auntie to come on so we can go ahead and get started trick-or-treating, but I love the clickety-clickety sound my shoes make on the kitchen floor. It sounds just like when Mama wears heels when she's all dressed up and pretty, so I feel pretty too. I mean, I felt cute anyway cuz I had Mama's lipstick and the dress, but the sound of the shoes on the floor just adds to it. I feel famous right down to my Barbie underwear and light pink tights, so I start tap dancing. I get into it and start jumping, kicking my feet out, and making big circles with my arms like I seen some tap dancers do on TV. I forget I'm just in the kitchen until Auntie tells me to sit down and be quiet even though she and Mama are yelling over something crazy like a pillow-case.

Sandra

I can't even believe Maxine was about to send Angel out trick-or-treating with that tacky-ass, leopard print pillowcase. Who does trifling shit like that? A fucking leopard print pillowcase. And a dirty one at that, cuz I know Maxine didn't wash it. She ain't been to the laundromat in God knows how long, and she ain't been home long enough to hand wash it and let it dry. Ain't nobody gonna care about how pretty Angel looks in her costume when she holds up that filthy thing, smelling all like hair grease and sweat. All people gonna be thinking about is grown people and all the nasty shit that Maxine done did on the sheets that go with the pillowcase, cause that's all that jungle print shit is about—somebody getting fucked.

They gonna think about old played-out ass Mr. Donahue always coming in our apartment, I'm not even gonna say like he owns the place cuz he does, but like he lives here and pays the LG&E and cable bills or something. Like he got the right to go up in the fridge and pour a cup of Kool-Aid like he did a couple days ago. Here lately, he's been getting extra comfortable, coming over here taking his shoes off, watching TV, and playing Candy Land with Angel like we're one big happy family. He needs to be home with his wife. I get sick of seeing him all the time, coming over here with fistfuls of old, melted pieces of candy and leftover fried chicken from Blue's. He's got all that property, but he spends so much money chasing skirts that he's got to get a part-time job at a restaurant with his crooked, perverted ass.

We don't need his charity. Don't nobody wanna be eating chicken every day of the week, and besides, ain't no telling where his hands and that candy have been. Soon as he slinks into Maxine's room, I make Angel throw all those warped Tootsie Rolls and Now and Laters in the trash. Sometimes she'll hide some pieces, and I'll have to take them from her. Lord, that girl got a sweet tooth. She don't care about a block of Laffy Taffy being smashed and curled up like a raggedy shoe from being in a pocket all day. If she had the chance, she'd sit just as patiently and pick off every little piece of paper sugar-glued to each and every piece of candy. Tomorrow's the first and I ain't got one cent of Maxine's half of the rent, so I know soon as Mr. Donahue throws his wife a couple funky breath kisses he's gonna be creeping around here today with something else I'm gonna have to wrestle from Angel.

Everybody else doing everything for Angel—bringing candy, buying costumes, spending time—and all Maxine had to do was get a bag. She could've gone to the dollar store and got one of those little plastic pumpkins while she was out all night doing I already know what and God knows too. But she couldn't even do that. I'm not surprised. I'm not ever surprised.

Maxine

Sandra got shit to holler about every damn day. I'm a grown-ass woman and I don't need it. She's always talking about how I don't do shit around here. Hell, if it wasn't for me, we would've been kicked out a long time ago. Mr. Donahue's tired of hearing complaints from Mrs. Kramer downstairs about Sandra's yelling. I calm him down, and he helps me with some financial ends and lets us keep staying here. Sandra's always looking at Mr. Donahue all cross-eyed, but he ain't done nothing for her to look at him like that.

He ain't nothing but a lonely old man who wants to be my sugar daddy. His kids are grown and moved away—I can't remember to where—and don't barely talk to him. They mad cause Mr. Donahue was cheating on his wife back in the day. I don't know why. I've seen his wife before. She's real pretty, but Mr. Donahue's handsome to be in his fifties. Clear brown skin, wavy hair, bowlegged. I don't know why most people do half the stuff they do, but I know most of the pretty men I've known don't know how to sit down. Anyway, she don't hardly pay him no attention, barely gives him any. I guess she still mad cuz he cheated back then, which makes sense cause he's still cheating, but I don't know why she don't just leave him. Maybe he said before, but I don't know. I be half-listening most of the time. I know he says he loves her, that he misses his kids. I don't know how he plans on getting everything together laying up around me, but his business ain't my business. I ain't like Sandy. Always rummaging around in somebody else's stuff. He brings me chicken and cheap perfume, and roses when he's trying to be romantic. He and I both know that ain't even necessary. I prefer cash, and it's hard trying to sell that funny smelling perfume. But he does it anyway, and I think it's sweet. He's good to Angel too. Brings her candy, toys, and sometimes clothes. Hell, Angel's daddy don't do half that shit.

It don't matter what the fuck I do in my room with my door shut or when I go out at night. Angel has a roof over her head, she always looks nice, and she has food to eat. Like I said, I'm grown, and the only mama I got died years ago.

I don't know why Sandra's making such a big deal about it. Ain't nothing wrong with that pillowcase. No, it's not fresh-from-the dryer, spring clean, but it ain't been dipped in shit and covered with roaches either. Sandra's always blowing something out of proportion. Like how she's saying I was gone all last week. Now, how did I do Angel's hair on Wednesday and make spaghetti on Saturday if I was gone *all* last week? Sandra's working my last good nerve. I wish Mr. Donahue would come on. I gotta get out of here tonight.

Angel

I'm not even thinking about asking Mama to go trick-or-treating again until I'm sitting and being quiet, looking out the window in the kitchen and I see Monet Stevens. When I asked Mama earlier, she said she was tired so I went on, but now Monet is walking up the sidewalk looking stupid, waving her hand like the Miss America she thinks she is for real. When I first saw her, I wanted to yell, "Psych!" out the window, but then I saw her mama.

Miss Stevens is standing in front of Monet, taking pictures like Monet is really somebody. I can't even call Miss

Stevens stupid cuz she's really nice. When it was Monet's birthday, she came to class and brought pink cupcakes 'cause pink is Monet's favorite color. She poured everybody cups of pink lemonade and sat in a little seat in the desk next to Monet. She stayed a long time and laughed and played games and paid attention when everybody was talking, even Stanley Bowers who's always saying dumb stuff. For my birthday, Auntie threw me a party at home and bought me a Barbie cake. And I know she paid more for it than Miss Stevens paid for her homemade cupcakes cuz I heard her fussing about the fifteen dollars that Mama never gave her for it, but that Barbie cake didn't taste as good as those pink cupcakes.

Miss Stevens is pretty too. Monet's always talking about it. I tell her my mama's pretty too, but my mama ain't never been to our school, and I don't like Monet, so she ain't never been to my house so I can't prove it. But I wanna show her today.

I run into the living room and Auntie is still yelling and cussing at Mama, first about Mama staying out all night and then about Mama eating the last piece of bologna and how come she had to go to Kroger and buy the bologna in the first place when Mama gets all those food stamps. Mama ignores her and holds her bologna sandwich in one hand. Her other hand is pointing all up in Auntie's face while she's telling her that she's grown and she'll do and eat whatever she GD pleases in her GD house.

I put my cup of Kool-Aid on the table and step in

between them, feeling the thump from Mrs. Kramer's broomstick under my glittery pink shoes, and I don't care about staying out of grown folks' business like Auntie tells me to or the stupid pillowcase or if I get any candy at all. Once I start thinking about it, I figure that Mama might really wanna go trick-or-treating with us now since she's up and eating and I heard Auntie talking on the phone to Miss Betty about how Mama's always out tricking on the street and trying to get something for free, but, just in case, I tell Mama that she can have all of my Snickers bars if she comes with us. And then Mr. Donahue comes walking into the living room with a hot pink plastic pumpkin resting on a big pan of chicken covered in aluminum foil.

Sandra

He didn't even knock. That's the shit I'm talking about. He owns this building, but he needs to respect our privacy. All Maxine cares about is getting her money, but I could have been walking around naked or something and, unlike her, I care about who sees what I got. Usually, I would have said something smart, but he's got the exact pumpkin that I wanted Maxine to get for Angel. I look at Maxine like, See? Even a low down, dirty adulterer knows that you don't send a kid out with a leopard print pillowcase. I can't stand him, but I'm not that rude so I thank him and tell Angel to come on.

I heard her ask Maxine to come with her, and I think it's a damn shame that Angel has to beg her own mama to go trick-or-treating with her, especially since Maxine's not even tired from work or about to go to work. She's just sitting up being trifling. It's an even bigger shame that Angel feels like she has to offer up her candy bars so that Maxine will say yes. Because I know how much Angel loves sugar, I know how much she wants Maxine to go, and I don't want her to have to hear Maxine tell her no so I try to get her excited about Sweet Tarts and Starbursts so maybe she'll forget about what she just asked Maxine, who's already trying to push Mr. Donahue, big pan of chicken and all, into her room. But Angel don't forget nothing. She won't stop asking.

Maxine

I'm getting ready to tell Angel that Mama has company, and me and Mr. Donahue have to talk, but he answers Angel before I can and tells her, "Why sure we'll go trick-or-treating with you." He puts his tray of chicken down on the coffee table and gives her the pink pumpkin basket. She reaches inside the pumpkin and smiles, pulling out a pair of big, red wax lips. She rips them open while Mr. Donahue digs into his pocket. He turns away from Angel, puts his hands to his mouth like a squirrel, then turns back around to show her a mouth full of fake vampire teeth. She laughs and kisses him on the cheek with her juicy wax lips. Mr. Donahue grins up at me with those vampire teeth. I guess he thinks I'm gonna laugh, but I don't see a damn thing funny. For the first time, I see what Sandy means about Mr.

Donahue overstepping his boundaries. Now Angel's all excited, telling me to come on. That we gotta hurry because she wants to show me something. How's he just gonna make plans for me and he don't know what I was getting ready to do? Mr. Donahue digs in his pocket and hands me a pair of vampire teeth, but I am not in the mood to play.

I tell Angel I'll be right back, then I pull Mr. Donahue into my room and tell him he's gotta get shit straight. He's not my man and he's not Angel's daddy. We've got a business arrangement and that's it. I reach for his pants so we can get down to business, but he grabs my hands and stares at me like he's never seen me before and didn't know what we were all about all along. He asks, "Can't it wait 'til we come back?" I guess he's talking about from trick-or-treating, and he's thinking *we*, all of us, are about to go trick-or-treating, and I know he's tripped and hit his head. I tell him I don't have time for this shit, that he's got a wife at home anyway, and I ask him if we're gonna do this. And that motherfucker tells me no and walks out of the room. When I go cussing after him, Angel grabs my hand and starts trying to pull me down the stairs. She's calling for Sandra and Mr. Donahue to come on, jumping up and down, telling me that it's about to be too late. For what I don't know. All that candy ain't going nowhere.

I got a headache for real now, dealing with Sandra and Mr. Donahue's bullshit, and don't feel like going to nobody's house asking for no candy. For a second, I consider going, putting on a mask and taking my pillowcase (fuck Sandy), and reselling all the candy I get, but you can't get nothing for some half candy bars and that cheap peanut butter candy. I figure if I break up the chicken, I can get more money quicker.

Angel

Mama said she's tired, but I know she's not. She just wants to go out, and I don't know why she doesn't wanna go tricking out on the streets with me, Auntie, and Mr. Donahue. Well, she's fighting with them so I know why she might not wanna go with them, but I ain't done nothing.

I'm so mad I won't kiss her with my fake lips, and I wipe off the kiss she puts on my cheek. I say, "Forget Halloween," and when I throw my pumpkin basket on the coffee table, my cup of Kool-Aid spills. Some of it gets on my stockings and shoes and I start crying.

Mr. Donahue runs out of the room, and Mama says "Oh" all slow like she's worried or sorry or sad when I know she ain't none of those things. She tries to come over to me, but Auntie pushes her back and tells her to go on. Mama starts yelling at Auntie saying I'm *her* baby, and Auntie tells her she don't act like it and steps over the spilled Kool-Aid on the carpet to sit beside me on the couch. Mama says, "Whatever, Sandy. FU," and goes to her room.

Auntie hugs me and tells me not to pay Mama no mind cuz she ain't got no sense. That I'm looking too pretty to stay in the house and not go get some candy. Mr. Donahue comes back with a wet dishtowel and a wet dishrag that he hands to Auntie. I see her look at him like, What the heck are you doing? But she takes the rag and while she wipes off my shoes and rubs at the splashed-on Kool-Aid dots on my stockings, Mr. Donahue wipes off the table, my pumpkin basket, and rubs at the Kool-Aid that spilled on the carpet. While Auntie is hugging me, the hair from her wig itching on my cheek, her Wind Song perfume all around me, and Mr. Donahue is scrubbing at the carpet, I remember what Auntie said and think about how now I can have all my candy bars. I promise myself I'm not gonna give Mama one. Not. One.

When he's finished with the carpet, Mr. Donahue takes the towel, all red with Kool-Aid, to the kitchen, comes back, holds up my pumpkin, and tells me we'd better get going if we're gonna get all the good candy. Auntie looks at him like he's crazy again and asks him if he's going for real. He says yeah. She says he doesn't have to. He says he wants to, and she huffs like she does when he's watching TV with us and laughing real loud or asking her if she can check the score on the basketball game, but then she says, "Yeah, I guess we'd better go."

Mr. Donahue says, "Come on, princess," and I know he's calling me a princess cause that's what I am today, but it reminds me of the shows on TV when the daddy calls his little girl a princess. Just then I remember that Monet Stevens ain't never seen her daddy cuz she said so when our teacher told us to make Father's Day cards last year. I know that Mr. Donahue ain't my daddy and Auntie ain't my mama, but Monet Stevens ain't gotta know that. Auntie ain't as pretty as Mama, and her wigs be looking crazy sometimes, but she's pretty when she smiles, and the wig she's wearing today is alright. It's big and curly, and if Monet say something, I'll say it's Halloween and she's Diana Ross.

I know Mama won't be home when we get back. Fine. So what. Let her go out by herself. I look down at my stockings. They're not dry and the Kool-Aid ain't gone all the way, but it doesn't stick out so much from the light pink. I don't think Monet'll be able to see it. I grab Auntie Sandra and Mr. Donahue's hands and tell them to come on.

INTRODUCTION

They're getting closer, and I can't believe she's going to say it even though I know that's what they do here. I came with Mama because she asked, and her future seemed to hang on my answer. I really just want to go to Mark's Feed Store with Zaria and celebrate the end of the semester with a fat plate of ribs, but I don't want to fuck things up. Mama's happy.

Earlier, when I went into her bathroom looking for some eyeliner, she was sitting on the toilet in her underwear, kneading lotion into her brown body—the implanted C cups and liposuctioned thighs. Both were fortieth birthday presents she'd given herself six years ago. I was fourteen, switch-thin, boy-hungry and struggling with the A cups she'd passed on, so I understood the desire for implants, but I thought it was crazy that she was so eager to knock down the brick house thighs that had my daddy talking marriage within a week, that she couldn't see her perfect parts.

The bathroom was steamy and smelled like her vanilla body wash, the cherry and almond Jergen's lotion. Sweat broke on Mama's forehead as her hands worked the lotion into her heels, feverishly as if making an urgent apology for the years of war.

I stayed in her bathroom to paint cat eyes onto my top lids, rim my bottom lids black. I don't wear much more makeup, but I picked up brushes and eyeshadow pallets from the basket she kept on the counter. I just wanted to be around her, to soak her up like sun.

She spritzed perfume onto the tender insides of her wrists that starred in my nightmares when she wouldn't answer the phone. They made me consider driving two hours from Bloomington to Louisville for the unsettling relief that she'd only spent days in bed trying to disappear into sleep. The radio in the kitchen blasted Bonnie Raitt's "Something to Talk About," and Mama seemed to be serenading herself in mumble-sing as she put on her makeup.

So, I know this is important, but being here makes me feel anxious and stupid that Mama and I dressed up in our Christmas gifts. And way stupid for almost crying in the car when Mama said, "I'm really happy you're coming with me, JayLynn." The Token Club, with its old tables and folding chairs that scratch and scrape against the dirty tile floor, is not the kind of place that should be cupping fragile moments like this. The room is blank, marked only with the Twelve Steps and Traditions. I'm dying for a "Hang in There" kitten, a field of sunflowers—something else. There should be someplace else for Mama to have to say, "My name is Claudia, and I'm an addict." Someplace carpeted so those concrete words don't thunk so loudly. Someplace with cushioned chairs that doesn't smell like smoke.

But nobody else seems to notice. Two-ton words are crashing all over the place, and nobody else is wobbled in their aftershock.

"My name's Jeremy, and I'm an alcoholic."

Jeremy stands on the back wall next to Vick, who's just introduced himself. Jeremy's legs are blue-jean sticks. His face is ruddy like he's been getting smacked around his whole twenty-something life, but he smiles and tilts his head back to take a deep swallow from his Coke, that looks like it's the best thing that ever happened to him. Jeremy, five introductions away from Mama, is next to a woman who says, "Ramona, addict–alcoholic," and whispers something in his ear before giggling, all shaky. Jeremy just nods.

I've been staring at Ramona since I got here. She looks like she's in her late forties, like Mama. She's wearing berry lipstick too severe for her pale skin, and her curly blond hair is frizzy, but she's wearing the baddest coat I've ever seen in my life. It's a rainbow of fur—red, burgundy, mustard, sapphire, jade—patchworked into one piece. It's so bad that I almost don't care if it's real fur. Mama noticed it too. It's just the kind of thing that gets us passing her *Us Weekly* magazines across the kitchen table to one another, sharing dreams.

But I don't like Ramona's introduction. It was quick and sparse with too many spaces—"Ramona, addict–alcoholic"—leaving it up to other people to make connections. It wasn't a declaration like Jeremy's. I can see Ramona at Kroger in the near future, placing her items on the counter: bologna, frozen lasagna, six-pack of beer, apples, peanut butter. The cashier stops the conversation about prom dresses with her friend in the next aisle to say, "Oh my god! Your coat is insane. Tammy, look at her coat! If I had a coat like that, I wouldn't wear nothing else, ever. I wouldn't even need a prom dress." She is barely paying attention as she calls for a manager to scan the beer that she is forbidden to touch. I wonder if Ramona's got a closet full of tricks like this, and then immediately I see a point beyond comfort in a woman named Kate's University of Kentucky sweatshirt and green sweatpants. When Kate introduced herself, she stood, waved, said, "Hello, everybody. My name is Kate, and I'm still an alcoholic," and I liked her right away. She's one of the loudest voices in the greeting chorus, and she smiles at everyone as if they're a newborn swaddled in her thick arms that she's seconds away from Eskimo-kissing.

I don't want my mama to have to say the words. I'd rather be eating barbecue and steak fries dipped in ketchup, laughing with my cousin, forgetting that my mother stands near a black edge every hour because she's addicted to pain pills, but since I'm here and she has to say the words, I want her to say them right. I pray to God the knockoff boots I bought her and all the compliments I threw when she was finally dressed won't get in the way of that. I was too afraid to tell her she was beautiful when she was stripped in the bathroom. Calling attention to what she believes to be her most unacceptable truths has, in the past, only led to more alterations, cover-ups, and withdrawal. When she and Daddy divorced, I was almost more relieved than sad. Daddy's love, like something straight out of the Bible—epic and long-suffering—read to Mama like a ghost story where the spirit never tires of chase. In spite of all this, I still want to punch myself for playing possum instead of nudging her to see what's real.

When Bert's done, it's Mama's turn. She looks at me and smiles a Kate-smile before looking back at everybody else and saying, "My name is Claudia, and I'm an addict" without even a deep breath—like the one I took—to prepare. I'm the loudest when everyone says, "Hi, Claudia!"

Then it looks like my turn because I'm sitting next to her. I didn't expect to have to say anything, but since I'm in the circle and everyone else has shared, it doesn't seem right not to introduce myself, so I say, "My name is JayLynn, and Claudia is my mother." The whole room, including Mama, greets me, and I offer a half-smile.

TO HAVE AND TO HOLD

Dude's grin is the first thing I see when I walk in the pawn shop. I can't even play it off and say the ring belongs to some distant auntie who lives out of town or something. As much as me and Sheila have been in this pawn shop lately giving our stuff away with the enthusiasm of kids asked to share their new Christmas toys, I know he knows it's hers. The first time we came into his pawn shop, I watched him watch Sheila's breasts plump up in her red V-neck sweater like Ball Park hot dogs right before his eyes as she folded her arms under her chest and leaned over his glass display case, waiting for his appraisal of the watch she'd given me for my birthday two years ago. I saw him lick his lips that were pinker than a man's lips should be, nearly fluorescent set against his skin that's the same brassy yellow color as the branches or vines or whatever the fuck designs those are on all of those played-out, wannabe Gucci, I'm-in-the-Mafia looking silk shirts that he wears with gold chains like his name is Guido and not Leroi. Even though he tries to make out like the name Leroi is something exotic.

He sits on a throne in his TV commercials.

"*Le roi* means the king in French," Sheila explained after I asked, "Who the fuck does he think he is?" crunching hard on a bag of potato chips that didn't taste as salty as I was feeling about just pawning my PlayStation. I watched Leroi hand some bad actress, with an even worse weave, a bag of money for turning in her "antique" vase.

"I know that, Sheila." I cracked into a big, burnt chip. Sometimes I think she forgets that I went to school too. That I could have gotten all A's and be getting my master's like her right now if I wanted. "If his mama had used a *Y*, he'd be a regular nigga just like everybody else."

Leroi stared at the ring on Sheila's finger like all the broke motherfuckers that walked into his shop stared at the shit they had to give up. He complimented her smile, the fat curls that bounced on her shoulders, her black boots with the killer dominatrix heels, that she insists on wearing even in snow when she could fall and bust her ass, as if he were offering nothing more than excellent customer service.

I would walk out, but he offers the best rates in town, and sometimes I really hate the motherfucker for it. He knows he has me and nearly everything I've ever loved. He knows I've become the loser I'm sure he told Sheila I was when he took her out for "Just a drink, Damon, damn" (as Sheila had explained in the below-zero tone she's taken to using especially for me) when I scoot the tiny, black velvet box across the glass counter. I don't try to hype up my merchandise like I usually do, working my hustle about so many carats of gold and silver and shit. My heart isn't in it. Besides, he knows how much that ring means to me.

Just the way he holds it in his thin fingers makes me want to jump across the counter and start whooping his ass. I plan to whoop his ass anyway, but after I get my money. I won't need him anymore after this. There's nothing left to sell, and I don't want the ring back. Not after his hands have been all over it.

"I'ma buy you another one," I told Sheila two weeks ago when she convinced me to take her engagement ring so we could put something down on the mortgage. I couldn't even look at her when I said it. I just rubbed her arms wrapped around my waist. We were standing in the kitchen, and I was looking out the window at the snow falling, lost between wanting her to leave so I could sniff away the tingling in my eyes and not wanting her to ever leave.

"I know you will, baby. I know." She kissed my neck, and I know she meant to be comforting, but it made me feel so weak that I didn't know what to do with myself. We probably would have stayed in front of that window forever, but something hissed, and Sheila went to turn down the heat on her pot of Ramen noodles.

I didn't take the ring that day, though. It was too much. Everything was too much. The brown overdue LG&E bills, parking my truck in my boy's garage around the corner to avoid the repo man, not having any cable, watching her stuff her purse with her own plastic bags to go to some ultra-cheap grocery store and come home with these sorry bags of nacho cheese tortilla chips that she's convinced herself are as good as Doritos. Two nights later, I was hustling again.

I gave my lawyer everything I had to keep from going to jail when I caught a case. Everything. All my savings. The money for me and Sheila's wedding. Shit. But I was like maybe it's for the best. Sheila had been on me for years about getting a "real" job, working all her sociology stuff about having a better life, like I'm one of her cases. She was kind of calm about it the first two years we were together. We were in high school and everybody was hustling. But five years later, even though everybody's still hustling, we're not in high school anymore and she's not going for that shit.

Right before I caught the case, she hemmed me up and gave me an ultimatum. Said it was her or the streets, which made me laugh because I was like, "What are we in some movie or something? 'The streets'?" It just sounded so dramatic, but she was dead serious and I should have known it. She's quick to ignite with an attitude, especially about someone's lost potential. I think the reason she goes off on me so bad is cuz she can't do that at work because the kids at the residential treatment center are so fucked up. Those kids have been beaten with irons and fucked with hot dogs, and you can't just yell at kids like that, so she comes burning through the house like a lit trail of gasoline, lashing at me. But she's right. I'm a smart brother, and I don't wanna be hustling when we have our kids, but I wanna quit on my own terms.

The money I made at Soulful Fashions wasn't shit. I was selling my ass off, hyping up all those fake plastic Nikes and cheap sweatshop Baby Phat jogging suits with threads coming loose on the thighs to brothers and sisters with something to prove and few resources to do it, until I found out we didn't even get paid on commission or with checks. You'd think the Korean people who own the store would be more progressive about business, but I guess they figure it doesn't matter since they're in the hood.

I don't know how Sheila knew where I'd been, but she did. Maybe it was the swagger in my walk, the confidence of a man with real money in his pocket. But she didn't even say thank you for the bag of Doritos that I tossed to her on the bed.

"Where you been, Damon?"

It was one in the morning. She knew I hadn't been at work.

"Over Dre's." I faked a yawn as I fell onto the bed next to her.

"You a lie, Damon. I talked to Stacey earlier."

Damn. I didn't know what to say.

Sheila sighed and attempted to roll over. "Get up," she commanded, and I reached for her because I thought she wanted me to get up and out of the bed, and I didn't feel like sleeping on the couch, but she tugged at the comforter I was lying on. "Get up!"

I obliged, and she cocooned herself under the covers.

"Baby, we need the money. It's just for a little while, okay? I'm gonna keep my job, but I just need to get a little stash so we can get out of this hole."

Through the comforter, I rubbed her back and kissed what I assumed to be the top of her head. I almost fell off the bed when she exploded out from under the covers.

She squinted her eyes into death rays. "That. Is. The. *Dumbest* thing I have ever heard. Damon, you . . ." she began. "Didn't you just *lose* all your money *because* you were hustling?" She sighed like I was a lost cause. "Just *stupid*." She flipped her sweatshirt hood over her hair scarf and pulled the covers back over her head.

The high ceilings that we loved in August are a bitch in the February chill. We walk around in two pairs of socks, waffle leggings, and anything fleece we can find. It takes nearly ten minutes to take off all the shit so we can have sex. The last time we did it, I didn't know if she was holding me so close because she loved me or because she was grateful for my body heat.

"You sure you want to do this?" Leroi looks me dead in the eye.

"Don't ask me stupid questions. Just do your job."

He raises his hands in a mocking pose of surrender. The hand with Sheila's engagement ring pinched in his fingers looks like he's giving the okay sign. "All right." He smirks. I know he's trying to make me look irrational. Like there's no reason for my hostility. Like I'm the angry black thug he thinks I am.

Fuck him. He doesn't know shit about me. I'm smart. Me and Sheila used to have deep conversations all the time about God, politics, racism, life after death, how we'll be as parents. Sometimes we'd be talking, and I'd say something that would make Sheila pause and smile at me the way people do after they taste something new and they like the flavors melting on their tongue—if they're the type of person to allow themselves to enjoy their food that way instead of grunting all over the place—and they think, "Where has this been? Why haven't I been eating this all my life?"

I've always been good in science. In school, I loved doing experiments and watching the chemical reactions. Elements combining to make new things. Stuff fizzing, dissolving, or crystallizing because of two drops of this or five minutes of heat; it's amazing to me. But how are you supposed to get a job as a scientist? They don't ever post those jobs. I check the paper sometimes. I have never heard a regular person say, "I'm a scientist." Especially never in Louisville, Kentucky. Even if there is a regular person scientist in Louisville, I can guarantee they're not black. You gotta be white to get jobs like that and be in their inner circle and whatnot.

Leroi reaches under the counter and pulls out one of those things. I don't know what they're called—the things people push up to their eyes to appraise diamonds. He's getting all up close on the ring, turning it around and looking from every angle like he really knows what he's doing. He didn't go to school for that shit. The more he's twisting and turning and inspecting the ring the more I can't wait to beat his ass.

"Two carats, princess cut, no scratches or flaws." He takes the thing out of his eye. "This is a good diamond."

I'm surprised because I was waiting for him to take the thing out of his eye and say, "This ring is flawed," all snooty so he could get in a jab, but I'm impressed by his professionalism.

"Where'd you learn how to do that?" My genuine curiosity catches me off guard.

Leroi shrugs. "Read a couple books, looked on the internet, got a certification." His blasé attitude makes me mad again. Like everything is so easy and I'm just lazy.

Last night when I was laying in the bed next to Sheila, who was tuning out my promises, I felt like one of those "I'm gonna" niggas who everybody knows are never gonna do a third of the shit they claim. Her best friend Anita's got one of them dudes. She's always coming over carrying her sack full of dreams—a metallic, granny-sized purse stuffed with celebrity magazines: *People*, *Us*, *Them & Em*. She'll flip through five magazines with the same exclusive photos from some famous couple's expensive wedding with extreme close-ups of the bride's ring.

"Look at that, girl." Anita will point at a picture with her store-bought, airbrushed nails that are always glued on crooked. "That is all that," she says excited like a kid before she realizes the kind of nigga she hooked up with, the kind who will never buy her anything like that, not even the cheaper knockoff advertised on the bottom right corner of the page. Yesterday, she was creaming all over some reality show star's pink diamond when I saw her eyes land on Sheila's ringless hand wrapped around a glass of grape Kool-Aid. She didn't say anything about it. She did, however, say something about our generic snacks and the fact that she had to keep her coat on during her visits, but not like she was pushing us out on Front Street, just calling attention to how close our situation had gotten to hers. She was like, "When'd y'all start buying Happy Snack oatmeal crème pies? I be tearing those up. I like those better than Little Debbie," and "I'm trying to keep my gas down too. Shit, LG&E better get out of my face talking about a two-hundred-dollar bill."

I guess she thinks that makes Sheila feel better, like she has a broke-ass soul sister in her struggle, but I don't like the way she tries to lure Sheila into her fantasy world and get her to hope for something better than I can offer her at this moment right in front of my face.

"Ooohwee, I want a kitchen like that. You see that? Your

girl from *Young & the Restless*'s kitchen? She got all that open space with the island. I don't even know what I'd do with a kitchen like that that wasn't filled with Lavar's dirty dishes. But I'd do something, I'll tell you that. I'd be one Betty Crocker baking, *Martha Stewart Living* bad bitch."

That's where Anita always thinks Sheila's going to take the bait and start dreaming about copper cooking sets and plasma TVs built into exposed brick walls, but Sheila always says, "I told you to leave his ass. You don't need him," and gets up from the table, usually to wash our dirty dishes, busting through all of Anita's fantasy talk.

And that's what scares me. Sheila does not take shit. Really, I'm surprised that she didn't leave me a long time ago. She's threatened thousands of times, and each time I'm just as scared as the first time cuz Sheila is not an empty threat kind of girl. She'll chop a string and never look back. That's why I never worry about her creeping out with dudes she used to date. The *X* in "ex" is way capital with her. Ain't no "I'm lonely" booty calls or flirting on the sidewalk with lingering eyes. When it's over, it's *over*. Not in a bitchy "I'm too good" or "I hate you" way, but in a busy, friendly "Let's just keep it moving. I'll holler atcha, partner" kind of way.

But Leroi.

She's digging him, and she hasn't officially made the threat, but it's as real and in my face as the white breath that came out of her mouth when she sighed at me last night.

I don't even know how she could like him. He's way lame.

Like I said, there's the played-out shirts and corny commercials. I guess she thinks he's cultured because of the whole French thing and the fact that he told her all about some expensive, antique Japanese tea kettle brought in by some Native American midwife. I told her he was an asshole for taking the kettle from probably the only barely working Indian midwife left in the South. Sheila's always talking about how drugs ruin lives, which, yeah, they do, but she never wants to talk about how King Leroi is getting rich taking from the poor. Heirlooms and stuff. History.

"It's not the same," she said. "They have a chance to get it back. Besides, most of the people that go in the shop are pawning things to get money for what?" She cupped a hand behind her three-hole-pierced ear, waiting to hear the answer that she delivered personally with a hard nod and a disapproving look thrown my way. "Drugs."

One point against me.

"But not the midwife," was my pussy-ass response. I said that Leroi was just fueling the problem by giving the crackheads money to support their habit. "But he didn't start it," Sheila answered.

Five more points.

Adding to the whole lame-as-hell thing is the fact that he's giving her information for her thesis on emotionally disturbed teens and running some old helping-her-with-her-homework-type bullshit. He's a big-time volunteer at Brooklawn, another residential treatment center for kids,

so he gives her the scoop on a whole building full of trou-
bled tales for her analysis, including his little brother, who,
as luck would have it, is a crack baby.

Score about a thousand points against me.

Sheila doesn't even care that Leroi has two daughters.
Their pictures are all up on the wall behind his counter.
Two copper-colored girls in puffy pink coats, smiling and
showing big Chiclet teeth. Sheila has never dated anyone
with kids because we've been together for seven years, but
I gather from her reactions to friends shacked up with baby
daddies that she wouldn't have it. "A son?!" she'll ask, stopping her friend in midsentence like she'd just said her new
man had a one-year-old swamp monster. "Aww, naw. That's
baby mama drama right there. *Fresh* baby mama drama."
But she's all "They are too cute" over Leroi's daughters and
asking how one of them did in the winter play and how
Leroi is handling the other one who's getting a little too
fast at nine, piling on the play makeup and giving boys her
number to call her on the phone.

"So, how much?" I ask Leroi with an attitude, watching
the ring pinched between his fingers, trying to get things
moving, but the words are covered up by all the shit in my
throat, so I have to clear it and ask again. I'm angrier this
time. "How much? Come on, man." I'm impatient, nervous, and fidgety like the crackheads that come in here with
TVs and DVDs. Leroi's mother was probably acting like
that in some other shop across town when she was big and
pregnant with his brother, itching to buy stuff from some

dude like me who had to leave the hot spaghetti dinner his girl made to answer her call.

I'm glad when his phone rings so I can get myself together, but I huff like I'm agitated.

"One second," Leroi assures me with one finger raised, all about customer service despite the tension thick in the shop air. The place always smells stale and dusty like every secondhand shop in the world, despite the hint of Windex that lingers from Leroi's efforts to keep everything in the store gleaming.

Leroi faces the wall in the corner behind the counter where he keeps the phone. He talks low. I wipe my hand down my face to clean the slate of this confrontation and start fresh—be cool, collected. Leroi's hand that's not holding the phone to his ear is tucked under his armpit. I hear him make plans for Saturday at seven-thirty. My blood is hot, making tiny bubbles just thinking that he might be talking to Sheila, then he says, "Okay, see you then, Sheila," and chuckles. A short moment of breathy bass, exactly the kind of laugh you use when you're running game.

He broadcasted her name just for me. Thousands of chemical reactions are exploding beneath the surface of my skin. I'm ready to end the waiting and start the beatdown right away, but I need the money. I gotta wait.

"Where you taking my girl on Saturday?" I ask, almost threaten.

"*Sheila* and I are meeting at the treatment center. Afterward, I told her we could go out for a drink if she likes. She seems stressed." He looks me directly in the eyes. "I'll give you twelve hundred for the ring."

I paid twenty-five hundred cash for it, but I nod.

"*My girl* doesn't need a drink. She's not a big drinker. I'll help her relax, alright?"

"She's not your possession." Leroi places the ring in its case, snaps the box shut, and places it on a shelf behind the counter.

My palms are sweating. I rub my thumbs against the slick skin, and my fingers, itching to fall into fists, curl tight over them as I watch Leroi move to the cash register.

He's right. Sheila isn't mine, and I'm becoming more aware of that fact every day, every time she walks out a door or picks up a phone like she did the other night. She was laughing hard as hell while I was trying to watch TV in the living room. I mean, holding her stomach, gasping for air, tears and all. I thought she was talking to Anita, so once she hung up I was ready for her to launch into something like, "So Anita was at work and . . ." And I was looking like the biggest jerk, man, just waiting to laugh, already smiling and everything when she started talking and hit me with the real punchline, "Okay, so Leroi . . ." All I heard was his name spilling from her mouth over and over while she laughed.

"Ain't nothing funny about the kids at that center," I said after Sheila had finally finished.

Sheila's face straightened. "I wasn't even talking about the kids. What are you talking about?"

"That's what y'all are supposed to be talking about—those kids—not all that other stuff." I fluttered my fingers to indicate the frivolity of "other stuff."

"Oh god. Don't start."

"Start what?" I asked even though I knew what.

"All that jealous stuff. I'm with you."

"You tee-heeing all on the phone with that nigga, I can't tell."

Usually, we're about ten minutes into an argument before I cross the line that makes Sheila explode.

"You can't tell?" Sheila asked in a disbelieving tone that let me know I was about to be begging for a retreat behind that line. "You can't see I'm staying with you in this cold house when I could be at my mama's?" She gestured to the window covered with clear plastic puffed out with freezing air. "You can't see me taking all my shit to the pawn shop for you—"

"I didn't tell you to—"

"—cause your dumbass caught a drug case when you should have been working a real job in the first place, theeen, you go back to do the same shit? You can't see this?" She thrust her empty ring finger in my face like she was flipping me off with her middle finger. "You can't see that? You won't find another woman who'll take that."

"You told me to take the ring, Sheila. It was your idea."

"I know. That's what I'm saying. That's love. That's me." She smacked her chest buried beneath a flannel robe. "And you're sitting there saying you don't see that shit."

But I feel it right then standing in Leroi's pawn shop

surrounded by all the things that people have given up for other things, habits, and people they wanted and needed more than guitars, game consoles, earrings, food, and memories. Sheila's not mine, but she's trying hard to be. She's fighting harder for me to become the person I've always wanted to be than I have ever been willing to fight for myself. She's been the one making sacrifices for a dream that she isn't sure will come true, but she's willing to risk everything for it. I feel the shit so strong, it's almost overwhelming.

"Damn," I say, and I guess Leroi thinks I said this because I'm torn up about giving up the ring and thinking about how I'm going to lose Sheila and wants to rub it in in his punk-ass way, so he picks up one in a stack of what looks like about a hundred daisy-shaped pieces of paper beside the cash register with the Brooklawn name on them and asks me if I would like to give a donation to help the kids go on a trip for spring break. This is his formal way of reminding me that I'm not shit because I might have sold the drugs that helped some of those kids end up in that home.

He's screaming for a beatdown that I wanna give now more than ever because I know I'll win in every way—the fight, Sheila. I know I'll take them both. But I can see him calling the police with the taste of his own blood thick and sweet on his tongue like the top layer on a homemade Popsicle, happily adding another case to my record. I won't give him that satisfaction. I won't do that to Sheila.

I guess Leroi thinks I won't say no to an invitation to

help the kids I may have helped fuck up cuz I'll feel guilty, but I've paid enough for the shit that I've done.

"Naw, man. I need my money," I say before I correct myself. "*We* need the money." In that "we" I hope he sees me and Sheila shivering in the bed together, eating bowls of Ramen noodles, and taking trips to the library because we'll both get tired of her shouting instructions at me to get the rabbit ears just right so we can get a picture on our TV without cable and really start liking reading books out loud to one another, even the ones about science, even though Sheila could not care less about science, and I will never get to read more than a paragraph before Sheila will straddle me and start shedding my layers.

Leroi puts the daisy back on the stack without a word and opens the cash register. Even though I don't want to, I open my hand and let him count out each bill and lay it in my palm because I know I need everything he has to give.

ANIMAL KINGDOM

Angel grabbed her house key, cell phone, cash. She was running away. Not in the troubled-white-girl-hitchhiking-on-the-side-of-the-road kind of way. It was just for tonight, Derby. Maybe all night. If she was going to leave, she might as well be gone as long as she could since she was going to get in trouble anyway, which would mostly just be Aunt Sandy real mad and loud for a while, hollering punishments she wouldn't enforce for long.

Aunt Sandy stayed chirping in her ear like Jiminy Cricket, throwing do's, don'ts, and bet nots. Despite her efforts, Angel had already done it—the biggest don't. She'd snuck her way to Cole's house, into his bed, several times in between all of Aunt Sandy's blowing up her phone. She called while Angel was at her register, after Angel had told her a million times—in texts while customers slapped gallons of milk and loaves of bread onto the conveyor belt, on the phone during her break, and in person in the car on the way home—"I'm *working*, Auntie. I can't talk." At first, Angel had thought Aunt Sandy was just being paranoid (what was she going to do at work?) but then Kayla, another cashier, told her she'd given Kenny, one of the managers, a blow job in his office, right across from the room where they counted their tills at the end of a shift. Angel had been shocked, not least of all because Kenny was married, and then she'd been disappointed and embarrassed by her limited imagination, especially since even boring-ass Aunt Sandy could fathom these freaky possibilities. No wonder Cole had broken up with her.

Aunt Sandy was on the couch, on the phone as usual. Her squeaking and giggling meant there was a man on the other line. Angel didn't know why she even bothered straining her voice like that. By Aunt Sandy's own doing, the guy would only be around long enough to take her out a couple times, at least once to her favorite restaurant with the soft, yeasty rolls that she glossed with cinnamon butter. Some of the deal breakers were valid—too much drinking, a pale stripe running below the knuckle of a ring finger, a short temper—but Angel thought a number of the others were dumb. Chest hair crawling from a shirt collar, old shoes, the mispronunciation of a word—these were superficial flaws easily fixed, no reason to give up on someone.

Angel had learned about the 80/20 rule while watching a talk show and thought Aunt Sandy's refusal to accept the 20 percent of a man's imperfections that come with the

80 percent of positive attributes was the reason why she would always be alone. No one would ever be 100 percent, but she wouldn't get that and wasted everybody's time trying to avoid the inevitability of people revealing themselves to be no more than human. Angel didn't understand how a woman who had bought and worn so many bad wigs couldn't forgive others' mistakes. Today's black bob swung around Aunt Sandy's cheeks and chin as she vibrated with fake laughter, shaking her head and gesturing pointlessly. Angel thought the inky color struck a harsh contrast against her golden skin.

The news was starting on TV. It began with Derby coverage at Churchill Downs—the favored horse, celebrities in town—but it wouldn't be long before the anchors launched into routine reports of who had gotten shot, stabbed, and raped and flashed mugshots of shady people looking their worst, reminding Aunt Sandy of all the bad that could happen in the world. This would make it harder for Angel to leave. She'd told Kayla and Jade she'd meet them at the store around the corner at six, and she was already late.

"I'm going to the park." Angel threw the words behind her as she stepped into her tennis shoes at the front door. "With Leanne," she added because Aunt Sandy liked Leanne and her deferential "yes" and "no, ma'ams."

Aunt Sandy placed the phone face down on the wide crest of her right breast. "For what?"

Angel hadn't thought she'd been paying attention. She could have walked out the back, but didn't want Aunt

Sandy to be call-the-police worried. If she knew Angel was out with a friend, she'd just wait at home angry instead of driving around looking for her.

Angel shrugged. "Just talking." She'd learned not to say "hanging out" because it sounded delinquent, reminiscent of "running the streets," which is what Aunt Sandy was always saying Angel's mother, Maxine, did.

"It's raining," Aunt Sandy said.

"Barely sprinkling." Angel flipped her jacket's hood onto her head and reached for the doorknob even though she knew the statement of the obvious was her aunt's way of saying no. She got tired of her not just saying what she meant.

"Where you going?" Aunt Sandy squinted at Angel like she'd shrunken into a seed sprouting something strange.

Angel sighed quietly, repeated, "To the park with Leanne."

"I said it's raining." Aunt Sandy's voice rose. "You'll get sick."

"It's seventy degrees."

"What'd I say?" Aunt Sandy's thin, frowning eyebrows scrunched tight over her glaring eyes. "It's Derby and it's too much going on out there," she said, softening her voice, likely trying to recover her delicate image in the presence of the man on the phone.

Angel fought not to roll her eyes. Their street was dead except for a faint thumping, a weak leak from the music playing at a backyard barbecue a few houses down. She was ready to be in Kayla's car on her way to the real party with music beating in her chest like a new heart.

"Okay. We'll just stay inside at her house." Angel opened the door and closed it behind her.

Aunt Sandy followed her, yelling down the porch steps.

"I'll be back by nine-thirty!" Angel lied and sped down the sidewalk.

Later, Angel imagined, Aunt Sandy would call one of Angel's other aunties and pace away the vacuum lines on the living room carpet that was still brand-new beige because she made everybody take their shoes off at the front door and set them on a black rubber mat. She would shake her head, yell, curse, and front about how she was going to beat Angel's ass when she came back even though she hadn't whooped Angel when she was little. She'd say she was going to take Angel's phone away, ooh just wait 'til she came home, just wait. She'd say Angel was disrespectful, ungrateful, hardheaded, hot—just like her mama.

Aunt Sandy stood in front of the house screeching, so desperate that Angel's pity soured to disgust and then hatred. For Aunt Sandy's wig with its blunt cut, straight edges. For her yellow face, a constant caution sign, that wasn't her mama's. For not going past that buckled slab of sidewalk in front of the house. For living like she was tethered and trying to keep her there too.

Angel silenced her phone, but it buzzed relentlessly.

"Look." She scooted to the edge of the backseat and

leaned into the front to show Kayla and Jade the screen lit with Aunt Sandy's face before laying the phone gently on the console as if it were a baby bird, a delicate and urgent situation she couldn't fix.

When Angel was six, she'd found a baby bird tweet-crying by the gnarled root of a sycamore tree in Shawnee Park and cried as Aunt Sandy pulled her away from the bird's struggle, its translucent pink body nuzzling against the grass. She'd told Angel if she didn't leave the bird alone, she would ruin it with her scent, and the mother wouldn't be able to bring her baby back to the nest. A mother abandoning her child for something as silly as a smell had seemed crazy to Angel. By then her own mother was flying off more days and nights than not, but she believed it was for good reason, that Maxine was "taking care of business" like she'd told her when she left her home with Aunt Sandy.

While Angel was running down the block and around the corner, leaving had been scary, exciting, and sucked the breath out of her lungs like the boom and colorful fizz of the first firework bursting from the river barge at Thunder Over Louisville. She'd watched the show on Waterfront Park's beaten-down grass two weeks ago with Cole's arms wrapped around her like he loved her, and then he'd broken up with her the next day. Now that she was sitting still in Kayla's car, all that adrenaline kept racing, and she felt jittery, anxious to the point of exhaustion.

"She won't stop calling." Angel felt young and stupid.

"Want me to block her?" Jade offered. Angel handed her

the phone and watched her fingers fly across the screen. "I gotta block a nigga, like, every day."

Jade's body was crazy swoops of deep curves, traceable even under her loose uniform polo and khakis. That body and her natural hair, often blooming in a fluffy afro puff, reminded Angel of Foxy Brown and other blaxploitation vixens of the not-so-distant past. She was eighteen, only a year older than Angel, but her savvy with men seemed to stretch that year into many more. Guys plucked bouquets from floral, fried chicken dinners from the deli. They lingered around her register, licking their teeth and lips shiny, asking when she would be taking a break, what time she got off. They scratched their phone numbers on the backs of receipts, and she called if they hadn't come in with a kid, paid for their groceries with an EBT card, or said something dumb right off the bat. Jade said you had to kiss a lot of frogs. She said the best way to get over one nigga was to get under another one. She treated finding love like the lottery; you had to play to win. Angel didn't think these were horrible ideas.

When she took her stilled phone from Jade, it felt like something dead. She buried it in her jacket pocket. Without Cole, Angel wondered how the thing had ever been worth keeping at her hip. He'd capped their four months by stuttering through a confusing mix of clichés that had dropped Angel's stomach. She'd ended up the way Aunt Sandy said girls who were too young and had no business having sex ended up—alone and hurt. Angel could have also ended up pregnant, with HIV, or an STD, so she'd used a condom. But the dangers didn't stop with sex. Aunt Sandy filled days warning Angel about the variety of ways she could ruin herself with a bad choice. If she wasn't careful, she could end up dead, broke, dead broke, spinning on a stripper pole, smiling from a milk carton.

Men often stood at the forks heading the paths stretching to these terrible fates, the wolf peering from a wool hood.

Angel's mother, Maxine, had made a bad choice more than ten years ago, and Aunt Sandy never let either one of them forget it. Maxine was the ultimate example. Don't get snapped by a crocodile smile. Smoke up a good time at a party and end up a crackhead, losing your morals, your values, your kid.

Yeah, Angel knew Maxine had been dumb, but life didn't work like that. One bad choice didn't destroy everything. People were allowed to make mistakes. Every day, a person made a number of decisions, and every day her mother chose drugs. *That's* how she'd ended up with no job, living in a raggedy apartment with a man she called her boyfriend like Angel couldn't recognize the difference between business and pleasure or their sickening mix. That's why Angel sometimes hated Maxine as much as she loved her, but she never stopped loving her.

There was a lot of good in Maxine that Aunt Sandy never acknowledged even though she was always grabbing at it in the presence of men, which was frequent despite her alarms about their life-ruining ways. Maxine floated through the world smoky-voiced, pretty-faced, and carefree, the way guys wanted you to be. Aunt Sandy attempted a version of this with her girlish tittering that always sounded forced and put on like her wigs and the parts of her face drawn on and colored in to look "natural." Beyond her fuchsia lipstick, Maxine met the world barefaced and head-on in her smooth, sepia skin. Unapologetically loud, brash as a boy.

Angel didn't know why Aunt Sandy was always on her, what had prompted her distrust beyond blood, the fact of being her mother's daughter. She hadn't seduced Cole; they were in the same AP class. He'd flirted so much she hadn't needed to do much but smile. Angel's brand of slick only helped her glide past Aunt Sandy's flimsy restrictions. She knew how to pitch her voice, which face to show. Most often it was the quiet, obedient, honor roll, Black Achiever face that slightly faded the Maxine laid over her high cheekbones and almond eyes like a mask she could never take off, even when her pride had been worn down to resentment.

Today, Angel was choosing instinct. She was tired of hiding, waiting for moments when she could just be whoever she was. Maxine rested in her mouth, a second tongue she couldn't speak yet but echoed in her laugh. Aunt Sandy's fear gave Angel hope that the words and ways would show themselves in time like the tip of a newborn's ear teasing their true color before its full bloom to brown.

Angel breathed easier the farther Kayla drove down Eighteenth Street. She sang with the music. Jade passed her an electric blue cooler. Angel had never had her own bottle of anything alcoholic. She liked holding it in her hands—the way it actualized and validated the fact that she had her own business to drink about—more than the taste, which was too sweet like everything made blue always was. She sipped slowly, controlled and semiconfident.

Kayla turned down the music. "Tamera's pregnant again." She sipped from her own bottle of blue.

"Well, that's his wife." Jade puckered her glossed lips, full of unspoken I-told-you-so. "When did he tell you?"

"This morning." Kayla took another sip. "They announced it today at their Derby party." She turned "Derby party" into a bitter song.

"How far along is she?" Jade asked.

"I don't know." Kayla's hair, salon fresh, rinsed to a smooth burgundy sheen, brushed across her shoulders as she shook her head. "A few weeks. I was so mad I don't remember. I been crying all day." She proved her point by spilling tears down her cheeks.

Jade passed her a napkin from the glove box.

"He still saying he's gonna leave her?" Jade asked.

"Yeah." Kayla tossed her head back, sending her long, side-swept bangs away from her face so she could wipe it dry.

"When?"

"Well, now it'll be after the baby's born." Kayla rolled her eyes. "He said he doesn't want to upset Tamera while she's pregnant."

Now, Jade rolled her eyes. "Then he won't wanna leave her with a newborn. Then he'll say he can't leave his kids, but whatever. Let's say he's leaving her. He left her, okay? She's gone. You get him and then what?" She doesn't give Kayla a chance to answer. "You're together, happy for a little bit, and then he leaves you. He's a cheater, Kayla. If he'll cheat *for* you, he'll cheat *on* you. And then you could be somewhere knocked up while he's out grinning in some other girl's face."

"It's not like that," Kayla said. "Kenny loves me. I know you don't believe me, but he does."

"He loved his wife too," Jade said.

"Yeah, he did—does." Kayla sighed and sniffed. "It's complicated.

"No, it's not." Jade chuckled. "What you think, Angel?"

Angel didn't like the know-it-all meanness tinkling in Jade's laughter, its disconnection from anything funny. She didn't know how honest she should be. Her friendship with Kayla and Jade was only five months long, a shallow thing that hadn't been tested outside of broken conversations between customers and breakroom gossip cut short by the time clock.

Even when they were clowning around, Kenny looked at Kayla with a tender sadness like he was beaming apologies for the woman he'd already married, the family they'd started. Angel thought a face filled with that much regret had to mean there was love at the core. Kenny looked like Maxine sounded on the phone sometimes.

"I believe he loves you, Kayla, but . . ." She'd taken Kayla's side because it was easier and nicer than telling her she was stupid and should leave Kenny alone, which Jade had done to no avail. ". . . he's married," Angel finally said and shrugged as if apologizing to both girls. Kenny had taken a vow to be faithful to his wife. Facts were facts. And Kayla's choice was Kayla's choice. She was nineteen, a dean's list sophomore at the University of Louisville, old and smart enough to decide what to do with those facts.

"I know that, Angel," Kayla snapped.

"Don't get mad at her," Jade said. "It's the truth. Like you said, you knew that. Months ago, and I'm tired of talking about it. We came out to have fun. Let's get you a new man."

"I don't want a new man." Kayla pouted.

Angel thought Kayla being spoiled was part of the problem, why she didn't want to let Kenny go. She was used to getting what she wanted. Her cashiering job was her parents' ongoing lesson about responsibility and the value of a dollar after she wrecked the first car they'd bought her on her way to Mall St. Matthews where she'd already spent well past the monthly allowance on one of her father's credit cards. She used to compete in beauty pageants, had won Junior Miss Something-Something (Angel couldn't remember), and flashed her beauty queen smile all shift, standing tall with perfect posture. She carried that poise even today—a sleeveless black linen minidress and plain, black leather slides upgraded her heartbreak into a sophisticated mourning.

"The dick can't be that good. He's only, like, five feet tall," Jade said.

"Height ain't got nothing to do with it." Kayla laughed, almost resentfully, to herself. "Those inches are where they should be."

"You're hopeless." Jade raised her hand to block Kayla's face. "We," she turned to Angel in the backseat, "are gonna find some new dick. Better dick." She raised her cooler. Angel wanted a whole man, but she clinked her bottle with Jade's.

Before the first time they'd done it, Cole had stood naked before Angel, also naked, her body buried beneath his sheet and comforter, both crisp with the scent of laundry detergent. She doubted Cole did his own laundry and wondered if his mother knew what he did on his sheets.

"You like?" His eyes flashed down past the smooth brown plain of his hairless chest and flat stomach to his erect penis, pointed at her.

"Mmhmm," she hummed slowly and nodded with raised eyebrows that she hoped looked flirty.

He smirked arrogantly as he slid into a condom (a Magnum, she's sure he wanted her to note) like the sight of his dick had left her speechless. But from what Angel had gathered from her limited experience, his penis was average, not the baby-leg trunks she'd seen in internet porn watched with her friends in true wide-mouthed awe.

"Tell me how much you love it," he prompted once he'd entered her and found a rhythm.

Angel was concentrating, trying to figure out what she was feeling, who she was becoming. She crooned a low, noncommittal moan, but Cole wouldn't shut up.

"Uh hunh." His breath was ragged. "You like that?"

She didn't think he really wanted an answer, but he insisted, "Tell me."

Angel ignored him, hoping he'd lose himself in the pleasure that sent him closing his eyes in efforts that appeared to be reining its advance or giving in to its intensity. She didn't know, wasn't feeling anything half as good as he seemed to be feeling.

"Tell me you love it," he huffed again. "Tell me you love this dick." The word was all hard consonants, punching Angel's ears.

"I love it," she whispered and he came, groaning, settling the weight of his chest onto hers.

Tell me how much you love it: his text to her that night.

Angel liked holding the secret of his desperation for validation, but hated its open splay in their privacy, the way its prick on her nerves likely signaled insecurities about her own desperation. How her heart lit with pride to read *U r so sexy*. It was easy to be freaky with words she didn't have to say out loud, without offering a sultry gaze for him to dissect, pick out her discomfort.

I want you in my pussy, she thumbed and tried to say it the next time they did it, but Cole's mother got off work at five, and it was never dark enough in his room for her to drop those words. She continued offering half-hearted moans and coerced declarations of love for his penis, but largely she lay still and quiet, listening for Cole's mother's possible early arrival through the chatter of TV or beg-singing of baby-making R&B. He wanted a blow job after Thunder Over Louisville, once they were back at his house, emptied of his mother who was attending a party, but Angel wasn't comfortable opening herself in that way, bending to her knees for him. She realized he was right when he accused her of not trusting him.

She'd been taught as much, and the wet snake of his tongue into her mouth, the urgent press of his hard-on at her thigh were consistent with Aunt Sandy's warnings. But boys will be boys. Cole was sweet. He gifted her bags of hot fries and bunches of flowery weeds. She didn't think it was fair to hold his nature against him.

He was too needy not to seek other girls willing to give him what he wanted, too cute for this search to take long. Still, Angel thought she might have enough time to get comfortable, loosen up. She thought their possible break would come from a slow peeling away. She could endure a short while of uneasiness for an 80 percent of good-morning and good-night texts, handholding, and Cole's jacket, thick with the sandalwood of his body spray, hanging a reassuring weight on her shoulders as she walked through school hallways. The ferocity of his want aimed toward her was worth it. The third and final time they did it, the night of the refused blow job, Angel tried to look into Cole's eyes, but they were targeting a fixed point on his headboard, his thoughts elsewhere as she hugged him closer.

Kayla took Forty-fifth Street into Shawnee Park, joining the traffic snaking from Broadway. She pulled away from the crawling caravan and managed to squeeze into a spot on the grass near an eggplant purple Cadillac Deville convertible shimmering with silver sparkles.

The guys in the front sat sideways, watching the two women dancing in the backseat along with the dudes swarming the car, stretching their arms to push video and cell phone cameras forward, pitch crumpled bills. The women's bare feet were planted on the black leather. One woman gripped the driver's headrest, the other the top of the backseat. Both of their asses were up, legs spread for balance and the cameras hovering beneath the tight skirts of their orange and aqua sleeveless minidresses.

"Well, that's nice," Kayla said.

"Don't be a prissy bitch and act like you wasn't on them knees in Kenny's office." Jade smirked.

"That was behind closed doors with someone I love," Kayla said. "They're letting strangers stick cameras up their pussies for money."

"You were behind closed doors with another woman's husband. Be real with yourself."

Kayla sighed heavily. "I know he's married, Jade, alright? I know. We *aaaa*ll know," she said, but once they'd set their folding chairs in the grass, she proceeded to text Kenny like she'd forgotten. Between her fevered thumb-tapping, she took dramatic, head-heaving, face-to-sky swigs of her cooler like she was hitting much stronger liquor. Angel and Jade watched the women dancing in the car, the doggish men acting like fools. The women rotated every few songs. The men in the front would pull two or three female volunteers from the crowd and have a brief, indiscernible conversation, a back and forth of lips to ears, beneath the thumping music before the women took off their shoes and climbed into the backseat.

Some of them twerked like the bases of their backs were motorized, bouncing at speeds that baffled Angel and left her feeling deficient on a number of fronts. Cole had called her "skinny thick," but Angel knew adding "thick" to a description of her body was all flattery without fact. Her ass wasn't big, and her B-cups weren't enough to draw the hoots and dumbfounded cursing that women who lifted their shirts and shook their tits received from the crowd. Her best assets were her intelligence and pretty face, but most boys didn't care about intelligence and couldn't be bothered with a pretty face unless it came with tits and ass for them to squeeze while they were looking at it. She'd tried twerking in front of her mirror but had given up after several attempts that felt awkward and looked stupid. Now, disheartened by the mute phone in her pocket and the likelihood of her ability to steal attention in so much booty-licious chaos, she wished she'd kept practicing.

In the backseat of the purple car now, two women giggled to each other as the bass beat around them. They folded over themselves, hid behind their weaves' bouncy curls as they sank lower into the seat beneath the weight of the men's boos. Angel was embarrassed for them and disappointed to know she was more like them than the women who rested their forearms over the backseat while their butts waved as easily as a flag in the breeze, the ones who grinned at their own asses, biting their bottom lips at the man in the passenger seat who'd said "Beautiful, baby," so often Angel had managed to read the words on his lips as they rolled from his mouth with the smoke from his cigarillo. He was sexy, the better-looking and darker of the men in the car with his mahogany skin magnified against his plain white T-shirt. To the driver's golden brown bald head, Angel preferred the rugged look of the passenger's trim beard and low-faded short afro that looked like some woman with shea butter-slathered hands had just roughed it up.

The driver smiled a lot, shining his glittery silver and diamond dust grill like he would happily chomp the women to a sparkly finish. The passenger nodded slowly, serenely in quiet appreciation. He looked to Angel like a guy who danced capoeira, quoted history and self-help books to friends while lounging on the green of an HBCU. As the previous dancers had exited the car, he'd placed bills in their hands, nodded finally in gratitude, a well-wish, but when the driver scooted the gigglers out of the backseat, they received the nod and no money.

"You got to play to get paid!" the driver boomed, standing to address the crowd. "Who's next?"

Jade jumped up, grabbed Angel's hand, and raised it with hers as she yelled, "We are!"

Angel yanked away from Jade.

"Yeah, you over there in the red shirt!" the driver called. "Come on up here!" He beckoned Jade forward as if signaling a large truck through traffic. Angel couldn't identify his heavy accent that suggested someplace new, but not too far away. It was country, Southern-ish, but slower than Kentucky, looser with the *R*s, turning his "over" into "ova," breaking his "here" into "hee-yah."

"Stop acting silly and come *on*!" Jade hissed.

Angel sat with her just-grabbed arm tucked behind her back, hiding it from Jade. When she looked toward Driver, she found Passenger's eyes locked on hers and remembered what today was about. Finding herself. Instinct. She was tired of living like a bird with clipped wings, grounded, even when Aunt Sandy wasn't around to hold her down. She stood and followed Jade.

Passenger smiled as she approached. Closer, Angel could see that he had a grill too. Just the bottom canines, a silver flash behind his lips that lit him a hip-hop vampire type of sexy that was otherworldly and familiar.

At the car, Driver shook his head at Angel. "Unh unh.

Too young." He stepped back to give Passenger a better view. "It's all in her face, see?" Angel cursed the baby still puffed around her cheekbones, regretted the loose spirals that framed and accented it. The jacket tied at her waist, caped over her skinny jeans, further suggested "minor."

"Yeah," Passenger spread the word into a long sigh. His eyes remained on Angel, whose breath had stopped, her heart fluttering in the stillness. "I see."

Driver's voice was gentle when he told Angel, "I can't, love," the twinkle of his smile shaded in his earnestness.

Angel found her legs and returned to her seat.

"It's for the best," Kayla said, finally looking up from her phone. "You don't want to do something you'll end up regretting and be stupid like me." She chuckled weakly. "Kenny's on his way," she said this staring away from Angel, past Jade dropping her tennis shoes into the purple car and climbing into the backseat. Kayla's gaze stretched off into the distance of women toeing through the grass like deer, their tails tipped high, men circling like bobcats, grills blasting smoke, the endless cars cruising through the park like unstrung gems, the rainbow of them gleaming in the weak sun. She raked a hand through her hair. "We've got some things to talk about." She tried to sound tough, but Angel didn't believe her or care. She was tired of everybody telling her what was best for her when they didn't even know what to do with themselves.

She got another cooler from the car and drank it while Jade danced with another woman. Of course, Jade was good. Of course, she knew what to do. She was the best dancer Angel had seen. The crowd hooted and barked. Angel's only consolation was that Jade danced with her ass, peeking from her denim cut-offs, toward the crowd, not Passenger's face. That would have killed Angel, though she knew feeling territorial was silly; he wasn't hers to claim. Still, he was a man with eyes, so he watched Jade. He told her, "Beautiful, baby," slid money in her palm and closed her hand around it as he nodded thanks, but Angel was relieved that he wasn't enamored like Driver who yelled, "Intermission!" throwing time out to the hyped-up crowd, tagging Jade as she made her way back to Angel and Kayla. The edges of Jade's face, around the slick filigree of baby hair, glistened with sweat. She was still catching her breath and huffed, "I'll be back" on an exhale with Driver behind her, sparkling over her shoulder. They went back to the car, and Passenger hopped out, heading toward Angel.

"Can I sit?" He gestured to Jade's chair.

"Yeah," Angel said quietly. She hadn't realized she'd been holding her breath again until she spoke.

Kayla's phone beeped as Passenger sat and Driver pulled off. She jumped up and directed Kenny into the vacant spot. He greeted Angel with a nervous smile, stuttering small talk. He asked if she'd won any Derby money, said a longshot named Animal Kingdom swept the competition. Angel had been in the car with Jade and Kayla, crawling through traffic when the race was run almost two hours ago. None of them had checked their phones to see what had happened. They, like most people at the park, didn't care about the race, and Kenny, who'd grown up in Louisville, must have known that.

"You gone be alright?" Kayla asked Angel, glancing toward Passenger, but it wasn't really a question. One arm was wrapped around Kenny's waist, and they were leaning toward the trees edging the green, lining the river walk. Their feet were moving before Angel had finished her response.

"Sorry 'bout that back there." Passenger rubbed his hands on the knees of his camo cargo shorts. Angel wondered if his hands were sweating. She liked to think she made him nervous.

"You don't owe me an apology," Angel said, though she appreciated it.

"My name's Bryce." He leaned forward in his chair to extend a hand. It was warm and calloused, not sweaty, when it wrapped around Angel's in a gentle squeeze. She'd received firmer handshakes from the principal while accepting awards, smiling for Aunt Sandy's flashing camera.

"Angel," she replied.

"That's pretty," he said, settling into his chair. "Whose angel are you?"

It was an odd question, but Angel answered, "My mama's," and immediately felt that to be a lie. She hadn't saved Maxine from anything. The glint of Bryce's silver fangs as he smiled and nodded like everything made sense steered her to other thoughts.

"Mama's baby . . ." he said. "How old *are* you, Angel?" He seemed slightly relieved to hear her response. "That's not as young as I thought."

"What did you think?" she asked.

He shrugged. "Fifteen."

There was a quiet pause before Angel threw the question of age back at Bryce. She'd assumed early twenties, but he was thirty. The alcohol helped her play it cool. "Yeah, it's all in your face."

Bryce busted out laughing, warming Angel with pride. She liked being able to surprise and amuse him. "Get the fuck out of here!" he exclaimed. "Chauncey said that shit, not me."

"You agreed."

He shrugged again. "True is true."

"Sure is, old man." She grinned.

"Whatever. Thirty's not old, and I look good." He stroked his beard and cocked a brow, posing for invisible cameras.

"You do," Angel confirmed, surprising herself.

"Oh wow." Bryce chuckled with embarrassment as he stared down at the grass. "Thank you." Angel resented his tone, like a teacher thanking a student for their effort. He pulled a cigarillo and lighter from a pocket at his thigh. Angel liked the smoke's sweet scent and Bryce's effort to blow it away from her. "Do you know that you're beautiful?"

Angel was startled by his sudden steady gaze into her

eyes and thought he was going overboard on the intensity for such a weak line. "You've been calling everybody beautiful," she said. She'd expected more, wanted more, from him.

"Isn't everybody beautiful?" he replied.

"To God, yeah, but y'all weren't picking ugly girls to dance."

"Okay, then why you doubting my words when I tell you you're beautiful?"

Angel had no response.

He pointed to her chest, the cigarillo's smoke curling over his finger. "Know that in your heart without a nigga having to tell you."

"I know I'm beautiful," Angel bristled. She felt like she'd been tricked and didn't want or need Bryce's little lesson. "I look like my mother," she added, though she knew Bryce didn't know Maxine.

"Why were you trying to dance?" he asked.

"Why did you want me to?"

"Girl . . ." He flinched as if pained by the insult of her suggestion. "I wasn't trying to see you dance. I was thinking of a way to keep you safe, tell you to watch yourself in a way that would mean something. I know I'm not your daddy."

"Sure ain't." Angel wanted this to hurt but doubted it would before deciding it was a dumb point to push him to regret. She was glad he wasn't her father. "Why you so worried about me? You were fine watching all those other girls."

"Not really. I keep imagining how I'd feel if my daughter

was dancing in some nigga's car." He continued to tell her about Nessa. "Short for Lioness," he explained. His tongue lost its laziness for her name and rose to the occasion of pronouncing the short *O* in its fullness instead of losing it to the *N*. He refused to let the short *E* fall into a nasally short *I*. Nessa had just begun pulling up on furniture, attempting first steps. The unraveling of a life lived before her, without her, stung Angel with an irrational sadness. She imagined this persistent ache beat in the background of the happiness Kayla snatched with Kenny. Angel felt something like this when she thought of her mother's days filled free of her, but that feeling was different, deeper because it was a reasonable hurt, justified. Jade was right. Kayla was stupid. For deciding to stand on the losing side of a choice that had already been made.

"Whose idea was that name?" she asked.

"Me and her mama wanted a strong name, something powerful."

Angel couldn't tell if the nameless address of his baby's mother indicated that they were still together. Either way, he'd painted them as a team, and Angel didn't like it.

"You know kids can turn that into 'Lie on 'is,'" she said.

"Kids are dumb; my baby's smart," he replied.

The distance between them spanned years and miles. Bryce and his cousin Chauncey were from New Orleans. They'd survived Hurricane Katrina and were both contractors rebuilding the city where they were born and raised, Bryce told her, not without noticeable chest-puffing. As he went on about the shitty levees, chopping through his roof to escape the rising water, and Chauncey's mother who re-located to Louisville with a sister, Angel felt like he was answering history report interview questions she hadn't asked. A chirp from his phone interrupted his description of the post-storm mold stink.

"Chauncey and your friend gone be a while," he said, returning his phone to his pocket. "They went to White Castle."

Angel nodded. Tenth and Broadway. The parking lot would be packed with thumping candy-colored cars, long lines in and out of the restaurant.

"I can't eat that shit." Bryce yawned. "It'll have me on the toilet all night."

"I didn't need to know that." Angel frowned at the image and Bryce's abrupt abandon of any pretenses to make himself sexy and mysterious.

"You'll know about it for yourself one day." He stood, reached over his head, and leaned back into a stretch. His shirt rose high enough for Angel to see the thick, black waistband of his boxers above his shorts. "I need to move a little bit. Let's take a walk." He pulled a blunt from another pocket and lit it as they headed toward the river walk.

"You smoke a lot," Angel said. She was bored and frustrated to find herself stuck again in a child's place. Attacking him in that small, niggling way lifted her spirits.

"I'm trying to quit the cigarettes and shit," he confessed self-consciously. "Cut back on the weed."

"Why not quit that too?" she needled. "What makes it so great?"

"You never smoked weed?" he asked.

She admitted she hadn't, feeling like she'd been tricked for the second time that evening. "Can I try?"

"You're a good girl, Angel."

She hated that he responded like Aunt Sandy, not answering her question. "I'm not that good. I'm not a virgin." The possibility of anything happening between them had dropped near zero, but in the event of that slim chance, she wanted him to know he wouldn't be the first, wouldn't spoil her.

"That's not bad, that's just living."

"Is that what you're gonna tell Lioness?"

"When it's time," Bryce said.

"Yeah, right." Angel rolled her eyes.

"I'm serious. I'm not saying I want her doing it at twelve, but I think I could handle seventeen."

Angel wasn't convinced and moved on. "Smoking weed doesn't make you bad either."

"Yeah, you're right, but . . ." He chuckled to himself. "You're just trying to get into something, like Nessa fighting sleep. What you fighting?"

The trees responded to Bryce's question with a grunt followed by a whimper. Ahead and to her right, Angel could make out Kayla through the brush. She was bent over, her dress around her waist, bracing herself against a tree with Kenny standing behind her in a puddle of his jeans.

"Ain't that your friends?" Bryce asked as Angel ran past them, yanking him with enough force to send him tripping into a jog behind her. "Shit! I almost dropped my blunt."

"Gross," Angel finally said, slowing to a walk. "I don't even know how she can do that. He was probably just having sex with his wife." She told Bryce about Tamera's pregnancy, the blow job in Kenny's office. It felt good to speak without censor, but that lightness quickly leadened to guilt. "He said he loves her," she offered in Kayla's defense.

"That's not love," Bryce said. "That's fucking, 'scuse my language. If he really loved either one of them, he would make a choice and be honest. Don't ever let a nigga play you with some shit like that."

"I feel like I kind of played my boyfriend. I didn't really love him." Angel felt shy revealing this truth she'd been keeping from herself. "I still cried when he broke up with me. He was my first. The only," she admitted begrudgingly as if coerced.

"That makes sense." Bryce nodded. "It's a lot of emotions tied up in sex."

Angel thought about Cole's flimsy ego and her stupid hope that sex would make her feel loved, wanted entirely in the way that Aunt Sandy and every woman in every song, book, and movie on the matter had assured her would be a letdown.

"You're really not gonna let me try it?" Angel's eyes flashed to the blunt burning in the pinch of Bryce's fingers. "I need something to help me handle these emotions and ease my pain." She choked out her words in a weepy, melo-dramatic fashion to make them sound like a joke.

She wanted to be talking to her mother, telling her about Cole. But Maxine didn't always have money to pay her cell phone bill. If the bill was paid, she'd probably be too busy to answer the phone. If she answered, she'd probably be too distracted to offer comfort or advice worth remembering.

"You're a mess." Bryce shook his head. "I'm not trying to have your mama mad at me," he said.

Angel almost laughed. Almost cried. "My mama's not gonna say nothing. Promise." She crossed her heart.

Bryce sighed heavily and passed the spliff. Angel pressed it between her fingers, imagining that twenty years ago Maxine had done the same thing. Maxine could possibly be in a rotation right now if that's the best high she could find; weed had become a last resort. Angel kissed where Bryce's lips had been and inhaled deeply, coughed.

"That's nasty." She frowned, pushing the blunt back to Bryce.

"Good." His smirk sparked Angel's disappointment to anger. She wanted to be closer to Maxine than her face melted onto hers, her blood in her veins. She wanted to understand the choices she'd made.

Kayla's laughter fluttered loudly in the trees' dark lace. Angel turned around to see her and Kenny, about fifty feet away, stumbling from the trees to the walking path. Kayla's head darted left. Kenny's white shirt, like Bryce's, glowed periwinkle in the fading light, and Kayla's quick flick to the right, hand on Kenny's back, guiding him in the opposite direction convinced Angel that she'd seen them though she likely hadn't recognized them. Kenny smacked Kayla's butt and she skittered. A jockey swatting a horse's hindquarters, the horse performing to the whip's command popped to the surface of Angel's drowsy thoughts. Kayla pushed Kenny weakly. A tease. A lie. She thundered to his call. In the pursuit of love and its lookalikes, girls became fillies, does, vixens, cows, queens, bitches, chameleons fading into the backseats and beds they'd fallen into with dogs, stallions, bucks, boars, bulls, cocks. Each person an entire animal kingdom. The name of that horse that won the Derby. Weird like most of the horses' names that sounded like titles, sayings, and jokes, not actual names for pets who were called, loved, scratched softly behind their ears.

Kayla and Kenny disappeared around a bend, into the growing shadows. A crisp breeze ruffled the trees, and Angel zipped her jacket, shivered.

"Cold?" Bryce asked.

"No." Angel lied before she'd realized it. "A little," she corrected, "but I'm fine."

"Come here." He wrapped an arm around her shoulder. She stiffly leaned into him, hands in her pockets, fingers fidgeting. After all she'd envisioned, attempted, she was struck anxious by this simple intimacy, her breath caught in her throat.

He rubbed up and down her arm as if starting a fire. His

vigor seemed exaggerated to highlight the utilitarian nature of his touch, its purpose to do no harm.

"Better?" Bryce smiled at her, his silver fangs sparking in the gray night.

Angel sighed, resetting her breath to its normal pace. "Better."

IN HER IMAGE

In the pauses between her retching, Claudia heard Jean's house shoes scraping to the bathroom, the creak of wood as she leaned against the door frame, a sigh.

"Dale know?" Jean spoke in short phrases riddled with gaps full of meaning often hidden from Claudia and her four sisters, though as the oldest, Claudia was the best at bridging the distance between what their mother said and what she meant. What she meant was almost always an order, it was just a matter of figuring out what made the most sense for the situation. "Greens are turning" meant throw them in a pot with some onion. "Tub's dirty" meant scrub it. "Rain's coming" meant pull the clothes from the line. Her words now, even as a question, were another fact made as plain as a gray cloud smeared across a blue sky. She'd been pregnant enough times to detect the signs, so Claudia wasn't shocked that Jean could tell at just two months along, but she was surprised that Jean had been watching her that closely. Now, and always, she wondered what Jean saw when she looked at her.

Dale had known for a month just as Claudia had, but Claudia knew this wasn't really what Jean wanted to know. Like greens wilting to waste, the fact laid bare in Jean's question was what she understood to be a problem, so Claudia sat back on her heels, gathering distance from the toilet's thick scent of bleach, and responded with the solution, "We're getting married. His uncle got him on at Philip Morris, and we're moving to Louisville in two weeks." She was happy to give this answer, have everything figured out.

"And you?" Jean asked.

Claudia stared. She wasn't sure if she'd missed a word in the noise of the toilet's flush.

"What *you* gonna do?" Jean seemed frustrated that Claudia had forced her to pull up more words. She crossed her arms. Sticks, the girls called them, called Jean, because she was so thin. Stingy and stiff in word, body, praise, everything.

"I'm having the baby," Claudia declared, stating what she thought was obvious. She swallowed, steadying herself for the work of lifting herself from the floor to continue the conversation away from the toilet stealing her dignity, but Jean left the doorway.

Claudia watched her feeling like she had that morning. When she stepped from the Glasgow High School auditorium stage in her cap and gown, she'd wanted Jean to hug her, expected her to at least tell her she was proud of her for accomplishing what she never had. Instead, she asked Claudia what she wanted for dinner before walking back to the apartment with Aunt Fredda, leaving Claudia with her sisters and cousins in their separate girl pack trailing behind them.

Claudia understood the meal and its plentiful portions as a gift. Jean never asked the girls what they wanted; they got what she gave. A roof. Chores. Abandoned clothing from the dry cleaners where she worked. Stiff men's pleated slacks that ballooned awkwardly at the crotch. Old lady dresses. Six months ago in January, Jean had come home and pushed a military-issued peacoat into Claudia's arms. The thick wool had rested heavy on Claudia's shoulders as she'd wondered whether the original owner was a husband or father who'd gone to Vietnam and never returned. Luckily, the coat was too big, and Jean had given it to Aunt Fredda, who'd given it to one of her coworkers at the nursing home. Otherwise, Claudia wouldn't have worn it, and Jean would have asked, "Where's that coat?" meaning, "Put it on," a hardness in her voice accusing ingratitude like she'd paid for the thing when she hadn't done anything but pick up somebody's left-behinds. Hadn't gone farther than a few paved miles from the dirt road where she'd grown up. Hadn't made it past the eighth grade before getting pregnant and dropping out. Had three baby's fathers and married not one of them.

A wave of nausea sent Claudia retching again. Soon,

her stomach was empty of the pork chops, fried apples, and biscuits Jean had cooked, and she was glad. She wiped her mouth, sat straight, and hated Jean for making her feel stupid for ever wanting that hug, for acting like she wasn't worth the breath it would take to say something nice like "I love you."

Two weeks later, Claudia married Dale at Glasgow's City Hall before an audience of her sisters, cousins, Aunt Fredda, Dale's family, and a few friends. Jean was at work, likely sweating in the weak, warm breeze floating from a dusty fan on the front counter of Finley's Dry Cleaners or sweating in the thick steam heat in the back, pulling stains from some white person's clothes. When Claudia told her the date and time of the ceremony, Jean had said, "I gotta work." She made no concessions about trying to go in late or take the day off.

In Dale's truck on the drive to Louisville, a grain from the sad handful of rice Maxine had stolen from the cupboard to fling in celebration fell from the crown of Claudia's afro and landed in her lap below her belly, which was still relatively flat. She left it sitting among the ditsy blooms of her favorite summer dress for the whole hour and a half ride before plucking and stowing it deep in the gilt-edged pages of the Bible Dale's mother, Mrs. Campbell, had given her.

The apartment building smelled like the old lumber that held it up, and her neighbors' dinners—liver and onions, fried chicken, polish sausage and sauerkraut. Dale's dress shoes rasped on the floor's grit as he ceremoniously carried Claudia across the studio's threshold into its suffocating heat where he cursed, dropped her, and darted for the windows. They were swollen shut and sealed with a new coating of white paint slathered over layers of old revival efforts. He peeled off his button-down, damp and wrinkled from the drive, and after a trip to the truck, he hacked at the paint with a butter knife from their new silverware set, another gift of many from his mother. Jean had given them nothing.

The opened windows offered little relief.

Dale frowned at the box fan he'd placed in the middle of the room. "It's just blowing the heat around."

"It feels a little better," Claudia said.

"Shit it does." Dale raised an arm, wiping his sweaty face across his shoulder, before pulling the murphy bed down from the wall to reveal a mattress decorated in a camouflage of stains. "I am not sleeping on that."

"I can get that out," Claudia said. She wondered if it was just the heat making the pissy smell so strong, old accidents made fresh.

Dale shook his head. "I knew I should've come up here and checked the place myself."

His uncle had found the apartment and convinced him that the cheap studio, recently vacated in a coworker's apartment building, was a good deal.

The place was dusty and stale with old appliances in the kitchen, rust spots in the tub and bathroom sink, but

Claudia didn't think it was bad. Dale was just easily frustrated and didn't know the power of good cleaning because he'd never had to do it. Mrs. Campbell, alone, kept their home shiny and lemon pine-scented.

"It just needs some time to air out," Claudia said.

The apartment building was on Forty-Third and Broadway by the western edge of the city pushed up against the Ohio River. They were only two blocks away from Shawnee Park so they walked there hand in hand, his left in her right. She couldn't help looking down at their fingers knotted together, his shining gold band.

After they crossed Broadway, Dale said, "Move, girl," and steered Claudia to his right side away from traffic, startling her out of her thoughts. "You so busy looking down you barely walking straight."

"I like the way we look married."

"I know you do, but I need you to be on the safe side if some fool gets to driving crazy."

Claudia felt herself getting weepy at the thought of a car jumping the curb, Dale pushing her out of the way. "I don't know what I'd do without you."

"Keep living," he said.

"I'm serious."

"I am too," he said. "What's the sense in both of us dying?"

Claudia noted Dale's clenched jaw, his thick eyebrows nearly stitched together and remembered Dale's father, gone since September. His mother's round face thinned to cheekbones and chin. At the repast, Mrs. Campbell had sat surrounded by tables crowded with food and refused to eat. Dale had pulled Claudia out of the church and into his truck.

In his bed, his slow, deliberate actions seemed to be defiance against the quick changes snatching the life he once knew, the eerie stillness settled over the rest of the house, his mother's shriek over her husband's coffin that had startled Claudia's blood into a tingle. She'd watched feeling as sad and helpless as the fake bird on Mrs. Campbell's hat shaken to the ground, the poor thing netted in black tulle. That day marked the first time she and Dale had made love, and the act brimmed with the greedy, nearly unbearable wanting just like Claudia had imagined it would. She understood love—life—to be wanting like that, the urgency that left Mrs. Campbell's stockings shredded from her attempts to climb into the coffin. Desire made life more than survival, and she wanted it all—the husband, the kids, the house—so much that other things often slipped past her focus.

"I just mean I love you," she said. She used these words sparingly for fear of ruining the gift of their return, but she wanted to make her feelings plain and share their warm, dizzying rush as an apology.

"I love you too," Dale said. "Stop worrying. Ain't nobody going nowhere." He squeezed her hand, but his face remained tight despite his soft words.

Claudia didn't know what else to say, so they walked

in silence. Once at the park, they settled at a picnic table beneath a tree with a trunk so bubbled and gnarled it appeared to be prehistoric. They kept up the quiet, and Claudia hoped it didn't feel awkward to Dale. It didn't seem to. He leaned back with his elbows propped on the table. His long legs stretched into the grass thinned around the bench. Claudia unfolded her legs beside his and made a show of lifting her face into the weak breeze as if content. They faced a playground and watched children running, flinging themselves into the air, falling. Beneath their yelling and laughter, the music of an ice cream truck, crawling through the parkway, began to rise. Kids abandoned swings to beg to parents. Some pleaded their cases with pointing and jumping.

Dale looked at Claudia. "You want something?"

She did but felt childish wanting something so needless and needing his permission to get it. When she'd decided to be a stay-at-home wife, she'd known that Dale would have to supply her everything but knowing and feeling were different. "No, thank you," she said.

"Wait . . ." Dale bent down, gripped her waist in both hands, and pressed the side of his face to her stomach.

"What—"

"Shhh . . . Yup . . . uh hunh." He sat up. "The baby wants some ice cream."

On the way back to the bench, Claudia used one hand to hold Dale's and the other to eat her crunch bar. She licked slowly, spreading the sweet across her tongue.

—

Claudia couldn't imagine Jean snuggled lovey-dovey with a man. Until she discovered the logistics of conception, she'd believed that Jean had, in fact, spat her and her sisters out, as Aunt Fredda was always saying she had. She'd known of fathers. Mr. Alton was Yolanda, Sandy, and Dee's daddy—not hers he seemed to emphasize every chance he got—and Mr. Mack was Maxine's daddy. Generally, Claudia viewed fathers much like dimples and money; some had and some didn't.

Mr. Alton came home from the ball bearings plant and sat on the couch in front of the fan with his pale, ugly toes spread and stinking. He demanded ice water, the biggest piece of chicken, some goddamn quiet. In the bedroom he shared with Jean, his demands were unknown, impossible based on the thuds against the wall, the tumbling on the floor signaling his dissatisfaction. He'd never struck Jean in the face, at least not hard enough to swell a cheek or black an eye. He kept his meanness tucked beneath her short-sleeve button-downs and slicked on a smile that fooled no one. At Aunt Fredda's apartment, away from Jean, Aunt Fredda asked Claudia if Mr. Alton had ever hit her or her sisters, and Claudia told her no because he hadn't. Aunt Fredda knelt on the floor and held Claudia's shoulders softly as she stared into her eyes, searching for truth. "You tell me if he ever does or even *tries*, okay? You tell me *right* away." But Claudia didn't tell anyone about the one time he dared raise his hand to her. Her straight back and the knife she grabbed from the kitchen drawer stopped him. She'd only been eight, but even then a burning inside of her had declared, *I am not my mother*, with a passion so fierce she'd kill to prove it. Mr. Alton dropped his limp hand and dribbled curses as he retreated to the living room. About a week later, Claudia and Yolanda came home from school to find a strange woman with brassy, frizzed-out hair burning fish in the kitchen. She pulled a cigarette from the pack Jean kept on the counter and planted a hand on her hip. "Y'all get y'all's stuff together so you can be ready when your mama comes."

Claudia packed quickly and happily despite Yolanda's crying, and although she spent months cramped with her sisters and cousins at Aunt Fredda's, she recalled that time fondly. Space was just as cramped in their new apartment, bunched up in one bedroom with her sisters and Jean on a pullout in the living room, but without Mr. Alton, the air felt lighter.

Maxine's daddy, Mr. Mack, was a butcher at Henderson's grocery. He gifted Jean beef and pork swaddled in thick, white paper and huge pots of stew thick with the day's leftovers that she complained were too greasy and gave her heartburn, but Claudia loved the stews and Mr. Mack, whose hands, big enough to cup baby Maxine in one palm, were always gentle. He called Jean and all her daughters "my girls," and Jean offered no reaction to his claim.

She didn't thank him for the stews and barbecue or let

him stay and watch TV or play a game of cards after he'd rocked Maxine to sleep. When she was ready for him to leave, she'd say, "It's getting late," even if the sky was hours away from hazing into its night colors. Claudia hated seeing him go, but she gratefully accepted the consolation of the warm, rib-squeezing hug he gave her and her sisters before he left. When he lumbered toward Jean with his tree-trunk arms spread wide, she'd shoo him away like a gnat and say, "Go on, Mack." Most days he played it off as a joke he was in on, but one day, not long after Maxine had grown two teeth and could tag him on wobbly legs, his face sagged with hurt. Claudia wanted to offer him the comfort of knowing Jean didn't hug her or her sisters either, but she suspected he already knew that. Jean seemed embarrassed by Mr. Mack and his dogged, sappy want, and Claudia thought it was because he reminded her that she could want, too—maybe need— someone else that way. Her weakness was undeniable in Maxine's existence. She seemed to resent Mr. Mack for exposing this vulnerability.

"Why you so mean, Jean?" His words, rhyming and sad like a country song, would have made Claudia laugh if the same question hadn't run in her mind all her life. She waited in the quiet, her heart beating so loudly she was sure Jean would hear and send her away.

"It's getting late," Jean repeated. Her hand rested firmly on the doorknob.

Mr. Mack sighed. "Bye, Jean."

But Jean never said goodbye. If she was on the phone, she'd hang up once she'd said her piece. If she was talking to you in person, she simply closed the door.

Each morning, Claudia went at the mattress with her small arsenal of cleaning solutions, recalling the laundry lessons that began after she started menstruating. For months, as she learned efficient stain removal, Claudia endured the excruciating intimacy of Jean unfolding her panties to point out blood ghosting on the cotton.

"Look," she'd say, working her hands around the wet fabric, a bar of soap, and water gone cloudy. "See?" And Claudia had no choice, but to nod at the magic Jean had just conjured that was as clear and invisible as the disappeared stain on the clean cloth.

All her mattress scrubbing was to no avail. She managed to cut the smell, but the stains persisted, and she surrendered this fight to others in her daily routine. The floor hosted a relentless parade of grit no matter how much she swept. She scratched sandpapery songs on the wood in her slippers as she washed breakfast dishes and wiped the sink and counter to a wet sheen that quickly dried a dull matte. Aretha Franklin, Mahalia Jackson, and Shirley Caesar kept her company while she scrubbed the bathroom, ate lunch, and cooked dinner. She'd found a gospel radio station like the one Jean and Mrs. Campbell listened to back home.

That music seemed to be the only thing the two had in common. It helped Mrs. Campbell extend Sunday morning church through the whole week. She spent evenings in the living room, rocking with her eyes closed, turning her couch into a creaky pew. "My Lord," she'd say, sometimes—more often after Mr. Campbell died—wiping tears from her face.

Jean didn't attend church, speak of Jesus, or cry. She smoked cigarettes, drank black coffee, and listened. Sometimes she sat still like she was searching for a message between notes in an organ's slow somber start, something loosed from a joyful shout that she was waiting to pluck right out of the speaker and stow for herself. At night, she watched TV in this probing way, almost daring Flip Wilson and Redd Foxx to make her laugh. She glowed alien, distant, in the blue light.

When Claudia turned the radio off, usually after she'd finished cooking dinner and was waiting for Dale, she was left with squirrels scampering on the roof, kids yelling in the courtyard, the pacing of her own footsteps. She missed her sisters and felt like she'd always missed Jean. The music reminded her she wasn't alone, but she was grateful for the week's end of dirty clothes that offered her a trip to the laundromat and the company of women who weren't just voices floating through her day.

She took in the gradient shades of brown; faces slick with grease and sweat; crooked smiles; lipstick worn down to a red rumor; nails glossed coral; dirt under nails; powder dusting the crease between breasts; sunglasses nesting in an afro; fresh cornrows tailed with fat wooden beads; hot-combed hair pulled back in a frizzy ponytail; the bronze gleam of one bold, bald head; prickly shading under arms; hair grown thick and shameless on legs; keloids on knees; legs shimmershining with cocoa butter; ashy feet scraping in beatdown flip-flops; lean-to walks; twisty switches; bellies sagging over waistbands; breasts swaying loose beneath summer dresses; nipples poking tank tops. Claudia wondered what songs these bodies held. She sat quietly, wrapped in the women's tsks, hums, and sighs like a blanket pulled from one of the dryers not condemned by a handwritten "Out of Service" sign. Their laughter broke in the hot, stuffy air like stained glass, a colorful thing close to the comfort of religion. They spilled gossip and confessions of stacking bills, kids stumbling down wrong paths, brothers/uncles/cousins back from front lines sweating sheets soppy with their nightmares, husbands leaving their bed-spots empty in the murky hours after midnight.

As Claudia listened, she caught two large brown eyes staring at her. A ragged-haired boy unfolded his hand to reveal a matchbox car as if he'd reached the finale of a magic trick. He was telling her how fast it could go, kneeling on the yellowed tile to show her when a woman entered hefting a stuffed basket.

"Jackson! I told you to go have a seat!" She pointed the boy toward an empty chair across the room. A baby girl stumbled behind her, grabbing at her leg. An older boy with hair just as unkempt as the younger boy's followed them, dragging another full bag of laundry.

"That one's on punishment," she explained to Claudia,

but Jackson only wandered toward the chair where he'd been directed before planting himself on the floor with the other boy, who'd abandoned his bag of laundry a few steps away from the washing machine where the woman dropped her basket. She began sorting through clothes as if she couldn't see the boys slinging their cars across the floor or hear their loud race commentary.

"When you due?" She looked at Claudia, and Claudia realized she was cupping her stomach. In the two weeks since the civil ceremony, it had grown into a firmer, though still small, bump under her T-shirt.

"Mid-December."

"You got that goofy grin. I remember that," the woman said like she'd lived a lifetime, though Claudia guessed she was only a few years older than her, about twenty-two or twenty-three. "You couldn't slap that thing off my face. I was—we were—so excited . . . and dumb." She looked down at the girl who was crying now and latched to her leg, slobbering a dark spot onto the hem of her pink tent dress. It was like the one Jean wore on the hottest summer days though Jean's was pale blue.

"Here . . ." The woman peeled the girl from her leg. "Go sit with Miss . . ."

"Claudia," she offered.

"Thank you. Stella." She nodded in greeting. "Go sit with Miss Claudia." She pointed, directing the girl, but the girl didn't move. To Claudia, she asked, "You mind? It's practice. This your first, right?"

"Yeah." Claudia stood. The girl's chest heaved with sobs as she approached.

"Go on, Aja." Stella nudged the girl, and Claudia lifted her into her arms.

"These kids been running me ragged since Cliff's been gone."

Claudia bounced and swayed Aja quiet as Stella told her Cliff was in the army and had been sent to Saigon four months ago. Her eyes drifted to Stella's left hand, searching for the ring she thought could have been left at home for a number of reasons.

"By the time we got married, we were low on time and money, so we didn't have a wedding or rings." Claudia thought Stella must have caught her eyes flashing down, her note of the naked finger. "We ran down to the court-house with Junior out to here." She held her arms in front of her stomach as if hugging an imaginary beach ball. "Girl, looked like he was ready to come walking out. My mama liked to died." She tossed some detergent into the washer and spoke over the clunk of her quarters registering in the machine. "I don't know when she gone learn I'm Christian, but I ain't no saint."

"We just got married." Claudia wiggled her ring finger on the hand cupping the baby's bottom.

"Congratulations," Stella said.

"The baby was part of it for us too," Claudia said, though she and Dale had been planning to marry after her graduation before she'd gotten pregnant. She felt a deep urge to be connected to Stella. Part of it was because of her beauty— slanted eyes, skin like a glass bottle glowing with brandy, lips so thick they had no choice but to rest in a soft pucker—but it was mostly because she longed to share something intimate with another woman. Back at the apartment, she had the same cheap flip-flops that Stella wore, but Claudia had worn her leather sandals, and this made her feel especially lonely, dressing up for such a banal occasion, and desperate for this meeting to become a friendship.

"Why'd you wait so long?" she asked.

"It wasn't me. Cliff was dragging his feet. Men don't know what they want." Stella shook her head. "He eventually got himself together." She began loading another washer. "And the babies kept coming, and they take money, so I had to wait for my ring. *Still* waiting on it. Your ring is nice, but I need mine to be huge. All the stuff I been through?" She paused, holding an armful of laundry, to raise her eyebrows at Claudia as if she already knew her stories. "Pushing out all these big-head babies? I'm gone need for that thing to walk in the room before me."

Claudia laughed. Aja was slack in her arms, her breath warm on her neck.

"Thank God you got her to sleep—and quick too." Stella raised her eyebrows again, impressed. "You got the mama touch. It ain't always that easy." She chuckled. "Get ready."

Claudia resented Stella's laughter. It rang with accusations of naivety that reminded her of Jean. "I've got four younger sisters," she said. "I know it's not easy."

"Siblings ain't the same. This one's gonna be yours," Stella said. "You can leave your sisters."

Two women stacking their laundry at the folding table nodded and hummed in agreement, a choir holding the same note.

Stella's kids were bad, and she knew it. She'd tell you herself.

Sometimes she declared it as a statement of defeat, "Girl, they bad," exhausted and flattened against her couch watching them scream, chase one another, and wreak havoc, free of her attempts to wrangle them with her own screaming and empty threats of punishment.

Sometimes she confessed it, chuckling with a touch of pride as if the children's badness was a beneficial life skill she was secretly and purposefully instilling to great success. "Girl, she is b*aaa*d," she'd said dragging Aja away from the playground and the cries of the little girl she'd bitten.

Sometimes she was amazed, like she'd just been dropped into her own life and made a sudden and sobering discovery. "Lord, they are bad," she'd say, summoning strength.

Always the children were powerful forces she'd never expected.

"They just miss their daddy," she'd say.

Claudia didn't tell her she'd missed her father her whole life but never knocked down a display case of candy because she couldn't get any or broken toys for spite.

The only picture of Cliff hung in the living room, below a ceramic cross, above the couch. "He hates the camera,"

Stella had explained. "Just stubborn." The first time Claudia visited Stella's apartment, across the street from the park, Stella had walked her right over to the chestnut-tinged five-by-seven as though she were making a real, face-to-face introduction.

Cliff was older than Claudia had imagined. He had at least ten years on Stella. In the picture, his pecan skin is smooth and carries the mystery of middle-aged black people that could place him anywhere in the wide range of possibilities from thirty-five to fifty-five, but his eyes, hooded beneath the brim of a flat cap, are bright with surprise and carry the weight of the years the skin doesn't show. He sits in a lawn chair facing away from the camera, pulled up to a folding table. The spread of cards in his hands, mostly clubs, is visible to the photographer. Stella sits beside him in a folding chair facing the camera. She smiles widely, full of teeth, and poses with a round, bald-headed infant Junior in the lap of her miniskirt. They appear to be at a barbecue, and the grill, out of frame to the left, sends thick smoke rising behind Stella.

"I just want him back home," she told Claudia today like she had every day they'd spoken since their meeting at the laundromat three weeks ago. They'd become fast friends and spent a number of the following weekday afternoons together.

Minutes ago, Claudia had climbed the stairs to Stella's third-floor apartment concerned by the absence of Junior, Jackson, and Aja's yelling that usually guided her to the door. When Stella said her mother had come by to get the kids and give her a break, Claudia was struck by a pang of jealousy. She couldn't imagine Jean being a source of relief or volunteering to care for children that weren't her own.

She and Stella sat on the couch, cluttered with dolls and action figures.

"It's so quiet when the kids aren't here. All I do is think about him," Stella said, her words breaking. "I can't stop thinking about him. I get so scared he's not coming back. I pray every day and I—" Stella grabbed Claudia's hand. "Pray with me."

"I don't know how to pray," Claudia confessed.

"Yeah, you do. It's just talking, like you're talking to me. It doesn't take special words. He can hear you; He's listening."

Claudia didn't tell her Mrs. Campbell had essentially made a job of praying, and it hadn't saved Mr. Campbell from his heart attack. But no one had seen that coming. Maybe Mrs. Campbell just hadn't prayed for the right thing.

Claudia clutched Stella's warm hand. She was scared for Cliff too. Last week, a laundromat lady's nephew had been blown across a field in South Vietnam with nothing to bring his wife but words she couldn't understand and a burial flag with no place to rest.

Besides this, Claudia wanted something, someone, to believe in besides Dale.

She loved him ferociously, that hadn't changed. But each

day it became clearer that he was just a man who left his dirty clothes on the floor and fell victim to his own moods. More often than Claudia liked, Dale came home with a paper bag that he sipped from all night. He kept the bottle wrapped tight as if ashamed to expose the liquor inside and his want for it. Some of those nights he played his records, turning up the volume until the sadness of those dragging, bluesy songs swallowed both of them whole and he lost himself to sleep, oblivious to the neighbors' beating on the floor. And some nights he lay on the bed beside Claudia, stared up at the brown clouds of the ceiling's water stains, and dreamed aloud about the baby on the way, the house he was going to buy for them.

Last night, he'd placed a hand on the small mound of her stomach and said, "I can't wait 'til he gets here."

She'd wanted to dream with him and pretend he wasn't drunk, so she'd grinned and challenged, "How you know it's a boy? You know my family's basically all women."

"It's not up to your family." The words slid around his tongue. "That's *my* boy. My father told me." His face unfurled into a wide, toothy grin that sent an icy rush down Claudia's back. It was the way he was and wasn't there in that smile and his eyes shining at her beneath heavy lids. She didn't not believe in ghosts or spirits but had personally never experienced the death of someone who'd loved her enough to keep coming around when they should've been gone or someone she'd loved enough to seek from other dimensions.

"I'm gonna be a good father," Dale declared. "I ain't going nowhere. Nowhere." He leaned over to kiss her, and his breath burned her nose.

Now, Claudia inhaled the lingering smell of breakfast sausage with her eyes closed, listening to Stella's words break through the apartment's silence.

"Lord, I don't have to tell you the obstacles placed before me. You know. I just ask that you let no weapon, God . . ." Her voice choked into silence before she sniffed and resumed. "*No* weapon formed against Cliff, me, or our children prosper. Guide, comfort, and keep us. Give Cliff strength and wisdom. Order his steps, God, to bring him home." She continued like this, her words rising in volume, her pleas more insistent until she exhausted herself into quiet sobs. Claudia opened her eyes to find Stella's face wet with tears, her head nodding, perhaps in response to an answer that she had missed.

"You okay?" Claudia asked.

"Yeah." Stella wiped her face before wiping her hands on her pajama pants. "I'm good. You go ahead now." She held out her hand for Claudia, who took it and closed her eyes again as she began.

"Umm, please keep Cliff safe."

"Yes," Stella whispered, encouraging her to continue.

"Bring him back home so he can be with Stella and the kids. Let them be united as a family in peace and love."

"My Lord," Stella said.

"Let them grow in that love and prosper. And live out

all of their dreams." Claudia had gone to church with Mrs. Campbell several times. She recalled a sermon about faith being the belief in things not yet seen. The pastor had urged the congregation to thank God for blessings not yet received. "We thank you for the nice house. All the bills paid plus extra. Vacations, good schools for the kids, college funds. We thank you for my healthy baby and the continued strength of my marriage. For growing closer and stronger every day. Amen." She was reluctant to open her eyes and step out of the life she'd imagined, but she felt a new lightness in her body that buzzed electric with hope.

Stella wiped her eyes. "Amen."

They prayed hand in hand on Tuesdays and Thursdays when the kids were with Stella's mother and Stella was granted the time to release her grief.

Claudia prayed hard and long, her voice swelling wall-to-wall. She painted a vivid future of her and Stella's children playing together, running through the yards in the homes they would own, past the swing sets and gardens, their husbands (also fast friends) talking by the grill, eventually joining them on the porch, where they would lean back in their chairs drinking iced tea while the day melted to a night decorated with stars and lightning bugs. Claudia could see it all.

She didn't like to think of God as a white man. She found this rendering of an all-powerful being who could have been anything, looked like anyone, stripped down to a white man a disappointing testament to weak imagination. Instead, she imagined Stella and her sisters and the ladies at the laundromat. Mahalia, Shirley, and the other black women on the gospel station with voices full and boundless as Heaven. Aunt Fredda, and, yes, even Jean. A God who really knew what it meant to bleed and sacrifice and turn nothing to something. She whispered to Her as she piled dust into the dustpan, wiped the counter, slicked a hot skillet with butter and watched the steam's rush to rise.

One Thursday after their afternoon prayer, Claudia turned to Stella. Claudia was two weeks into her second trimester and had given up on the high-waisted jeans that she could no longer zip or button over her stomach. She wore a yellow tent dress nearly identical to the one Stella was wearing the day they met and was wearing again today. They matched down to their feet in the same cheap flip-flops Stella always wore. Maybe it was the sudden discomfort of this twinning, seeing herself in Stella's sadness caused by an absent husband that prompted her to say, "Dale brought me the most beautiful flowers yesterday." It was a lie, but she didn't see it that way. She didn't want to wake from the dream she'd built in prayer and saw her words as more declarations of faith, vocalization of her certainty in the not yet realized.

Stella stood and began tossing toys from the floor into a milk crate in the corner of the living room. "That man." She shook her head. "You got a good one."

What had really happened yesterday is that Dale had woken up in the middle of the night still so drunk that he'd peed all over the floor. Claudia had cried this morning telling him about it, pointing to the towels, bunched in a corner of the bathroom, that she'd used to clean the mess.

She'd wanted to tell Stella about the way he'd looked right through her as she'd screamed helplessly against the dull thud of his piss streaming to the floor, but it was too embarrassing.

When Dale came home that afternoon with a bouquet of roses, Claudia almost couldn't concentrate on his apology. She caught that he was sorry and ashamed. He didn't know what to do with himself. He missed his father. It was hard, but he was going to do better.

She hugged him. "I know you will," she said, feeling the power of her words.

She spent the following Monday afternoon telling Stella about her Saturday dancing in the apartment with Dale, their Sunday walk to the park for picnic lunch. Tuesday evening, Dale came home with that familiar burn on his breath, but that was a private hurt she only shared with Mahalia, Shirley, and the others from the radio—a sacred circle who moaned and wailed for her.

She met Stella on Wednesday and kept watering her mustard seed, daydreaming a reality of Dale drawing her a bath, his warm hands massaging her feet.

"God, you make me miss Cliff," Stella said. She was

standing at the kitchen counter, spreading peanut butter across bread for the kids' lunch. "That support and love, a body to melt into at the end of the day." She sighed. "What am I gonna do?"

"You'll wait," Claudia said from her seat at the kitchen table. "He'll be here."

And the next day he was, just as they'd prayed for him to be. Not in Stella's apartment, but on the corner of West Market and Shelby. Claudia was at the bus stop after leaving the grocery store and saw him driving by in a brown Oldsmobile. He glanced toward her with those old eyes in that young face. Then, the light turned green and he was gone. She knew it couldn't have been him, but it was a sign.

She thought it would bring Stella comfort and assurance, but it made her more anxious. She worried Claudia for more details. What time was it when she'd seen him? Was anyone else in the car?

"Did he look like he missed me?" She stared at Claudia with wet eyes.

Claudia didn't know what to say. It was like a ghost had looked through her, but she knew she couldn't say this, so she said yes because she imagined that wherever the real Cliff was, he really was missing Stella and the kids. She said yes because this was her prayer.

She had no words for what happened the next day. None were needed. The sheets, red with her blood, told the whole story even though in Dale's truck on the way to the hospital, racing through a night too black for prayers to take hold, Marvin Gaye kept begging from the radio, "What's going on?"

She didn't tell anyone she was coming, so she wasn't expecting a warm welcome, but she still had the nerve to hope.

Maxine was the first one at the door. She ran to the truck, and her squealing drew Yolanda, Sandy, and then Dee outside. Jean peered through the screen door before disappearing back into the kitchen.

"What y'all doing here?" Sandy asked. She and the others' faces were gathered in the frame of the open passenger window. Maxine, seven, was at the bottom, standing on her tiptoes. Dee, eleven, and Sandy, thirteen, hovered above her, and Yolanda, fifteen, stood the tallest, though Sandy's head blocked most of her face.

"Can I pretty please go back with y'all?" Maxine begged.

"Get out of the truck so we can see your belly!" Dee said.

Claudia looked at Dale as she opened the door. "Come back around seven-thirty." It was four o'clock on Sunday. They'd lain around the apartment for much of the day unsure what to do with themselves, how to move forward, when Claudia had made the suggestion: home. A return. A reset.

"Where's he going?" Yolanda asked as Claudia stepped from the truck.

"To see his mother." She felt bad about leaving him alone

to deliver the news to Mrs. Campbell, piling more sadness into that house so soon.

"Your belly still ain't growed!" Dee complained.

Claudia was wearing her tent dress again. The cotton floated over her stomach, hiding the tiny bump that hadn't yet receded.

"The baby's gonna be little," Maxine said.

"She ain't far along like that y'all," Yolanda explained. "You gotta give it time."

The girls trailed Claudia into the apartment.

"She gotta eat. You eating right?" Sandy asked.

"If anybody else wanna eat they need to go to the store. I'm done once these pieces finish." Jean set her fork on the stove and took her seat at the table.

"I'm not hungry," Claudia said.

"See?" Sandy said. "That's why she's small. She's not eating right."

"Where's Dale?" Jean asked.

"He went to see his mother." Claudia emphasized *his* as if to remind Jean that she was her mother.

Jean sipped from her coffee mug. "Why y'all here?"

"I lost the baby." Claudia wanted to throw the words at Jean and, finally, stand strong, but she broke down.

"What?" Maxine asked. She was genuinely confused, but Claudia's crying was triggering her to the verge of her own tears.

Dee gasped.

"I wanted my mother," Claudia sobbed. She was tired of pretending. She just wanted Jean to be nice.

Yolanda and Sandy wrapped themselves around her. The soap and sun scent of her sisters' shirts, a reminder of the hours Jean worked at the dry cleaner, the care she took to keep their clothes and bedding spotless, was the closest Claudia felt she'd ever gotten to her mother. When she lifted her face from Yolanda's shoulder, Jean was standing at the stove, staring at the roiling grease.

"These things happen, Claudia." Jean pulled the drumsticks from the skillet and told the girls to get their plates. "You too." She nodded to Claudia.

"I'm not hungry."

"Get a plate." Jean frowned. "You need to eat," she said softer.

By eight-thirty, Dale hadn't returned or called. Mrs. Campbell said she hadn't seen or heard from him. She was surprised they were in town.

"How you feeling, baby?" she asked Claudia.

"Fine," Claudia answered because she was tired and worried and didn't want to drop any more of her problems onto Mrs. Campbell. She knew both of them would be up wondering and waiting.

Claudia and Yolanda sat outside on the porch in the chairs usually reserved for Jean and Aunt Fredda. Sandy and Dee were squished together on the tight porch steps, and Maxine flitted around them like the lightning bugs. The girls were trying to distract Claudia from her grief and worry. She could tell by the way their stories climbed over one another, vined around her, growing a barrier against silence and the pain that rested there. They didn't seem to know that pain was patient. It had time. It would be there when all the words dried in their throats. But she appreciated their effort and savored the simplicity of their problems like a drop of butterscotch. She was stars and skies away from their who-likes-who-and-what-to-say sagas.

Jean called them in at nine o'clock as usual, but she waited until the younger girls had gone inside before stepping outside with Claudia.

"Stay if you need," she said.

Claudia's throat tightened as she nodded. Jean went back to the couch, and Claudia waited until she'd wiped her face dry before she joined her sisters in their room.

When the phone rang at eleven, Jean was still awake. She stayed up late most nights though she woke at six in the morning for work.

"Yeah?" she issued her standard gruff greeting before handing the phone to Claudia, who'd popped anxiously from the bedroom.

"He's here, baby," Mrs. Campbell said. She told her Dale had been stumbly drunk at The Barrel and the owner had taken his keys and called her. "He told me about the baby." Her voice wobbled into a higher octave as she whimpered, "Honey, I'm so sorry."

Claudia nodded, tearing up again. She forgot Mrs. Campbell couldn't see her.

"He's a mess and won't come in the house. He fell asleep in the car."

When Claudia hung up, Jean asked no questions. She smoked and stared at the television, but Claudia could feel her begging the inquiry from months ago, "What *you* gonna do?"

What Claudia did was climb into the truck when Dale came to get her the next afternoon. His eyes were red, hung with heavy bags, but his face looked scrubbed, his hair was brushed, clothes smooth. She imagined his mother ironing his clothes while he showered, telling him to get himself together. When he reached for her, she grabbed his hand and held on.

She stayed while he said he was going to stop drinking and didn't. While he spilled himself onto her stomach, her back, the sheets when he was fast enough. While she waited anxiously for her blood to show, unsure if she welcomed its visit. While she wrestled with God in her lonely hours and prayed tentatively, begrudgingly with Stella until one hot Thursday in early October when Cliff returned with a knock at Stella's door.

"Oh my god!" Stella leapt onto him, but he peeled her arms from his neck.

"I need you to stop calling my house."

"Let's just talk." She pressed a hand against his chest,

near an indecipherable logo on his navy shirt, urging him into the hall.

"Me and you are over. We've *been* over," he spoke slowly as if he questioned Stella's ability to comprehend. "I'm married. You know that." He peered over Stella's shoulder at Claudia. "And your friend and whoever else can hear it too."

"This is none of my business." Claudia stood. "I'm gonna go."

"Let's just talk," Stella repeated, reaching for Cliff's hand. She didn't acknowledge Claudia squeezing past them, but Claudia didn't mind. She was so embarrassed for Stella that she couldn't meet her eyes.

"Come in," Stella pleaded. "I miss you. The kids miss you."

"I gotta get back to work," Claudia heard Cliff say as she fled down the stairs.

After nothing from Stella for days, Claudia showed up at her apartment on Tuesday.

Stella rushed to explain. "I'm so sorry. I didn't want to lie to you. I just wanted somebody to understand what I'm going through without judging m—"

Claudia cut her off. "Dale has a drinking problem." She offered this because she needed a friend, and she had to restore the balance to make it work. She'd heard that the truth could set you free, but she didn't really believe that. Freed or hidden, most people's truths ate them alive.

"Oh, girl." Stella sighed. "That's nothing to be ashamed

of. That's not your fault." She shrugged. "You can't help who you love."

But Jean had lived a life proving that you could. When she died at the beginning of the new year after a quick, quiet fade from lung cancer, Claudia and her sisters cried, but not like one would expect a daughter to cry after losing their mother. Not inconsolably, as if they would not be able to move on, and Claudia wondered if this reaction had been a purposeful intention guiding Jean's life and the complicated relationship she'd built with her children.

The pastor patched a sermon out of riffs of Psalm 23:4, John 3:16, and anecdotes of Jean as a child attending church with her mother and siblings. He'd tried, but to him and nearly everyone else who came and commented on the arrangements Aunt Fredda had made, the way Jean looked so peaceful, like she's sleeping they said, though she'd never looked peaceful in her sleep, she was as mysterious and unknown as the god the pastor went on about. The god who leads to green pastures and still waters also sends men to war to die, leaves children fatherless, mothers grief-stricken, spins wives into widows. She pushes us into the world alone and pulls us from it the same way. Who knows Her reasons? Jean would have hated everything but the music, and Claudia's certainty of this made her grateful to realize she'd known at least some small part of her mother. The choir's lead singer was Mrs. Washington, Claudia's fourth-grade math teacher. Her voice was like the hand she'd placed on Claudia's back when she'd grown disheartened by wrong answers, a warm presence helping her understand how the world adds up.

Dale sat beside her in a front pew of Aunt Fredda's church glaring at Jesus hanging above the pulpit. He didn't stay at the repast. Claudia told him he could go. Neither understood the full extent of what she'd meant, the door she was opening for both of them until he showed up the next morning, and she told him she was staying. He was too tender from the embarrassment of another night at The Barrel, reported to Claudia by Mrs. Campbell, to accrue more humiliation by begging with her sisters peeking at the door. So, he left without incident.

For the first few nights, she slept in the room with her sisters as she always had. She was afraid of venturing into the living room's darkness, the dead silence, emptiness wide as an open mouth. But she grew tired of spending her nights untangling from limbs that weren't Dale's and made her bed on the pullout. She hoped, prayed for a hazy figure. A whisper. A breeze. Flickering lights. But there was only the smell of smoke in the couch cushions that had always been there and her own breathing or her sisters' chattering. And she wondered if Dale had really spoken to his father. She wouldn't have been mad at him for lying, just as she hadn't been mad at Stella. Nobody wants to be left, alone. She kept vigil late into the night, bathed in the celestial blue of the TV. She was now the subject of the stoic image she'd observed all her life.

EVERYTHING YOU COULD EVER WANT

When you get out of the car, you feel wet and sticky. You rush, twisting your neck, to scan the back of your long, floral sundress. You fear blood blooming among the fuchsia and yellow hibiscus, but there is nothing.

"You're fine, baby," Nigel, suddenly at your side, assures you.

The July heat trapped in his car for the three days he spent in bed curled around you like a comma, paused, has made your thighs sweaty, soggied the overnight maxi you're saddled on. The doctor said the bleeding would only last a couple of days, but the nurse handed you a bag of pads like you would be bleeding forever, her face made ugly in its contortion to express sympathy for you and Nigel.

He rubs tight circles on the small of your back, guides

you out of the parking lot and up the sidewalk lined with wooden rocking chairs. There's a wait for a table, and you head to the bathroom to change your pad before wandering the store attached to the restaurant with Nigel trailing along. You pry the tops off jarred candles, sniff, and pass them for him to smell. You try to imagine scents filling the apartment in Chicago where you and Nigel will eventually settle, just the two of you as you originally planned.

You visited in March during your spring break, eager to find a place that would offer more career opportunities for the degrees you would earn in May, his BS in computer science and your BA in English. Wrapped in a wool scarf and down coat, you stood on Michigan Avenue craning your neck to take in the length of the Tribune Tower. You hoped to work there, climbing to a *Chicago Tribune* office somewhere in the sky, maybe fact-checking and copy-making until you could write feature stories. At a Hyde Park café, you drank hot chocolate and saw yourself sitting at the corner table during your off-hours, writing short stories and novel chapters, losing yourself to words in the hum of other patrons. Afterward, on the way back to the hotel, you and Nigel admired a duplex and spent the evening dreaming it yours, but you can barely remember it now. You can't shape the rooms or the stuff you filled them with to make them a home. There's only a generic red brick building with a closed door and the words and pictures on the candle labels forcing their manufactured images. *Fresh Roses* conjures a fat, pink bloom. *Country Apple* evokes a wicker basket spilling shiny, red fruit. Everything places you right back where you are: in your favorite restaurant in Bloomington, Indiana, which is one hundred and five miles away from your mother in Louisville, Kentucky.

Tomorrow morning, she'll be hundreds, thousands of miles farther as she makes her way to Hawaii. The display of decorative model sailboats and porcelain conch seashells makes you think of her at home packing.

As you approach the toys, large water guns, and yarn-haired dolls in the far corner, the hostess calls Nigel's last name and announces your party of two. She stands at her tiny station before a chalkboard scratched with the day's specials and tells you, "I love your dress." You thank her and smile.

Six weeks ago, when you sat on the toilet staring at the two blue lines drawing the scariest, biggest news of your life, you thought about clothes. You were wearing your favorite jeans and almost cried as you imagined your stomach ballooning, pushing you out of them forever. You'd found them at the Salvation Army for three dollars. Your dress, another one of your favorites, is loose and billowy around the midsection. Your pregnancy or not is inconsequential to its fit. It floats around your ankles as you follow the waitress. You look breezy and carefree.

You conceived on a rainy Saturday after you and Nigel had gorged on sitcom reruns and pizza delivery and ran out of condoms. You were still cruising on the high of graduation, all the previous week's speeches about success and taking chances, and had dared to use the pull-out method. Of course, Nigel didn't successfully pull out in time. You knew about the morning-after pill, but the possibility of pregnancy that had haunted you all night evaporated in the sunshine like most ghosts do, and you convinced Nigel not to worry, as if you had sovereign control over your body.

You'd both been lazy and dumb. It was no way to bring a child into being so you were sure that you wouldn't.

Ultimately, you were right.

The waitress circles to your table twice before you order. You can't choose between breakfast, lunch, or dinner, can't be trusted with decisions. You didn't even choose this place. When you slipped into your sandals, said you needed to go, Nigel grabbed his keys. You hadn't been specific but meant you wanted to drive until everything here and now was a dot miles and miles behind you. As Nigel approached the expressway ramp, you thought he understood, but he made a right turn and brought you here. You weren't hungry when you arrived, but you haven't eaten all day, and now that you're out of the apartment, watching and smelling passing plates full of corn muffins and country ham and gravy-slathered food that tastes like it was made by somebody's mama, you want everything.

Your waitress's name, Heather, is stitched onto her brown apron with gold thread. She is petite and spritely. Her brown ponytail bounces as she nods, confirming your and Nigel's orders, assuring you the food will be right out. She looks like she's never had a sad day in her life. You like her and her bright energy. After she brings your drinks, Nigel reaches across the table to hold your hands, says, "You need to tell her, Jay," and ruins your first sips of lemonade by reminding you that the pleasant wanting, asking, and receiving you're doing here with Heather is a limited miracle.

You are too tender to argue with him, so you nod.

You were eleven, twelve, thirteen, fourteen, fifteen, sixteen, seventeen. You waited. Patiently. Quietly. Reading your book. Watching TV. Letting your mother rest out all her sadness so that when she got up she'd feel better and be ready to go.

Does it matter where you were going? The movies. The fair. The park. The mall. Your cousin's birthday party. The grocery store. The pizzeria. The library. The living room to play Monopoly. The kitchen to eat dinner. Your bedroom for good-night hugs. The point is you never got there together.

Your mother is going to Hawaii with her boyfriend, Mike. She met him seven months ago in AA, but his first *A* is for *Alcoholics*, not *Addicts* like your mother's. Mike has been sober for fifteen years. To your mother, you exclaimed, "Good for him!" Your face was sunny with fake enthusiasm and sincerity. You said the same thing to your cousin Zaria as you sucked your teeth and turned the bright bitter with your full-bodied sarcasm. You want your mother to be with somebody with no *A*'s to call their own.

Mike is full of AAisms like "One day at a time" and "It works if you work it." You appreciate this because it can keep your mother on the straight and narrow path she's been walking for the past year, but Mike is white, pink-white actually, and you're resentful of the white saviorism of it all, highlighted by the fact that he's rich. Your mother has regained her nursing license, lost after she got caught stealing opioids from work, so she makes good money on her own, but it's not Mike money. Not lawyer money or I'm-friends-with-a-Derby-running-horse-owner money.

One day, when Mike was just a name that kept rolling off your mother's tongue, she said, "You know his wife died last year."

"Oh," you said and made it sound sad, but you weren't thinking about that lady, who your mother continued to tell you was forty-seven and had breast cancer.

You didn't know Mike's wife, and she was already dead, unlike your mother who sometimes wishes she was. But she hadn't called you crying in a while, and you didn't want to be a downer by bringing up the possibility of her being a rebound chick or whatever they call the woman who follows the dead wife, so you kept your mouth shut. You listened when she told you about cruising Lake Cumberland on Mike's boat and eating dinners at such-and-such fancy restaurants in stories that would have been boring if they didn't carry the ending of her laughter or a smile you could hear curled in her words. You didn't say much about much though you had plenty to say. You were nervous about the approach of postgrad life, but happy to hear your mother's happiness without your life getting in the way. You'd gotten used to its ring in your ear when she called crying.

Mike said things were moving too fast.

A familiar guilt and empty aching burrowed in the pit of your stomach, stretched, rose, and pushed your breakfast to the base of your throat. The baby—who you didn't know was there yet but had suspected and feared—pushed your oatmeal the rest of the way up, made you excuse yourself and tell your mother something you ate wasn't sitting right when you called her back. She told you to get some rest, ginger ale, and crackers. You bought a pregnancy test and spent all day reading those blue lines, stuck the stick in your purse, and carried it to work like one of the library books you spent hours scanning and shelving, but it was more like a story you were writing—incomplete and frustrating as you reread the opening and wondered how you would get to the ending you'd envisioned.

Your mother called again that night.

"How you doing?" she asked.

"I'm good," you lied. "Feeling better."

Nigel sat beside you on the bed, smiling with all his teeth. He thought you were about to tell her what he called "the good news," which made you think about Jesus and the cross and bleeding for the sake of children. He'd called his parents almost as soon as you'd ended a maddening round

of him grinning and asking if you were serious as you held
up the test and told him you were heart attack, dead-ass,
swear on the Bible, your mama, your dead grandmama serious.

You held the phone against your ear and watched his
chest rise, filling with some celebratory shout about to bust
from his lungs, and you put a finger to his lips, buttoning
them shut. "Not now," you mouthed, shaking your head.

"How are *you* doing?" you asked your mother, steeling
yourself against her sadness.

The little girl at a nearby table snatches a french fry from a
younger boy's plate. He whines in protest, and you can't tell
whether his high pitch is words or the universal mewling of
children. He seems to be about three, the girl six or seven.
You assume they're brother and sister, that the man who sits
beside the girl, resting his sturdy arms, dark with farmer's
tan, is their father and the woman who you've caught staring at you is their mother.

The woman is young, old enough to be a couple years
out of college if she took that route, and pretty in the way
of popular white girls who shine in their small rural high
schools and dim in the bigger world against millions who
reveal their ordinary beauty for what it is. Her orange tank
top reads *Fun and Sun* in big, teal letters that stretch across
her boobs, but when she raises her arm, thin and toned, to
tuck a long plank of wheat brown hair behind her ear with

bulky white French-manicured tips, her skin carries the indiscernible tan of shaved almonds so you guess she isn't getting much sun, and she's too busy looking at you to suggest that she's having much fun.

The man tells the boy to hush and offers the girl some of his green beans, but she shakes her head, closing her eyes and sending her fine, butter-colored hair sailing.

"If you don't want the green beans, then you're not hungry." There's a harshness in the man's voice that reminds you of the chill bumps the air conditioning has blasted onto your arms. You put on the jean jacket you brought. You are always prepared to be uncomfortable, make adjustments.

The little girl is on the small side of fat. Her cheeks, elbows, and shoulders rounded. Her purple T-shirt presses tight against her middle. She plucks another fry from her brother's plate. He howls and slides down in his chair to kick at the girl under the table. Her screams break the woman's stare and draw eyes from other diners, including Nigel who turns around to look.

"Hey!" The mother snaps her fingers in the girl's face, grabbing her attention, before lowering her voice to a whisper. "Shut up and stop it," she hisses through thinned lips and gritted teeth.

"He kicked me!"

"She keeps taking my food!" The boy starts crying with real tears and the kind of wailing that opens with a wide pause from a deep inhale before it gains volume.

"I'm hungry!" the girl yells.

The woman scoops the boy upright in his chair before collecting him in her arms. "I'm hungry too," she says. She rocks the boy aggressively, a quick ticking back and forth. She clutches his head to her chest, but the point of the hold appears not to be comfort or care, but strategy, a move that will muffle his cries and maybe put him to sleep. The huge wedding ring on her clutching hand suggests that the man loves the woman a lot. It makes you think they had a big fairytale wedding and she didn't see this life—she and her husband arguing with their fat daughter about french fries, wearing a bright lie on her chest—around the corner from that magical day. "I haven't even gotten a chance to eat my food because of y'all's carrying on."

The girl says nothing and moves a thin tassel of hair from her shoulder into her mouth as if she can find what she needs, wants, in her own fragile strands.

A piece of you that isn't already broken splinters and a big, ugly cry builds in your stomach, balls up in your throat. You take another sip of lemonade to push it back and squeeze Nigel's hand tighter.

"My parents would have just left," he says. "Called the waitress for a to-go box, paid the bill, and whooped my ass in the car."

You see Nigel as a boy, chopped into half of his six feet, acting a fool in a restaurant. You have imagined a little Nigel many times in recent weeks—shrieking a shiny cord of drool down his bare chest as he waddle-runs, his diaper swishing between hammy legs churning to escape big Nigel's creeping tickle-monster hands. You have smelled the boy's hair, damp and coconut-scented from washing, as he lay against your chest while you read him a story he already knows by heart. The two of you duet the dialogue. You know his voice, have begged him to be quiet, keep it down, please stop while you sit at your desk trying to write. You have resented his calling, crawling over you, burrowing into the covers beside you, talking, talking, Mamamamamama-mamamamama, when you just wanted to sleep and wake to the day on your own.

When the woman's eyes return to you, you're staring back at her. She quickly drops her gaze and adjusts herself in her chair. Her hand, clawed around the boy's head, relaxes into his brown curls.

You immediately feel the urge to apologize. You hadn't meant to shame the woman, not really, just remind her to be gentle with her daughter and remember she's just a kid and kids want and want and want. "Don't make her feel guilty," you want to tell the woman. You think she'd understand; the want in her eyes when she looks at you in your sundress, sipping lemonade at your table centerpieced with your hands laced with Nigel's is not that different from the hunger apparently tearing through her daughter.

"McKenzie," the woman says, "take your hair out of your mouth." And then, as if you said what you wanted and she understood like you thought she would she tells the man, "Get her another order of fries."

"She's not hungry, Jackie."

"How much is an order of fries? Two, three dollars? Just get the damn things so we can eat in peace." She pauses before saying to no one in particular, "This was supposed to be a nice day out."

"I'm hungry," the girl insists quieter.

No one responds.

"That's what my parents would have done," you say. "Just given me what I wanted." You mean that's what your mother would have done because when your parents were together, your father did whatever your mother wanted. You don't admit that the woman said the kind of passive-aggressive shit your mother probably would have said or confess your fear that, in a similar situation, you would do the same.

"Spare the rod, spoil the child," Nigel says.

"But you're still spoiled," you say.

"Yeah." He laughs and the sound makes you feel lighter. A flimsy smile spreads your lips.

Behind Nigel, the woman asks, "Why are you crying? We're getting the fries, McKenzie. Jesus Christ."

You are an accident. Your parents don't use this word, but you are a writer and it is concise and accurate. Four months before they made you, your parents met in a hospital room. Your mother was your paternal grandfather's nurse. She didn't think she could conceive after she'd lost her first baby nearly ten years before.

Your father calls you a surprise, like you're a great gift God pinched from a cloud just for them. Your mother calls you her baby. This is sweet too, but also concise and accurate in a way that doesn't indulge in cute excuses or cover-ups. It is a fact; you are her baby. Blood of her blood.

Whatever the words chosen to explain you, you pushed your mother with the baby carriage before she was ready. Before marriage and maybe love. At least not the forever kind of love your father gave freely, unabashedly, in mushy gushes, until your mother didn't want it anymore.

You've read that depression doesn't require a reason, no sad story beyond the anticlimactic account of chemical imbalance, but you don't believe this. Everything comes from somewhere. $X + Y = Z$. This begets that.

Your mother was an accident too, and you're pretty sure your grandmother, who had her when she was fifteen, wouldn't have had a problem using the word. She couldn't afford sugarcoating in time or money; your mother was the first of five daughters. Your grandmother let the roof she kept over the girls' heads by sweating over stains in other people's clothes at the dry cleaner where she worked for thirty-five years; the food bought and served on chipped, scratched plates express what she never said, what your mother has told you she never knew for sure.

In all the pictures you've seen of your grandmother, she is already middle-aged, a grandmother. You've stared at these pictures and tried to trace the girl before the babies in her grave face, the hard stare of her dark eyes, the straight line of her closed mouth.

The father flags down the waitress and orders the fries, but, in the end, he cancels the order and pushes away from the table. The mother does the same and grabs her purse. She doesn't ask for a to-go box and leaves her plate full of a beige pile that you guess is chicken and dumplings with mashed potatoes. She cuts her losses in favor of a quick exit. The girl's crying is alarming. It pours from her in low, gravelly peals. Her face is the deep pink of the baby girl onesies and flimsy tutu skirts you considered weeks ago at Walmart after detouring from buying toilet paper and dishwashing liquid. You browsed bottles, car seats, diapers, strollers, and cribs until you were dazed and overwhelmed.

The man lifts the girl from her chair, and she keeps crying, perched straight-backed in his arms, as they leave the dining room.

"Well," Heather says upon her return, "somebody's not happy." She sets the platters on the table. You ordered pancakes. They're topped with a dome of butter that looks like a scoop of ice cream, like it's a celebration.

Two weeks after Mike broke up with your mother, he changed his mind.

"He said he can't spend his life pining over Annette," your mother told you. "We're getting together for dinner tonight."

"That's good." Your words were unconvincing, but your mother didn't notice.

"A*aaa*nd he wants to take a trip to celebrate our reunion." She gave the phrase *celebrate our reunion* air quote emphasis, as if to highlight that these were Mike's words, not hers. As if they, and the whole idea, were silly. You knew this was a form of defense, not wanting to be too excited. You are expert at building these kinds of guards.

"He said I could pick. Anywhere. Anywhere!" she repeated.

"Oh wow," you said.

"I'm thinking of Hawaii. Is that too simple?" she asked. "I feel like Hawaii is the place where someone who's never been anywhere would pick, but I haven't really been anywhere." She laughed and sounded far away.

You still hadn't told her you were pregnant. Now that she wasn't crying and could process the news, you wanted to tell her, but didn't know how, couldn't determine which words you should use to interrupt her dreaming.

She considered other destinations, flitted from Hawaii to the Bahamas to Italy, France, and Spain, growing farther and farther away like she was already gone and you'd never reach her.

"Travel. See the world!" This is what your mother urges instead of motherhood, what she told you after your graduation when all your aunts were gathered around you asking about your postgrad plans. Months later, as you stared at those two blue lines, her words resonated. They were intended to be encouraging, but you read between them like the degree you'd spent four years earning had taught you to do and found another meaning. You are always listening for the unsaid resting in your mother's tongue, the thoughts that drag her down.

She was telling you what she wished she had done, what she probably didn't do because she had you, and kids need stability, foundation, home. You grounded her in a life you can't even be sure was second-best. That's why you feel responsible for her depression and trying to keep her happy. That's why you've always been an honor roll student and done the right thing (most of the time). That's why you didn't tell her you were pregnant. Even in her best mood, you were afraid she'd be disappointed and say you were making a mistake, imagining herself at twenty-seven and pregnant with you.

You can still hear the girl crying from outside, though she is quickly fading. You tell Nigel, "I would have never acted like that." You're not bragging, you're thinking, remembering.

"You wouldn't have had to if just a little whining would have gotten you what you wanted."

"No, I mean I wouldn't have tried it. Even when I was little like that, I just wanted to make Mama happy. I just wanted to be good for her. Even when I was mad or sad. It's like I could feel all the sadness she was holding inside."

In the days since the emergency room, you have not

stopped imagining your daughter. The baby was a girl, you are sure of it. It's why she didn't make it. She would have grown curled beside all your fears and sadness, known the indistinguishable taste of all your wants before she had a chance to develop her own cravings.

You ask Nigel, "Do you think we were spared somehow?"

"No," he answers and looks you deep in the eyes, but you don't believe him. He's like your father. He would never call your kid an accident, will never admit that the loss was for the best. "That was one moment for one family," he says.

"That's not what I meant." You sigh because he will never get it, get you. His mother thinks all babies are blessings, angels, perfect. Your mother is less generous. You have watched her look at a magazine photo of celebrity parents with their newborn, shake her head and say, "That baby is *not* cute," before flipping the page on that baby's face. His mother thinks motherhood, like multivitamins and exercise, is good for all women, character-building like wellness retreats and self-help books. While she was regaining her nursing license, your mother worked briefly at an abortion clinic.

When Nigel told his mother you were pregnant, she was a series of squeals and chirps through his cell phone. "Oh, I'm so happy for you!" she exclaimed and somehow managed to make her words sound like a squeezy hug. You couldn't imagine your mother reacting that way and wondered how you would grow that level of enthusiasm.

266 / MAMA SAID

"Nevermind," you say now and push the melting ball of butter around a pancake.

"Why don't you want to tell your mother?" Nigel asks.

"I told you it's not about not wanting to tell her. It's not a good time."

"It wasn't a good time when she was broken up. It wasn't a good time when they were back together." He sets his hamburger down and wipes his hands. "There was no good time for good news and now there's never gonna be a good time to say what needs to be said."

"I told you, you don't get it."

"That was our child, JayLynn. Our baby. Her grandchild. And she doesn't even know about it. She deserves to know."

"Keep your voice down," you say."

"Somebody needs to speak up for them. They deserve acknowledgment. They didn't make it, but they were here. Even if it was only for a little bit."

You keep forgetting it was his baby too. Mostly because you feel like your girl is so like you—uneasy and unsure how to insert herself into the world. So timid that she didn't try, didn't want to be a bother.

Nigel nods when you ask to leave. He gets Heather to bring the check and to-go boxes. You pack up your pancakes. When you get back to your apartment, you call your mother. Nigel steps outside on the porch.

Your mother's greeting is chipper. You gather your breath

and waste no time. The story of the two blue lines and the ugly emergency room nurse rushes out of you.

"Why didn't you tell me sooner?" she asks, sounding hurt.

"I was scared."

"Of what?"

You start crying.

"I wouldn't have been mad at you," she says. "I just want you to do everything you want to do before you have kids. They're a big responsibility."

"You couldn't do everything you wanted to do because of me?"

"Everything I have or haven't done is my choice. Being a mother makes things harder, but I could have done things differently if I wanted. I just wanted to do what was best for you. I mean, as best as I could. It's not like I've been the world's greatest mother."

"You did the best you could," you offer.

"Are you okay?" she asks. "That's stupid. Of course you're not okay. But you will be. You hear me? You're gonna be okay."

You let your courage build in the silence before you blurt, "Can you come up here?"

"Now?" she asks.

"Nevermind," you say. "I know you've got a flight in the morning."

"It's just . . . I . . ." she stutters. "I can't stay long."

"That's okay. Don't worry about it." The big, ugly cry from earlier returns to your throat. You want to get off the phone to let it out.

"No. I'll be there," she says. "I'll finish packing and come up, okay?"

"Okay," you say.

You don't believe her, but a strange car pulls up to the curb after you're done watching TV and reading and are sitting on the porch staring at the space between lightning bugs. A white man sits in the driver's seat, and you realize it's Mike before your mother gets out of the passenger seat. You rise from your chair, and she springs across the street, up the porch steps.

"Come here, baby," she says so quietly that you aren't sure the words are real, that you haven't imagined them or the jasmine scent of her. But she gathers you in her arms, and she's really here. Your mother is here.

ACKNOWLEDGMENTS

My deepest gratitude to the entire staff at West Virginia University Press, including Derek Krissoff, Sarah Munroe, Sara Georgi, and Natalie Homer, for the care and enthusiasm they've shown for this collection. You've made a dream come true! Thank you to Sejal Shah for helping to make this match.

Thank you to the editors at the literary magazines who previously published some of the stories in this collection: Mensah Demary, Athena Dixon, Maris Finn Endres, Becky Hagenston, Robert Moreira, and Jennifer Walkup.

Special thanks to Cate Marvin and Z. Z. Packer for taking me to breakfast at Lynn's Paradise Café all those years ago and showing me that a life with writing is possible. I'm forever grateful for your encouragement.

Thank you to Alyce Miller for taking time throughout the years to offer advice about what it means to be a writer on and off the page. I appreciate it more than you know.

Thank you to my professors at Indiana University with

shoutouts to Crystal Wilkinson and Margo Crawford, who were the first to read, critique, and support work that eventually became part of this collection.

Thank you to the SUNY Geneseo English Department for providing time and funding for professional development that helped me complete the book. Thank you to my students for the lessons you've taught.

Thank you to Diem Jones and Elmaz Abinader for the opportunity to learn and connect at VONA. Thank you to Michael Collier for the chance to attend Bread Loaf.

A windy body roll to the ladies of We All Write: Selena Fleming Cochran, Reenah Golden, Tokeya Graham, Lu-Tonya Highsmith. Thank you for your support, kettles of ginger lemon tea, soul cries, and laughs. Y'all are the dopest!

A huge shoutout to the ladies of the Bolder Collective: Rachel Hall, Gail Hasking, and Sonja Livingston. Thank you for being there (literally) as accountability buddies, friends, and mentors. Who knows if this book would have been done if I didn't have your company during the rough stretches.

Thank you to my homies Aisha Sharif, Keshia Swan, Courtney Harris, and Caroline Beltz-Hosek for helping me navigate the ups and downs of life while writing these stories.

A lot of time, feedback, conversations, and support helped produce this book. Thank you to the following people for their offerings throughout this long journey: Catherine Faurot, Mariposa Fernandez, Jess Fenn, Liz Van

Hoose, Antonya Nelson, Will Boast, Amina Gautier, Kyle Semmel, Leslie C. Youngblood, Sally Bittner Bonn, Banke Awopetu, Monique Harris, S. Erin Batiste, Beth McCoy, Maria Lima, Albert Abonado, Olaocha Nwabara, Sonya Bilocerkowycz, Mark Broomfield.

For being a bunch of perfectly imperfect characters, I give thanks to the Sublett family, especially Heaven, Kim, Stephanie, Donna, Andre, Karen, Sharon, and Kayla. Rest in peace to Tyus and my grandmother Richie. I love y'all, we matter, and our stories are important.

Thank you to my brother, Donald. Being your older sister has allowed me to experience the struggle, sacrifice, and reward of caring for someone else. That insight shaped a number of these stories.

Thank you to Grandmother Gilberta McKoy who taught me how to lead with love and be a beautiful person inside and out.

Thank you to my cousins, Paulette Sublett and Jonika Dulin. Y'all are my best friends. Y'all will ride for me, fly for me, listen to me rant when I'm down, lift me back up, and help me construct a plan to get back right. I love y'all for real.

Thank you, Daddy Joe, for trusting me to make my own choices. Thank you, Daddy Donald, for crooked parts in my hair, cream of wheat and bacon mornings, and teaching me independence.

To Joe, the love of my life, thank you for believing in me when I doubted myself.

Finally, special thanks and the biggest hug to my mama. From you, I got my face, my stubbornness, and my love for reading.